BLACKROCK ISLAND

International Standard Book Number 13: 978-1-60452-128-3

International Standard Book Number 10: 1-60452-128-7

Library of Congress Control Number: 2017936816

BluewaterPress LLC
52 Tuscan Way Ste 202-309
Saint Augustine FL 32092

http://bluewaterpress.com

This book may be purchased online at -

http://www.bluewaterpress.com/blackrock

Please note that address information is subject to change. At the time of printing, the address was correct, but may have changed since. Please check our website for the latest address information for BluewaterPress LLC.

Book Dedication

Christine, Morgan, Evelyn and Baby Jones
Mark, Eloise and Lauren Hackman-Brooks
Thomas J. and L. Elaine Burke
Christine Villas-Boas and Linda Carrick
Carole J. Greene and Suzi Weinert

Acknowledgements

I am grateful to the following family, friends, students, writers, graphic artist, photographer, and editor who gave me the opportunity, education, and incentive to pursue my writing career. Honorable mention goes to my children Christine and Mark, also to my editors and readers, who have shared ideas and given me inspiration and support both personally and professionally. To my parents, Tom and Elaine Burke, who gave me the opportunity, education and incentive to pursue my writing career, and for that, I am forever grateful. To Elmore Leonard, who helped me endlessly with the writing of the first draft through the last draft. His inspiration and encouragement drove me to my best efforts in writing the novel. I cannot be more grateful to have such a patient and encouraging mentor.

To my friend Lt. Commander Robert Paskulovich, U.S. Navy, who encouraged me to write. To Elizabeth Kane Buzelli, Suzi Weinert, Brenda Hiatt, Cynthia Harrison, Gerry Hempel Davis, and Jean Harrington, who have inspired me and provoked my thoughts to make me a better writer.

Also, to Chuck Sambuchino, Claire Gudefin, Michael Kiefer, Calvin Khemmoro, Nancy Young, Maggie Mc Clellan, Deborah Newcomer, Dorta Kosa, John Nelson, Ken Prather,

John Van Ophem, Judith Searle, Geraldine Hemple Davis, Patricia Currence, Abigail Stonerook, Tom Klieber, Elizabeth Klieber, John Minnis, Matt Klug, Kevin Walsh, Dr. Bonnie Ellis, Maureen and Andy Coubrough. And thanks also to ADM William J. Fallan, U S Navy; CAP Terrance Bronson, U S Navy; Zach Ogden USCGMB3; Captain USAR Alan Anderson; Rev. Peter Donohue, OSA; Robert O' Neil, and Robert Capone. All of these wonderful people inspired my creative thoughts and ideas.

To my publisher, Joe Clark, who has given me the opportunity to bring my book to print, thank you. Finally to my literary agent, Carole J Greene, for the encouragement and time spent enticing my creativity. I cannot thank her enough.

I am forever grateful to all.

CHAPTER 1

BLACKROCK ISLAND
IRELAND

The blond woman in the pilot's seat fastened the shoulder harness, preparing for takeoff. Holding in the starter button, she engaged the helicopter's generator, slowly releasing it. After a minute, flipping switches on the instrument panel, she stared at the green lights illuminating the cockpit and completed the start sequence. The white glow from the Bell Jet Ranger's strobe lights pierced the darkness.

Placing her hands on the controls, she forced them into position while the straps held her upright. The whirling blades beat the air. Simultaneously, the turbine whined to a high pitch for takeoff. Rotors thumped as the skids bounced on and off the landing circle, dirt flying. The dim red light in the cockpit stood out against the dark forest behind it, silhouetting her figure.

Soldiers equipped with heavy weapons and body armor held their positions surrounding the helicopter. The leader of the Irish peacekeepers shouted at the woman through the bullhorn, "Halt or we will shoot!" He punched his fist upward at a forward angle.

The woman's head turned sharply toward him and then swiftly back to the instrument panel. The engine revved to a high pitch as the controls were forced into gear. Scraping the tarmac, the skids lifted off the launch pad.

Troops were lined up for the kill shot. Kneeling, facing forward, weapons at the ready, men clad in black steadied their fifty-caliber sniper rifles into their shoulders, waiting for the command.

"Fire!" their leader screamed. In one swift movement, he brought his fist down toward the ground.

A barrage of bullets riddled the target. The helicopter exploded, sending shards of metal in all directions as the bright orange flames scorched the black sky.

CHAPTER 2

A MONTH EARLIER
MANHATTAN, NEW YORK

Laine Sullivan stared at the caller ID. Max, her former boss. She knew why he was calling. Her mind drifted to the undercover operation in Cuba the previous year. She grappled multiple times with what she could have done differently during the assignment. Discovering the bomb in the casino storage closet minutes before it exploded had not provided her enough time to warn the crowd. It demolished half the casino. Flying debris penetrated the Canadian Embassy next door – the real target. Many high-ranking officials died. Quick thinking on her part had miraculously kept her alive. Locating a nearby stairwell, she hid under the concrete steps when the walls blew out. The space was enough to keep her relatively safe, but it took the rescue crew hours to dig her out from under the damaged structure. Her memories blurred.

The sound of the cell phone vibrating on the desk brought her back to the present. She froze, unable to pick it up before it stopped ringing. She fingered the classified document Max had overnighted to her that morning, and frowned. The electronic copy of the same document waited for her on her laptop. It was protocol, and she knew it.

Sitting at her antique French desk, she felt safe in her New York studio condominium, but it was not enough for her. Creating architectural interior and exterior designs made her feel alive, but something was telling her to get back to the job she loved and had worked in for the last ten years — the spy game.

She remembered the visit from Mr. Trenchcoat, a CIA agent who came to her parents' home while she was studying civil engineering in college. He recruited her when she was only twenty-one — the year before she graduated. She learned fast and moved up the ranks, and then moved on to what she called Spooksville. She loved being a CIA undercover agent, up until a year ago — until her husband's death and the incident in Cuba. Her work in New York as an architect and designer was an excellent cover. She was taking a leave of absence, but now Max was coming for her.

Central Park hummed with activity outside her window. Max's call reawakened her to a life she was trying to forget. This was the part that caught in her throat, shoving down what she really wanted to say to Max. The danger excited her and she knew it, but she was not sure if she was ready. She let the phone stop ringing before making her decision. She dialed his phone number and logged into her laptop.

"Hello, Max," she said softly into the phone. "Haven't talked to you since John's accident." She pushed the speakerphone button and grabbed the pen on top of the classified document.

"I've got an undercover assignment for you."

"Yes, I know. I read the file."

"Will you take it?"

The computer screen in front of her filled with images.

"I don't know."

"It is time to move on."

"I am not so sure." As she scrolled down, a photo of a handsome man came into view—not really her type. Next to him, a jockey held onto the reins of a sleek black horse. "Who is the person of interest?"

"Miles Bourke, thirty-five-year-old bachelor, privately educated, and one of the wealthiest thoroughbred racehorse owners in Ireland and France."

"Young for all that," she said. She scrolled to another image. "I see a thoroughbred horse in one of the photos." Max knew she knew and loved horses. He was well acquainted with all of her weaknesses—he had trained her.

"It's Midnight Madness, his most expensive horse. That's Lucre—his private racetrack in Blacksod, on the west coast of Ireland."

She continued scrolling. The next image pictured fans in the background of the racetrack, waving programs and pointing at the horses on the track. "Quite the state-of-the-art racetrack. Who builds something like that along a seashore?"

"Like I said—lots of money in the Bank of Ireland—a Euro billionaire. His buyers include sheiks, princes, international breeders, U.S. 'big boys'—you name it. But… it's more involved than that. That's why I called you."

"I've been out of the spy business for almost a year." She stared at the beautiful black horse, the man, and the racetrack. Her instincts were good and she saw beyond the photograph. He'd sent her the image for a reason, and she knew it. Clever Max, she thought.

"We've got a situation. You are the best person for the job."

"I'm taking time off, since Cuba and …"

"I know, but you were never discharged. And you owe me," he said in a firm tone. "It's simply a listening and gathering information operation."

"Right." He was playing her.

"Take a look at the next picture," he said in a gentle tone.

"What happened? This is sickening."

She could not take her eyes off the sleek thoroughbred racehorse sprawled on its side on the racetrack—black, dead eyes staring out at her, white foam seeping from its nose and dripping onto the dirt. Its back knees were buckled under its belly while the front legs jutted out at odd angles. A jockey, dressed in full bright colors, wiped his hand across tears streaking down his dirty face as he knelt near the horse's head, rubbing the steed's regal neck.

"The official verdict is 'milkshaking.' It's an energy boost injected in the horse's nostril before the race to make him run faster."

"Like athletes on steroids?"

"Yes, but the effects are lethal."

"What kind of psycho would do that to a horse?" She leaned closer to the computer screen. She could see veins popped out on the horse's neck. Horrified, she scrolled down, removing the scene from her view.

"We don't know, but we want to find out. The horse was running in first place at the Kentucky Derby until this happened. Never made the finish line and dropped dead in front of all the fans. Saudi Arabian Sheik Abdulla had a lot of money riding on that horse. Bourke sold it to him, but he said he had no part in the injections. The sheik is seeking revenge for his dead horse. Not a good situation, especially on U.S. soil."

Maimed horses—she didn't know if she had the stomach for it. She attended charity events to raise funds to protect horses. This was too much to imagine. She couldn't stand animal abuse. Max knew he'd hooked her with all this horrible background information—damn him. "Is there more?"

"Same thing happened at the *Abu Dhabi Irish Guinness Festival.* The Irish and the Emirati come together—over money, that is. A lot of money changes hands—a lot more than we've been led to believe. That horse really suffered. And..."

"I bet it did," she said in a hard tone. "What else?"

"There was another 'milkshaking' incident in Ireland. Bourke's horse was running in the *United Arab Emirates Cup*. His purebred Arabian horse stumbled to its knees, throwing the rider over his head in the last leg of the race."

The bitter scene rose up in front of her. She pressed him to continue. "What happened? Could they save the horse?"

"Its knees buckled to the ground as the jockey cleared his leg from under him just before it rolled over. It was sweating and lathered behind the saddle; foam was oozing out of its mouth. It died a few minutes later."

"Who does this?" Pushing her chair back from her desk, she stood to relieve the tension in her back. The graphic scene was too much for her. She had to find a way to stop it.

"They shot him on the track in front of the crowd— same action as in the other incident. The race committee was shocked. Fans were screaming and out of control, so the officials had to shut down the race." He liked telling it so much he ran his words together at Mach speed.

"Okay, I get it. What do you want *me* to do?" she said, making no effort to hide the anger in her tone.

"Take the assignment. Get to the bottom of it, and find out who is doing it. Stop it."

"How?"

"We have the tools and the technology. I can fill you in on all the details later. We operate under contract for a private agency: National Operations Venture Advancement Systems—NOVAS. We have a silent agreement with the CIA."

"A new title but the same business?"

"Yes, unofficially and off the record. We don't exist. You know the drill."

"Yes, I do, unfortunately." Slipping a loose dark hair behind her ear, Laine looked at the photos again. Poor defenseless creatures, she thought.

"What's my agenda?" Her muscles tensed.

"We want you to stay on Bourke's island. It's fifteen minutes' flying time from Blacksod to Blackrock. Bourke's seventy-year-old caretakers, Eamon and his wife Patricia, live there with him."

Again, the injured, doomed horses burned images in her mind. "I got it. You know I have a weak spot for horses." Anger replaced the nauseous feeling in her stomach. She could make a difference by stopping the abuse.

Focusing on her laptop, she noted the aerial view of Bourke's island; she saw thick forests trailing along the black rock cliffs behind the cottage. The Atlantic was a rough, choppy sea of green surrounding the island. The cottage, lighthouse and helicopter pad were situated near the northwest forested area near the cliffs. It was isolated. She memorized it.

"You'll be undercover. Bourke wants to renovate his lighthouse. He knows you are an internationally renowned architectural designer, so it's perfect. You can do both. Design a party room. Listen for information that might lead us to a killer or killers in the horseracing business. How you get it is up to you."

"When do I start?"

"We got Bourke's confirmation today. He hired you to redesign a party room in his lighthouse tower on the island."

"Today?" Laine said in an angry voice. "In case you've forgotten, I need to practice at the gun range. I've been out of the business for almost a year, since John's accident."

"Call it what you want, but it was not an accident."

CHAPTER 3

MANHATTAN

"It was an accident, Max. How can you say that? My husband was the number one solo sailor in Michigan. He knew Lake St. Clair."

She remembered the first time they met—at a charity event in New York. She liked what she saw. John Rafferty was dressed in black tie, a triple-starched white dress shirt, and sporting a red and black-striped bow tie; he looked like a movie star. Long, dark hair curling over the collar of his jacket framed a suntanned face and dreamy blue eyes. Instead of sipping champagne, he drank Scotch.

During the bidding of the live auction, Laine went back and forth with him on an expensive lithograph until she won it. He congratulated her on the buy, smooth talking the way she liked it. She'd needed the attention back then, she thought. She was a lonely target after her parents died in the plane crash—not herself, the covert operative, but a needy woman searching for love. John gave her his dazzling smile and offered to take her to dinner. Sardi's restaurant was his favorite. They went, but she'd paid the bill when he discovered his wallet was missing.

Max was waiting. Giving her time to think.

"So what did you find out that you aren't telling me?"

"That's another story for another day."

"I would prefer to talk about it now."

"Are you sure you can handle it?" Max said.

"I can handle it."

"Your boat was smashed on the rocks in the shallow part of the South Channel near Squirrel Island in Canada."

"Tell me something I don't know."

"The Border Patrol and the Coast Guard combed Lake St. Clair for over a month. There was no body—no trace of any foul play. Nothing. They did everything they could to find his body."

"I know all that."

"Even NOVAS came up empty-handed. We combed the area for over a week right after it happened. I never told you because I wanted you to put it behind you."

"I see."

"We sent in divers and planes from Selfridge Air Force base. They used head sensors looking for clues. No John— no trace of him, or anything else for that matter."

"It doesn't make sense."

"There's a cover-up and your husband is part of it. It was no accident, so that's why there's no body. The boat was wiped clean of fingerprints. Your husband planned it."

"You're wrong. There's got to be another answer. He had everything—including my money."

Or did he? she wondered. Thinking back, she realized he had conned her down the aisle six months after they met at the charity auction in Manhattan. His easy manner and carefree style were deceptive—the actor always "on." In the beginning, he was a lot of fun, but what a surprise to find out on their honeymoon he had no job—zero in savings. He told her his identity had been stolen, and he was working it out. He said he was living at a friend's place while he was looking for a new condo. It was all a ruse. Later, she found out there was no condominium—just a room in a bed and breakfast in Yonkers. She confronted him about the lie, but he had a million excuses—and a lot of unpaid bills.

"He couldn't be that bad—fake his own death. Come on."

"I see it differently. He didn't tell you what was going on half the time. He was a con artist. Womanizing, gambling, drinking, lying, running through your money—"

"Yes, his debts were horrendous. I found out so much of it after he died, but this—"

"You have a good memory. Think about it."

"I trusted him. Shame on me. I'm in the business to know things. I didn't even know my own husband."

"We can't know everything. Some people are good at hiding their true self. There were things you couldn't know. Don't beat yourself up over it."

"You're right, Max."

"This assignment is good for you."

She pondered that for a moment. "It may be what I need. I'm fine." She gazed out her window. Droplets of water slid down the pane, making zigzagging trails on the glass.

"A few questions, if you don't mind," Max said. "I have to ask."

"Yes."

"The Coast Guard confirmed the place where your boat was found. It's the drop-off point for drugs coming into the United States and Canada. Did John ever mention anything about drugs?"

"No. This is the first I've heard about it."

"Did you ever suspect he took drugs or sold them?"

"That would be a stretch even for him. Womanizing and drinking—yes. He was a conniving and convincing hustler—but drug dealer? Definitely no."

But...what if she was wrong?

"I had to ask," he said in a low voice. "I know it's hard. The things we don't want to accept are hard to know."

"It's the nothingness that's hard to know."

"Yes. I'd like to brief you on the assignment. Are you ready?"

"I'm fine. It's clear to me what I have to do now. Go on."

"The lighthouse is Bourke's secondary residence. He owns a vast estate and a massive farm called Lucre along the west coast in County Mayo, not far from the island. Got a slew of expensive thoroughbred racehorses in Donegal. It's the perfect setup for money laundering and drug dealing."

"So you think Bourke's part of it?" She tried imagining the operation and being in Ireland — not so bad.

"That's what you'll be able to tell us."

"Okay."

"I am sending more photographs now."

She waited as they loaded.

"The satellite images are of Bourke's property where he keeps the horses. Note the racetrack, farmhouse and the stables. And of course, the horses."

"I'm impressed. Beautiful horses — hundreds of them."

"All for sale. He flies his helicopter back and forth to the island from the farm and also from Blacksod."

"Nice life."

A helicopter popped into view. Behind Bourke's farm was a sleek black Bell Jet Ranger 450. To the right of it, several barns sparkled white under red-shingled roofs. Stonewall fences penned in hundreds of grazing thoroughbred horses.

"If anyone can gain his confidence, it's you. You can design the plans for his party room in the lighthouse. Get close to him and find out what is going on behind the scene."

"Why focus on him?"

"He might have misappropriated funds from the sale of his horses, but it is unlikely, given his current financial standing. Could have skimmed off the top when he sold them — but it really doesn't make sense."

"You think there is some type of undercover operation going on?"

"All the information points to it. NOVAS was hired to find out who or what is behind it. There's a lot at stake. We're trying to keep our government out of the spotlight."

"What else have you found out?"

"Saudi Arabian Sheik Abdulla is upset over the 'milkshaking' incident at the Kentucky Derby. His prize horse died on the racetrack in front of the fans. He is also Bourke's wealthiest customer, and Bourke sold him the horse. He is making all sorts of accusations against Bourke and condemning the security at the Derby. The major newspapers are giving it a lot of press. We need to shut it down. It's destroying our relationship with the Saudi government."

"What's Bourke's take on it?"

"Bourke is giving it back to the sheik in no uncertain terms. The papers are full of their accusations against each other. It's a ro*yal* mess. Excuse the pun."

"He has a death wish then," she said, studying Bourke's angular jaw, chiseled cheekbones — a Marlborough cowboy type with an attitude.

She had been around plenty of those and avoided them. That was what made her husband John different — *or so she had thought*.

"We also discovered there is an American concern or an unknown person or persons interfering in the brokering of Bourke's horse sales. The numbers are not adding up. We dug deep to try to uncover a paper trail, but we are coming up empty-handed. Whoever did it was good at it."

"Right. They usually are."

"NOVAS accepted the contract and our government wants results, but technically we do not exist in an official capacity. On the political scene, it's of paramount importance for the U.S. to keep an open line of communication with the Saudi Arabian government. The 'milkshaking' incident looks like a strategic move to make the sheik look bad. The U.S. does not want to upset the ongoing negotiations with the Saudi government. A lot of money is invested in the horseracing business, and it brings the countries together somewhat like the Olympics. The sheik wants reassurance it won't happen again on U.S. soil. I can't emphasize how important this is."

"The horseracing business is a good place to set up this conflict between our governments, subject to even more pressures with the murder of an innocent horse."

"Yes, it is. We have to put a stop to it."

"Get in close to the source?"

"Yes, and that's where you come in."

"Go on."

"NOVAS has been conducting an undercover operation for several weeks near Bellmullet Peninsula in the Atlantic Ocean. They've been looking into our situation, but they haven't had any success. A group of scientists is conducting 'research' in that part of the Atlantic under the guise of protecting marine sanctuaries on the west coast of Ireland. They are under the cover of a special project to study the whales in the County Mayo area. The trawler is really a communication spy station. It carries high-tech electronic surveillance equipment designed to update us on new developments, but strong winds and seas have slowed our progress. It's not working.

"The prime minister of Ireland will give us whatever help we need, but again, we're not operating in an official capacity. We have to find out what is really going on inside the racing business, something we hope to do through Bourke's connections."

"I see." She focused on a photograph of several men with Bourke who were seated in the stern of a ninety-foot wooden Trumpy yacht. It was similar to one she had refurbished in the Florida Keys.

"You can do this," he said.

"Yes, I can. Murdered horses, drugs, money laundering, a Saudi sheik, a rich Irish gentleman—the whole works. Risky, if you ask me. I do not want another Cuba."

"None of us do."

"Make it worth my while."

"Already did. I tripled your fee. It's being wired into your Swiss bank account as we speak. Plus Bourke is paying top dollar for your design expertise."

"I see," she smiled. "You know how to charm a girl. Any new toys?"

"Absolutely. Techno has a kit for you. Show your gun at the airport. They will clear you. Also, check the false bottom in your luggage after you land. Everything you need is there."

"Who is my contact here?"

"I am. You'll brief me every couple of days."

"I've always had a handler."

"This is different, but we use the same procedure—a secure cell phone. Your code name is Labrador. Wait for my call. If something comes up, my number seven on the speed dial will connect you directly to me."

"Things have changed."

"Better technology, but we still need the on-site intelligence. Report to me every couple of days. Keep a low profile."

"Got it. When do I leave?"

"The car is scheduled to pick you up in half an hour. You leave from La Guardia airport and land in Donegal, Ireland, tomorrow morning. Bourke is picking you up at the airport. He has your picture—the one taken for the magazine feature."

"Okay. Who is my backup over there?"

"No one," he said. "You will be on your own."

CHAPTER 4

MANHATTAN STUDIO CONDOMINIUM

A fter hanging up the phone with Max, Laine pulled her 9mm Glock out of her desk drawer. She slid out the clip, loaded it and snapped it back into place in less than thirty seconds. She set the safety and slipped the pistol into her purse. If there was one thing she was good at, it was her talent for hitting the target. She was a top marksman and enjoyed practicing when she could, regardless of her time away from ops training.

She walked into the front hallway, opened the closet and pulled out her Louis Vuitton suitcase.

She carried the case into her bedroom and placed it on the bed. Walking over to her closet, she selected her black high heels and her black St. John's business suit. Next, she chose a coat, slacks, skinny jeans, sweaters, blouses and undergarments. She lined them up neatly in the case. In her bedroom, she gazed at several designer gowns from her closet and reached for one.

This will do, she thought. She put the tight-fitting black Chanel cocktail dress in the case along with the rest of her garments. From the rosewood jewelry box, she took her pearl necklace and earrings. She put them on and smeared clear lipstick on her lips. Next, she snuggled a Dior makeup traveling kit into the zipper compartment of her tote bag. To top off her attire, she sprayed herself with Coco Chanel, stashed the tiny bottle between her clothes in the suitcase, and zipped it.

After changing into her travel ensemble, Laine looked at herself in the mirror. The dark blue Ralph Lauren suit fit her perfectly—just right for the long flight.

Looking at her reflection in the mirror, she noticed the dark circles under her eyes. She dabbed on a little more makeup. It reminded her of her sleepless nights. Shaking her hair free, she swept the brush through her wavy dark hair.

The curtains on her bedroom window shut out the light from the street when she closed them. Next, she wheeled the zipped case out of the room into the center hallway and entered the living room. She turned down the air conditioner then closed the blinds facing the park. She grabbed her classified papers and placed them into the Michael Khors designer portfolio. The iPad Mini and Kindle were arranged in her tote, next to her weapon.

There was a loud knock on the door as she set the security timer on the alarm.

"Coming," she said. Running to the kitchen, she grabbed her favorite *Earl Grey* tea in a small tin. It slipped easily into her carry-on bag. At least I can practice my interior design skills in another country, she thought, and at the same time, help the horses.

On her way out the door, she snatched the picture of her husband John from the table and dropped it into the trash bin. She twisted her wedding ring off her finger and flung it there too. The door slammed tightly behind her as the man in the dark suit took her bags and handed her a secure cell phone.

CHAPTER 5

DONEGAL TOWN, IRELAND

After exchanging greetings in the airport, Laine and Miles Bourke sped out of Donegal airport in his white convertible Mercedes Benz toward Donegal Town. In a short time, they bounced over the cobblestone streets. As they passed the large stone fountain in the center of the square, water flowed from the top, over the edge of the second tiered bowl to the lower basin, and splashed onto the street. Water pooled around the stone base and seeped into the cracks. Pedestrians mingled on sidewalks and peered inside colorful shop windows under a cloudless blue sky.

Miles Bourke handled the car like a race driver. He glanced over at his passenger. "You are quite the designer. I read in *Architectural Digest* about the yacht you refurbished. I'd like you to take a look at my Trumpy," he said, shifting his gaze from Laine to the road ahead.

She noticed his strong hands gripping the wheel as he smoothly maneuvered the car through the narrow streets. "Sure," she said. She wondered if he really liked what she did or if he was trying to impress her. Max must have sent Bourke the magazine article, but he forgot to tell her. It bothered her. The little details like that could blow her cover.

As they drove slowly past the harbor, she noticed the charter boats lined up along the docks. "Good fishing here?"

"We're known for good fishing."

"I love to fish, and enjoy being out on the water."

"Fantastic. We'll pick a day and I'll take you salmon fishing."

"I'd like that," she said, studying the layout of the town. All she had to do was look and she could memorize it. It was the one thing she still had going for her.

He steered past a rustic place with a colorful blue-and-white-striped awning over an outdoor deck facing the marina. The upper deck was jammed with people who were laughing and singing with a small group of Irish musicians. Down by the dock entrance, the sign *Donahue's Pub* hung loosely on chains from a wood beam. People flooded into the lower bar to sit at iron tables, drinking and eating.

"A drink, dinner, and the harbor view are things you might enjoy later in the week at Donahue's Pub. We bring our freshly caught salmon to the chef and he whips up his own recipe for it. Never had a bad meal there."

"I'd like that," she said. "Speaking of salmon fishing, we catch freshwater salmon in Michigan. I used to fish with my father during the summer months on Lake Huron."

"I fished with my father too, as a lad, but I've never had freshwater salmon—only saltwater salmon. Do you like it?" he said, navigating the car through the crowded street.

"Yes, very much so." She laughed and patted his arm in a friendly manner. She felt the strength of his muscles and quickly removed her hand. She was warming up to him.

"On another note, I've gone over the photos of your lighthouse, emailed to my office. I've been toying with the design of the window that faces east. We need to increase the size. Let in the light."

"Good idea," he said as they drove to the end of town near the church.

It was warm and the breeze felt good to her. "I am enjoying the many varieties of architecture in this town."

"And so it is, quite varied. We're passing St. Patrick's on your right — tourists come from all over the world to see *that* architecture." As they drove past it, the Sunday church bells chimed. Parishioners were grouped in front of the church, listening to the heavy bells tolling from the tower.

"It sounds beautiful."

"Aye. Legend says Christ showed St. Patrick an entrance to hell on that very spot, before the church was built.

"Oh, my God!" Laine said. "It can't be."

"That it is," said Miles, as they sped past it and headed out of town.

"No, I mean…stop the car! Please stop!"

He braked and pulled over to the side of the narrow road just out of town. "What's the matter?"

"This is crazy, but I think I saw my husband in front of the church."

Miles stared at her. "Your husband?"

"Yes, I think he saw me too." She spun partway around in the seat, but the seatbelt stopped her from looking back. Then it was too late because the road behind them had twisted around the bend, blocking her view.

"I'm not sure I understand."

"No, you wouldn't. How could you?"

"Want to talk about it?"

"I thought I saw my husband with a woman. It gave me a shock."

"I'm sure it did," he said, shoving blond hair from his forehead. "Want to go back?" He began to turn the wheel, but she put her hand on his and stopped him.

"No, give me a minute."

Creases lined her forehead. She stared at the farmland flanking either side of the road. Tall green hedges and low stone walls surrounded hundreds of sheep that were marked with blue and red stripes, peacefully grazing within the enclosures. It was a trick she learned on the job—focus on something else, then make a decision. She had to pull herself together or he would think she was crazy. "I must be mistaken."

"I'm listening." Unbuckling his seat belt, he turned off the ignition and leaned toward her.

"I'm not sure how to begin, so I'll just say it. My husband died in a boating accident in Michigan—a year ago." She felt her muscles tense. She was on full alert and her training kicked in. *Remain calm. Modulate your voice.*

"I'm sorry for your loss."

"Thank you. It doesn't make sense. I couldn't have seen John."

"It is puzzling. Maybe the man you saw resembled your husband." He took her hand in his hand and held it firmly. "Things are not always what they seem."

"You're right." She saw the man in her mind. *I'm certain that was John.*

"No worries. We can be back in town in a few minutes." He continued holding her hand. His eyes captured her face.

"No, I have to be imagining it. Let's go on. Like you said, the man I saw looked like him." She felt the warmth of his hand and something stirred inside her. She let go of his hand, opened the car door, and climbed out.

This is confusing. Why would John be in Donegal? If he were alive.

Miles was looking at her, expecting something. She had to shake herself out of it. He was staring at her.

"I'm fine."

He walked around the car and stood next to her. "Mind telling me what happened?"

"I don't really know. He went solo sailing and I never saw him again." She twisted a strand of her dark hair. His gaze was comforting, but she knew her place — the operation loomed above everything else. She looked away from his comforting blue eyes.

"That's troubling." He took a step toward her.

"Yes, but I'm fine." She wanted to forget, but the painful memories exploded inside her head. "Really, I'm OK." She leaned against the car and moved a short distance away from him.

Now coming down the road, an elderly sheepherder tipped his tweed cap, while his walking stick tapped the road. A feisty dog raced alongside him barking at the sheep to herd them into place.

Miles nodded at him and turned back to her, waiting for her to continue.

The mass of animals and the man slowly eased past their car parked on the narrow road in the shadow of the trees.

Laine was happy for the distraction and took her time to think about what she would say. "It's hard to tell what happened to him."

"I'm a good listener," he said.

She watched Miles watching her as he leaned toward her, interested in what she had to say. A cold thought came to her. She could gain his trust and get something from him in return later on. Max's voice echoed in her mind: *Get the intel.* This decision was going to be a calculated guess on her part, but she'd give it a try.

"It may help to tell it."

"Yes, it may. John disappeared in a sailboat accident a year ago. He was sailing in the South Channel near Squirrel Island in Canada. That's across the lake from where I live."

The memories sickened her. She looked away from him, blinking back tears, and continued. "The hull was smashed to pieces on the shallow rocks near the shoreline. There was no body, life jacket, wallet, money, or clothes. Not even keys. The whole thing is strange. It doesn't make sense to me. The United States Border Patrol and the Coast Guard were called in. They ruled out foul play. The Canadian authorities weren't any help either. He just disappeared... without a trace."

Miles leaned back on the car next to her. He nodded his interest, urging her to go on.

She felt her pulse quicken. "He sailed alone a lot. There was no sign of a struggle or any proof he had even been in the area where they found my boat. He told me he was going solo sailing a few days before it happened. We were going to do it together, but things changed. It was like that with him. Nothing was ever consistent."

She wondered if she had given too much information by the way Miles looked at her—caring, compassionate. She was not used to anyone like that.

"Does seem strange," he said in a gentle voice.

"Maybe he got knocked in the head with the boom—fell overboard and got caught in the current. It could carry him all the way to Detroit and no one would ever know." She turned toward him.

"Hard to say, but I know currents can be tricky," he said.

"The officials gave up the search. So did I."

"Sorry for your loss."

"Thank you. It's hard to lose someone you love. We were married for only a short time. It still hurts to think about it."

"Yes."

"I didn't really know him like I thought I did—seems I didn't know him at all. There's no resolution."

"It's hard to know someone." They stared into each other's eyes for a moment.

"Yes, especially since we lived in different cities. I worked in my studio in New York. Flying back and forth to our home in Grosse Pointe wasn't ideal."

"Sounds like you led separate lives."

"We did. I was busy with work. When I had time off, he wanted to party all the time—big drinker. Not my kind of life."

"It can be a curse. The drinking, that is."

"Yes."

Should I tell him? She plunged on. "I asked him for a divorce a few days before he went missing."

Miles shifted his gaze away from her, quiet for a moment. "How did he take it?"

"Don't think he really cared. Partied with his friends and drank more Scotch at the club."

"Not a nice man."

"The marriage had been over for a long time. But drowning—I wouldn't wish that on anyone."

He held her eyes with his. "Loss from a death is permanent. It's the one thing we can't take back."

"I never saw him again after that last conversation." She surprised herself at how comfortable she was, telling him her tragic story. "I thought taking this job would help me forget the past, but when I saw that man in town, it all came back to me. I'm sorry to burden you."

She wanted to win him over, even if it was the truth. This was something new to her—she was not used to the feeling.

"Sometimes we need to get it out. The bad things that are making us sick."

"Yes, the bad things seem to take up all the space."

"Aye, that they do."

They stood for a few minutes in silence.

"A change of view may take your mind off things."

"Good, I could do with a change."

Dark, thick clouds hovered in the west. She kept her eyes on the trees in the fields, bending under the wind, scraggly, and broken in parts. The clouds above them grew ever darker.

"You should decide what you want to do. I've got a Bell 505 Jet Ranger — safest helicopter made — waiting to take us to the island, or we could go back to town. Check things out. It's up to you."

"We should be on our way. Looks like we have weather coming in."

"Right," he said and opened the door for her. "That we do."

He went to his side of the car, climbed inside, and left the shadow of the trees. "Down the coastline road, not far ahead, we'll come to the helicopter launch pad in Blacksod. Beat the weather, if we're lucky."

The road ahead curved and twisted through the lush green hills of farmland bordering the Atlantic Ocean.

"Yes, if we're lucky." She felt the wind shift. It chilled the air.

Miles is a different kind of man than the type I know, she thought. There is something about him I've never experienced. I have to watch myself — concentrate on the job — I can't let my emotions get the best of me.

CHAPTER 6

FLIGHT TO BLACKROCK ISLAND

In a short time, Miles swerved into the Blacksod Lighthouse parking lot and pulled into an area near the helicopter launch pad. He went around to the other side of the car and opened the door for Laine.

"It's ten minutes to the island from here," he said, lifting the luggage from the boot.

Laine's eyes widened as she followed him to the sleek white helicopter. "We're not taking *that!*"

"We are," he laughed. "I picked it up yesterday. It's a Bell 505 Jet Ranger X." He stored the luggage in the helicopter compartment.

"It's gorgeous!"

"I have had others, but this is the newest one in the group. What drew me to it was the unobstructed visibility from the cockpit. It's spectacular. It does 125 knots, giving it a fuel range of 350 miles." He helped her in.

"I can't get over how well-designed it is." She could see the reflection of her face in the tinted glass windows of the gleaming cabin. She smoothed her windswept hair back over her shoulders. The egg-shaped cockpit was open to the sky and the surrounding area. She turned toward her pilot. "It's remarkable."

"Aye, that it is. All leather—in any color you want. I prefer a white interior." He eased in closer to her, pointing to the flat floor. "More leg room in the back, too."

"Can't wait for us to go up in it." She saw Miles looking at her with quiet awareness. It was the best equipment she had ever seen, and she had seen plenty on her undercover assignments. The gauges were top notch. She nodded, smiling at him with new respect.

"I'll take you for a ride along the coast, but not today."

"Sounds good. I've had a few flying lessons, but I've never flown one of these—not that I've had *that* many lessons." She suppressed her excitement. Her undercover flight training was current, and this was one of the helicopters she had wanted to fly. It would be easy for her. But that would remain her secret.

"You fly?" His eyebrows shot up in astonishment.

"A little. I learned a long time ago. I haven't kept up my license, but this makes me want to renew it." It was a lie, but it would make sense to him. She gave him an encouraging look.

"We can work on that. I am a licensed instructor." He took a step toward her and she could smell his cologne. "I logged a thousand hours of flight time over the last ten years. Those were the days. Flying took my mind off business."

"I bet you're an excellent instructor. I am ready to go if you are." Her eyes penetrated his and she liked what she saw. There was a genuine softness in those bright blue eyes that seemed to look inside her—making her feel emotions she had not felt in a long time. She broke his gaze and abruptly turned away, climbing into the cockpit.

"All set?"

"Yes."

He didn't seem to notice the change in her demeanor and kept talking while she fastened the harness. He waited next to her seat to help her, if she needed it. "A few of us from town took flying lessons many years ago. There was Wilfrid, Tommy, Marla…"

He stopped talking. A blank look covered his face.

She could see he was remembering something. His face turned hard. She cautioned herself to keep the conversation going. She wanted to hear about the townspeople, but it could wait. Changing the subject, she said, "Do you work a lot?"

"Too much. I enjoy breeding and selling the horses, but at times, it is all-consuming."

He was quiet now, contemplating something.

"Then it's time to change it. Live the life you want."

He laughed and closed her door.

In these few moments, she knew something was off. Taking a small notebook from her pocket, she scribbled the word "townspeople" on the page. While he climbed into his side of the helicopter, she quickly put away the notebook.

Miles flipped switches, punched buttons. "Patricia and Eamon, my caretakers, will have dinner for us on the island. They practically raised me like second parents." He was back to his jovial self.

"I'm looking forward to meeting them." She adjusted herself in the seat.

"I see rain," he said, looking west.

"Yes." She pulled on her headset. "I'm ready."

"We're off."

He continued checking the instrument panel and flipped more switches. His skilled hands manipulated the flight instruments as they lifted off the launch pad and headed toward the island.

She noted his skills were honed to perfection when he expertly maneuvered the controls. Liking what she saw, she relaxed.

The flight was enjoyable as they soared over the dark green Atlantic Ocean. Under the gray clouds and buffeted by high winds, the small aircraft bounced along.

Miles interrupted her thoughts. "If you look below, you can see whales and dolphins."

"I spotted them a few minutes ago." She spoke through her microphone in an excited voice.

"Lovely they are."

"What a nice surprise." Scanning the water, she saw rolls of dark skin emerge from the waves then disappear.

"A grand treat for you today."

"Yes, it's fine. Just fine. Fine as anything can be."

Miles reached over and gave her arm a squeeze, but she gently pulled away. Taking her cell phone from her pocket, she turned toward the window to photograph the dolphins vaulting out of the water alongside the whales. They shot upward out of the rough sea and quickly nosedived back into it. The white crests of waves crashed over their tails as they slipped below the surface. Shortly, they surfaced again, leaping high in the air and arcing their way back into the water. The whales ignored them as they rolled along in the ocean.

"We'll be there shortly," said Miles.

"I'm going to enjoy designing the party room in your lighthouse."

"That's how I feel about it myself, so it is. Whatever you need will be made available for you."

"A deal is a deal," she said in a quiet voice. She continued snapping pictures of the whales and now the lighthouse, which she spied a short distance away.

Her thoughts were clear. Memories of John returned to her from earlier that day. There was no doubt. She knew it was her husband. He was alive and well. What happened to him on the lake at home? Why didn't he contact her? Why would he want to disappear, to have the world think him dead?

She would have to find answers to those questions — and more — but be careful not to involve Miles. Her first phone call would be to Max. She could do nothing to check on her husband's personal records at home, but Max could. She wanted him to find the trail that would lead her to him in Ireland. He wouldn't be able to hide for long now that she knew he was alive — in this new life he was living without her.

Anything that would give her a clue, to make him want to disappear from her life, was going to be her number-one priority. Passports, banking accounts, bills, and anything she may have ignored after his "death" — and before it — would be thoroughly examined until she found something — whatever he was hiding.

She would start by asking and listening to people in town when she was with Miles. John would not get away with whatever he was mixed up in without her finding out — she was sure of it.

Her anger turned to pure, cold-blooded hatred at being duped — he was not going to get away with it. She would find him soon enough — make him talk — whether he liked it or not. She set her mind to it, thinking she couldn't wait to find him again. Nothing was going to stop her from learning the truth.

CHAPTER 7

DONEGAL TOWN SQUARE

"What the hell, Marla, I saw *her*," John said. "*My wife, Laine!* What's she doing in Donegal?" He ran his hand through his dark shock of wavy hair. "Give me a cigarette. Maybe she knows I'm alive." He lit the cigarette, drew a deep breath and sent out a smoke ring. "This is the worst. I can't believe it."

"You're imagining things," Marla said, high heels clicking as they walked down the street to his old Ford truck. "You read your own obituary to me, Johnny—*John Rafferty*—died on Clair Lake… or whatever it said. She had a memorial for you, didn't she? Good thing you changed your name to Jack Lafferty."

"She's a lot smarter than you think, Marla, and it is Lake St. Clair." He rubbed his chin, looking at the place where the car went by him with her in it. "I know her. She's here for some reason." He inhaled and blew another ring.

"So what if she is 'smart'?" Marla leaned in and gave him a peck on the cheek. "We can take care of that."

John liked the way she bent into him, kissing him, smelling good. He threw his arm over her shoulder as they walked to the car. "What do you mean? Take care of what?"

"Take care of her," she said in a soft, low tone. "You've got a plan. I know you do. And I'm the one who is going to help you with it. We'll have to see where she's staying. That was Bourke's Mercedes she was in, so she can't be too far away."

"Hold on, Marla. I don't have a plan. I don't know what you're thinking, but it can't be good. Can it?"

He dropped his arm and turned to face her. He thought back to when they'd been together for a few hours this morning — those long legs and soft lips.

She noticed his eyes moving up and down her body. "Are you listening to me? Pay attention to what I am saying. Yes, it will be good. You'll see. Give it some time. You always come up with something."

"Yeah, I'll think of something." He turned, pulling her into him in an embrace.

"Not here." She forcefully shoved him away. "Look how you handled that overblown sheik. He'll be eating out of your hand on the next horse sale."

"Yeah, I was pretty clever, wasn't I?" He shrugged, flipping his cigarette to the ground.

"You sure were. How many races did he win with that horse you sold him a few months ago?" She took his hand, squeezed it, and quickly let it go.

"Three races I know of. Yeah, you're right. Lots. He won piles of money. That sheik owes me now."

"He does. And you made a fat commission on it, too. It will keep us for at least a year. Don't screw this up."

"A year! Marla, are you nuts? It will keep us for five years after the money I skimmed off the top. The sheik will never figure it out. I am the best broker in Ireland."

"Yes, you are. Let's keep it that way."

"It was easy. The next one will be even easier. I know exactly how to play him. Heard there's some action with the horses in Mexico."

"Mexico?"

"Yeah, they need good brokers. I'm the best, so I have been working on an angle. If I can get a Mexican connection, we can make a lot of dough. Made a ton on that sheik and he's good for more, but I have to expand. Keep things moving and keep it going."

"Yes, that's true. Good thing you stashed the last sale money in a safe bank," she said, climbing into the truck.

He slung his body into the driver's seat. "Wiring the money into that Swiss bank account of yours was brilliant. They'll never find out. It's not even in my name."

"I did what you asked me to do. It was all your idea. You're the mastermind." Marla pulled out her cigarettes and offered him one. "It's our little secret."

"Yeah, I am the mastermind, aren't I? Let's go back to my house—think up a new plan. Have a little fun."

Jack pulled into the street and headed north along the coast. The clouds hung low above the horizon, blocking out the sun.

"I'll come up with something. Maybe we can get rid of her. Scare her into leaving." He flicked the cigarette ash out of the window, smiling as he drove.

"I knew you'd think of something." She pulled down the car visor. Looking into the mirror, she ran her fingers through her long blond hair. Grabbing the tube of red lipstick from her bag, she carefully swept it across her full lips. "Drive fast, Jack, I can't wait. Remember, I have to be home early today. My mother is sick. I wish I didn't have to go home to let the caregiver go. We only have a few hours."

"Yeah, I know. You told me over and over."

"It's the way it is."

"We'll figure something out. Laine is not going to mess up our plans. I've got a lot of money at stake in my business here. She's in the way now, but not for long." He jammed the accelerator to the floor.

"That's how I like you to think. Straight ahead." Marla watched the road from her rear view mirror. No one was following them to Jack's place.

CHAPTER 8

A YEAR EARLIER
GROSSE POINTE, MICHIGAN

John paced in front of the window. It was a fine day for sailing. "I'm going by myself, Laine. I'm sailing alone. We'll celebrate your birthday on another day." He gazed through the window at the lake.

"No, I don't think so, John. I haven't been happy with us for a long time. I've decided...I want a divorce."

"Yeah, right. You'll get over it. It's only a birthday — we'll find an hour to go when you're in Grosse Pointe for longer than one night." He hung up on her.

Laine stared at the phone. Maybe things could have been different if they'd worked harder on their marriage, but not anymore. Thinking back, she realized they had grown apart. She also admitted to herself that she was totally frustrated with his smooth talking. His outrageous social behavior at the yacht club was an embarrassment. Enough is enough, she thought. She didn't know how to describe how she felt, but she was clear on one thing. It was over. She'd call a divorce attorney on Monday.

"Bitch," he said as he slammed the phone on the table. He felt like saying worse to her but held back, shrugged it off. She would get over it—she always did. Now he poured Scotch from the crystal decanter. Gazing again at Lake St. Clair, he slugged it down. It made him feel good. It always did.

It would be a wonderful sail—alone, without her. Maybe he'd sail up to Port Huron and do a little fishing. Have some fun.

The doorbell rang.

"Damn it," he muttered. "Who could that be?" He stomped to the door and flung it open. His eyes took in an elderly, white-haired man holding a small suitcase. "What do you want?"

"Sorry to bother you, but is this Laine Sullivan's home?"

"It is." John heard an accent in the man's voice. His sport coat was worn at the elbows. Standing on the front porch of their French provincial house, he looked like a man who knew his business. Maybe he was selling something. He did not have time to listen to a sales pitch.

"Um," the man hesitated. "I've come to see her."

"She's not here. Who are you? Or should I say what are you selling?"

"Not a thing. I'm her Uncle Norbert Sullivan. From Ireland, I am."

"Oh yeah? Laine's never mentioned any relative in ... where'd you say?"

"Ireland. She's never met me."

John leaned against the doorjamb. "Oh?" Interesting.

"May I come in?"

"Why not?" He stepped aside and motioned him into the house. It struck him funny that this old man had come to see his wife, claiming to be related to her. He wondered how long he would be taking up his time. The wind might die down before too long and he would miss the best part of the day. "This way," John's voice slurred.

Norbert set his bag near the door and took off his cap. John watched him eye the marble foyer, suspended spiral staircase leading to the second floor, the intricate French railings, and crystal chandelier.

"I was having a drink. Want one?"

"Sure, I might as well. I was up all night. Can never sleep on planes."

John led him to the library and the bar, where he chose a crystal tumbler from the shelf. "Neat or with ice?"

"Neat is grand." Norbert admired the mahogany bookcases, an authentic Louis XV antique desk, and leather chairs. "'Tis a beautiful home you have here, lad."

"It's Laine's home, actually. I moved in after we got married — guess it's *our* home."

"I didn't know she'd married."

"About a year and a half ago — maybe more. Who knows, these days?"

Norbert stared at him, saying nothing, frowning.

"Take a seat." He pressed the drink into his hand and grinned. John sat and threw his feet on the polished coffee table, slumping into the chair opposite him. "What can I do for you?"

"When can I see her?" He sipped the drink, looking at John's deck shoes, and waited.

"Another week or so. She's in New York finishing some project. There's always some project — she's never home. I guess she is designing the inside of a yacht or something. I can't keep track."

"Feckit. I came to the States expecting to see her. Didn't know she worked in New York — could've flown there instead of coming here to Michigan." He stood up, wrung his hands, as if waiting for her to walk into the room.

"She has a studio apartment on Park and Fifth. Hardly ever see her myself. Relax, relax and finish your drink. You can always go to New York, if you really want to see her."

"I suppose I could get the next flight out."

"I suppose you could."

Norbert sat again and picked up his drink from the table, eyes squinting in thought. "I wish I'd known. I came to give her a present—surprise her. I should have called before I left Donegal. I have a ticket home day after tomorrow."

"No problem. I can give it to her."

"It's most important that *I* give it to her."

"I can tell her it's from you." John emptied his glass, got up and refilled it at the bar.

John eyed Norbert and watched him mumble to himself. "Can you tell me what it is?" He threw back a large slug of Scotch and swished it around inside his mouth. It made him feel good.

Norbert thought a moment. "You look like a sound man."

"Laine trusted me enough to marry me."

"Ah, sure. I suppose I could mail it to her in New York, but I should give it to her in person. I want to make sure she gets it." He rubbed a finger over his upper lip and looked over at John again. "How about you give me her address before I leave?"

"No need to do that. Whatever it is will be safe with me." John walked to him, topped off his glass, splashing some of it on the end table.

"I suppose you're right. It seems a long way to come for nothing. I *wish* I'd known she wouldn't be here." He sighed while he stretched out his long legs and sipped the drink.

"I'll tell her you were here. She'll be sorry she missed you."

"Possibly, but we've never met. Her father and I were brothers, you see. We had a misunderstanding. That's why he left Ireland and I stayed there in our family home." Reaching inside the breast pocket of his suit coat, he pulled out a fat white envelope. "'Twas a long time ago. Laine is the last of our family line. I want her to have this." He opened the document and smoothed it on his knee.

"What is it?" John was very interested in the old man now. A document could mean only one thing—*money*—a *lot* of money.

"A deed for her property in Ireland." He handed it to John.

"Property? Laine has never mentioned property." He grabbed it a little too quickly. He'd have to lighten up or the old man might get suspicious.

"Aye. She doesn't know she has it. I'm giving it to her." He straightened in his chair, drank a little more of the liquor.

"Where is this property?" John was feeling happy now. Better than he had in days.

"Blacksod—on the west coast of Ireland. Not far from Donegal—if you know where that is."

"Vaguely. How much property?"

"Oh, quite a lot along the coastline. Enough to secure her future, so it will."

John skimmed through the pages, devouring the contents. "This is a very generous gift. Nice of you to give it to her."

"Look at me, lad," Norbert said with a chuckle. "I'm an old man. I don't have many years left, no kin save Laine. And like I said, she is the end of the Sullivan line. The property rightfully belongs to her—not to the State, where it would revert if I didn't give it to her."

"I couldn't agree more," John said, concealing a smile. "I'll put it in the safe, if you want to leave it here for her." He popped up from the chair with the deed and went behind the bar, before the old man could change his mind.

"That's grand."

He slid a large photograph to the left, exposing the safe. He crooked his thumb toward the picture. "This is Laine's sailboat crossing the finish line during the Port Huron to

Mackinac Island Sailing Race. Her boat took first place. I was the navigator. It was a spectacular finish. The blast from the cannon echoed throughout the harbor in the early morning when we crossed the finish line. We beat all the records."

"'Tis a fine day, so it was, for you."

John was feeling fine. "Sailing is hard work. Too bad Laine couldn't be there for it. Working." He dialed the safe's combination, opened it, and slipped the deed inside. "Done," he said, slamming the door and readjusting the photo. He realized he might have said too much by the look on Norbert's face, so he added a small lie. "They put her name on a trophy at the club. She was really pleased."

"I see. Well, it is time I should be on my way." Norbert struggled from his seat. "Thanks for the jar."

John remained silent a moment. He could not let him leave before he found out more about the property. "What are your plans for the weekend, now that you've delivered the deed?"

"None. I thought I'd be spending it with her. My ticket home is not till Monday night." He started toward the foyer. "Can you call me a cab?"

"If you want one." John gulped down his drink. "Say, Norbert, I was about to go for a sail. Why don't you join me? Yeah, since Laine is not here, why not go? You don't leave for a few days anyway. C'mon."

"Sounds tempting, but I should really be —"

"The boat is at the yacht club down the street," he said, blocking the front door. "It's fitted out for a short cruise and ready to go. I was going by myself for a couple of days, but it would be much nicer with company." He thought about how he had just told Laine he wanted to go alone — what a joke on her. He had stepped into a gold mine — he'd take the old man sailing — what a sail it would be. To hell with her — he had the deed to the land now. Property in Ireland she knew nothing about. "Well, what will it be?"

Norbert said, "I don't swim. Wouldn't be much help to you."

"We're not going swimming, we're going sailing. Besides, I can take care of that. Plenty of life jackets aboard."

"You looking for company, are you?"

"I am." A thought occurred to him. He might be able to get more information from him about the land. All the things he wanted were at his fingertips — his hatred of Laine burned inside him — she wouldn't get rid of him as easily as she thought she would. He would get rid of her! Funny how it was going to work out after all — he saw it clearly.

Then, the old man spoke quietly to him, bringing him back to the moment. "I don't have the clothes for sailing, lad. I didn't expect to stay but a few days."

"You'll be back in time to catch your plane. It's only for the weekend. What time do you leave?"

Norbert fumbled in his inside coat pocket, pulling out his glasses and his ticket. "Looks like I leave Monday night, half nine. Me friend Margaret's pickin' me up when I land. Usually I call her when I change my plans. No need for that if you're sure we'll be back in time." He put his glasses back in his pocket.

"I'm sure. Wait here." John tossed down his drink then dashed up the stairs. A few minutes later, he returned. "Here," he said. "Try on these sailing clothes. I know they will fit you."

"No, lad. I would only slow you down."

"Try 'em on," John said in a loud voice. "There's the bathroom." He showed it to him.

"You're crazy. I've not been sailin' in I can't tell you how many years. Even then, I was terrified of the water. I don't think this is a—"

John patted him on the back. "It's a great idea. Don't you worry. I can handle the boat alone. You can enjoy the ride."

Norbert thought a moment and took the clothes. "I'll give it a go."

While the old man changed from his travel clothes, John opened the safe, pulled out a roll of bills, plus his American and Canadian passports. He smiled as he removed the deed. He quickly stuffed it and the rest of the items into the small travel bag he kept in the drawer of the bar. Next, he washed the glasses and cleaned up. No one would ever know Norbert had been there. It was going to be the sail of his life.

He went to the garage, pulled out the car and threw his duffel and Norbert's suitcase into the trunk. He left his cell phone on the kitchen counter, after deleting his calls.

Together, they walked out of the house, climbed into the car, and headed to the club for two days of sailing. The sun was shining. A light wind was blowing—a good day to be out on the water.

The cruise on the lake and through the South Channel was uneventful as all sails functioned amazingly well. John plied the two of them with plenty of liquor and snacks. The winds were favorable and John's simple cooking was at its best in such close quarters.

During the afternoon, they anchored near Harsens Island in a small inlet, never touching land. The freighters passed by them, sucking the current in and out of the channel. In the distance, the tall, brown grass lined the rocky Canadian shore. Seagulls dipped and soared overhead. They passed the evening playing gin rummy. John let Norbert win most games.

Norbert commented many times, "John, me lad, "'Twas a great idea of yours. I've not been so relaxed in many a year."

"We've had good luck," Lighting a cigarette, he inhaled deeply. The toes of his deck shoes rested on the opposite seat as he leaned back against the wire railing, while guiding the wheel with his other hand. "Want one?"

"No, thanks just the same. Never got in the habit."

"I tried to quit but never could. Wind is picking up, but not much to worry about."

"That's good. I have to catch that flight tomorrow."

"You'll be home on time. Don't worry." He sucked the smoke into his lungs and felt himself relax. "My last one," he said and chucked it into the lake. "You're a good influence."

"Glad you be likin' it." The old man sat against the wall nearest the galley with his legs sprawled in front of him along the seat. His hand gripped the safety rail while the other hand balanced him on the cushion.

The rest of the day was smooth sailing. They made good progress until John changed course. Topside before dropping off to sleep, they admired the wonders of the stars.

He liked the old man. And his land.

CHAPTER 9

LAKE ST. CLAIR, MICHIGAN

On Sunday morning, the boat arrived opposite Squirrel Island. A strong wind blew out of the south so they were forced to tack several times to stay in the channel. John hadn't planned to go as near to the rocks as they were headed, but an idea came to him. He wondered if he could get close enough to the shore to —

Norbert cleared his throat, interrupting John's thoughts. "We'd better be headin' back, lad. The wind is makin' my stomach a bit queasy."

John was surprised when the old man spoke up. By all rights, he should have been half-drunk by now, but he seemed to have sobered up. Jack sensed he was silent because he was observing him and the surrounding area.

"We're almost to the place I think you'll enjoy. Hold on a bit longer. We can do a little fishing, if you like. I think you'll find it relaxing. Take your mind off things. I've got all the equipment on board."

"What kind of fish do you catch?"

John could see Norbert was pale, taking on a greenish hue. Seasick.

"Perch. A lot of perch."

"The rocks look like arrowheads sticking out of the water up ahead. You sure this is deep enough?"

"Yeah, we're fine. The fish love to hide in and around those rocks. We'll steer clear. I know a spot to catch a few good fish. We'll tack in a few minutes and then drop the hook."

"Never caught a perch, lad. Always a first time."

"Fine fishing."

"The last time I fished was a few years ago in Ireland. We caught a few salmon."

"Lake Huron is the place for salmon—not here in these waters. It's too shallow. We can spend the night on shore, if you're not feeling up to staying on the boat."

Norbert was quiet now.

"I have an idea," John offered. "It may settle your stomach to be on land tonight. I have camping gear below, so we could pitch a tent on the shore. Or better yet, we can check into the motel on the island. It's located just past that grassy point. Head back to the club in the morning." He pointed ahead. "What do you say?"

He lied smoothly now, waiting for the old man to make a mistake and say yes.

"It might be a good idea to stay on land. We could try a bit of fishing too."

"Like I said, it might take your mind off your stomach."

"If you're sure we'll make the plane tomorrow, it's good with me."

"Will you stop worrying about your plane? I told you I'd get you back in time. We'll go to the motel after we fish." John focused on the tree-lined rocky shore. "I've got some juicy night crawlers in the cooler."

He grabbed a bag of crackers from the side compartment of the boat and tossed it to Norbert. "Eat a handful of these saltines. They may be a bit stale, but they'll settle your stomach." He watched him cram a few crackers in his mouth.

He did not expect everything to go as planned. When Norbert agreed to go sailing with him, he had no plan. It came out of nowhere. He'd have a bit of fun at Laine's expense.

"It is getting very shallow here," said Norbert while biting into crackers two at a time. The small pieces flew onto the deck.

"We want shallow. Get the bigger perch in this part of the South Channel." John needed to distract him, make things up, or he might have a problem. "I have it under control. Trust me. We'll fish and then head in for the night. We'll sail home in half a day. The marine forecast said the wind would be coming out of the north tomorrow — at our back. We can always motor back, if you want to — up to you. I think the sail will be fantastic."

"If you say so, lad. You're the captain." Norbert eyed the deserted shore. He gripped the wire railing and held on tightly.

The waves swirled around the enormous boulders near the surface of the water as the boat zipped past them.

John could see that Norbert's face was creased and scorched from the sun, peeling. "Yes, we have to get you out of the sun too. You're sunburned."

"It hurts a bit. I could use a little ground under me feet, too."

John aimed the boat for the rocky coast ahead. He shivered under his flannel shirt when the sun hid behind the clouds. "Take the wheel a sec, will you? I'm going to get jackets for us. There's a lot of debris today. Watch for submerged telephone poles or drift wood — sail around it."

"Take the wheel? Sail around it? I don't feel I can," Norbert said.

"You'll be fine. I'll only be a minute."

"Not so sure about that, I am." He did what John asked, slid over to the wheel and gripped it between the spokes. "I can't see the best without my glasses."

"You can't really see much anyway. The entrance to the motel is just around the bend. The sea grass blocks our view of it. Head for the large, pointed black rock ahead, and we'll be on course."

"Head for a rock?"

"Steer dead ahead. It's getting cold, so I'm going below to get the foul weather gear. Hold the wheel straight."

John disappeared into the galley. He returned momentarily with the jackets. Norbert had stopped smiling some time ago, gripping the wheel, frowning, eyes squinting.

"I'll take over. Take off your life jacket. Put that on; it's warmer." He threw the jacket over to him.

Norbert struggled out of the life jacket, dropping it on the deck. At the same time, John spun the wheel, heeling the boat on its side while riding on top of an enormous wave.

"For the love of..." Norbert grabbed the rail, his feet skidding on the slippery desk. His hard look met John's eyes. "What are you doing, lad?"

"Take it easy. We got caught up in that wave. I didn't want it to hit us broadside." John spun the wheel back in place, heading the bow off the wind.

"Getting a bit rough for me. Can you slow it down? I need to put my life jacket back on."

"Yeah, we need to adjust the sails a bit."

He wondered what it would be like to own property in Ireland. The thought came to him in a flash. The wind engulfed the sail again, heeling it dangerously close to the water on its side. A stream of water rushed its way to the stern, filling the area where their feet were planted.

"We're taking on water. I think I've had enough for one day, I have." Norbert screamed into the wind, panic in his voice. The water sloshed inside his shoes. "Let's call it a day."

"It'll drain out. Don't worry. We'll be in calmer waters soon."

He grinned at the old man. Kept thinking he could own that property all by himself — his own land. Why did he have to tell Laine? She'd never know the difference — it could be his little secret. Yeah, he didn't need to tell her.

He stared at the only thing stopping him.

"Do you feel up to lowering the jib, Norbert?" John said in a loud, excited voice. "We can make better time. Then we'll motor in if you want to go to shore. We need to get it down, so we have less stress on the boat." His lies were coming smoothly. He was feeling good.

"Och, not so sure. I can try." He hesitated. "Hand me my life jacket."

"Skip it. You can put it on when you are finished dropping the sail. I need that jib down. Hurry, will you? The wind's picking up."

He steered into the wind, making it easier for Norbert to climb on top of the deck of the cabin. "Take your time."

"Aye." The old man frowned. Inching his way onto the foredeck, he crept on his knees along the slick white deck. As he went, he slid his hand along the thin wire rail, gripping it each time the boat lurched, and eventually made it to the mast. "This one?" He pointed to the jib with his free hand.

John nodded. "Unfasten the line on the cleat near your hip."

He did. It slid down the track in one swift movement. In the next instant, the tip of the jib caught the wind and swiftly billowed outward, away from the boat, filling with air. Sail and the lines wound around Norbert's feet, trapping him. Letting go of the mast, he bent to free himself of the silky mess, but at the same time, the boat lunged forward and waves crashed over the bow, throwing him to the edge of the boat.

"I'm going over," he screamed. The massive white jib twisted around him and pulled him half off the boat.

"Hang on," John yelled.

Now the waves hit them broadside. Norbert's legs dangled in the water. Tangled in the sail and lines, he found himself trapped under the railing. The lake rushed over him in torrents as the mainsail continued to pull them closer to shore.

"I'm stuck," the petrified old man cried. "Help! I need help!"

"I'm working on it." Jack smiled and steered the boat to starboard to catch more of the wind.

The jib continued to fill with water as it trailed alongside the boat. Jack's navigation was superb. It was all happening to his advantage. Another wave surged against the side of the hull and Norbert finally flipped overboard.

The sail became an anchor pulling him down into the lake. He clawed at the white of the fabric as it pocketed the cold water around him. The line was still attached to the boat. He hung onto it with what little strength he had. By chance, it had wound itself around his waist and kept him afloat.

"For God's sake, John, get me out of here!" Norbert bobbed up through the mass of white-crested waves. The line and sail were slipping through his hands.

"Keep your hands on the line!" John shouted to him, never leaving the wheel. "I am coming to you. Hold on!"

"Hurry!"

Waves forced him under the water. His head disappeared under the icy cold blanket. He pulled himself back up. Coughing and spitting water from his mouth, he sucked in what little air he could in the churning water.

"I will be there shortly. Just hang on. I am working on it." John watched in fascination as wave after wave rolled over the struggling Norbert. The old man twirled in the waves and eventually began losing his grip on the line. He bobbed up and down continuously.

Finally, the sail stretched out like a thin white wire. The current and waves made it appear like a long ribbon being pulled away from the boat. Filling with water and pulling the old man under, the sail created the only solution — to help him claw his way back to the surface — to survive.

"I have to cut the sail so I can come around and get you," John shouted through cupped hands. "This isn't working."

He lashed the wheel down, scrambled over the foredeck to the line that held Norbert, and cut it. The knife he kept in his jacket pocket freed Norbert from the boat and set him adrift in the rough water.

"I can't hold on much longer!"

The current took him farther and farther away from the sailboat under John's watchful eyes.

"I'll be right there. I'm coming. Hang on," he screamed into the wind. He climbed down from the deck, planted his feet in the stern, and took the line off the wheel.

His thoughts returned to the land — the property — now his land. It would be really nice to have a new start. Alone.

He spun the wheel in the opposite direction, away from Norbert. He watched the last of the line and the sail slip quickly away from the boat. While he gazed back at the old man, another wave rolled over the white hair. John shouted again that he was coming, as he sailed in the other direction.

Norbert bobbed up and down, but John was too far away to see what was really happening to him.

The Canadian shoreline was dead ahead. If he sailed into the shallow part of the water, the beach was within walking distance of the boat. John envisioned the property in Ireland — green and beautiful. He could broker horses there like he did in New York. He knew the business — yes, that's what he'd do. Live in Ireland and broker horses. Have a fine life.

Setting the automatic tiller dead ahead, he made his move without a backward glance, smiling.

Poor old man, John thought. He's lived a good life.

CHAPTER 10

SQUIRREL ISLAND, CANADA

Within a short time, John disappeared into the woods along the Canadian shoreline. There was no path, so he forged his way through the brush until he came to a dirt trail leading toward a small shanty. Grape vines covered the roof and part of the windows. It was definitely deserted. Huge weeds made it difficult for him to reach the front porch steps.

The wood squeaked as he walked across it to the door. Locked. He spied a rusty piece of pipe to his left by an old ladder-back chair. Perfect tool to pry open the door. It groaned and the hinges popped.

He stepped carefully inside and looked around. The rough cabin was sparsely furnished and dusty. A small cot with a stained mattress stood on the left in the single-room. Straight ahead, a wood-burning stove sat squarely mounted to the floor in the middle of the room. A wide black pipe shot up from the heater and out through the roof. Next to it was a single rattan chair with torn cushions. Beyond it, he spied a small kitchen. A white enamel counter with red trim surrounded a small sink beneath a rusty faucet. A single cupboard perched above it. One door hung open, exposing chipped dishes. In front of the counter sagged a worn wood table and two equally worn stools.

John thought this had to be a hunting cabin. He turned around and saw the equipment. Leaning against the wall behind the door was a bow and arrow set, snowshoes, fishing poles, bucket, long-handled fishing net, and a large oil slicker.

"Indians," he said out loud, looking carefully at the items.

He needed to figure out what to do next. Even though the dust was thick, he decided to stay and make a plan. He dropped his bag on the cot and went outside to explore the surrounding area. He found a canoe resting against the side of the house under the bushes on the right. In the backyard, an outhouse and a large shed nearly blended into the forest. He swung the shed's double doors open and went inside, discovering an old black truck hidden under a tarp.

"My lucky day," he muttered. Opening the creaky door, he climbed inside. "Yes!" he shouted, excitement in his voice. The key was in the ignition.

He gave it a twist. The engine coughed, sputtered and died. He turned the key again, and the engine roared to life. The gas gauge said half empty, but what did he know? It may not even work. He let the engine warm up while he ran back into the house for his bag. He was good to go — he just did not know where.

Backing out of the shed turned out to be easy. The truck's engine purred along as he clunked down the dirt ruts that passed for a road. Eventually, he came to a wide road and took it along the coast highway. Then he saw it: an airport logo on a sign, pointing straight ahead. He'd been smart enough to bring his passport, so he would head there and take a plane to Ireland. Getting out of the country as fast as he could was his main objective now.

A plan was falling into place.

The old truck chugged along the winding road. At the next town, he jumped down from the cab and filled up the gas tank at the old general store. He had to go inside to pay; he'd find out how far the airport was and be on his way.

An old Indian woman looked up at him as he came through the door. Her eyes, set in a wrinkled face, stared into his. "Forty dollars." She spoke perfect English, frowning at him.

He handed her the money. "How do I get to the nearest airport?"

"I need fifteen more. Your American dollar is not worth a whole lot. Take the road north for the airport. Can't miss it." Then she gazed out the window at the truck. Her mouth turned into a straight line as she waited for him to give her the money.

"Okay," he said, shoving the money in her withered brown hand. She gave him a hard look and said nothing.

He walked quickly out the door. He could feel her black, beady eyes staring at him through the window, watching his every move. He picked up the pace to the truck and roared out of the gas station.

She gave him a strange feeling—like she could see inside of him, knew what he'd done.

He sped down the road to the airport with an uneasy feeling. It was best if he left the country today. Left it all behind.

CHAPTER 11

SQUIRREL ISLAND, CANADA

Claire and Michael Gudefin strolled along the beach path lined by tall grass on their lakefront Squirrel Island property. The trill of a marsh wren punctuated the June evening, while sandpipers poked their long beaks into the rocky shoreline, searching for food. As the warm summer breeze turned the leaves of weeping willows over and over, the current on the rocky shore swept pebbles along their path onto the beach.

Squeezing Michael's hand as they walked, Claire said, "We have all summer to ourselves. Seems strange without the family."

"I know. We'll miss them. But they have their lives too, Claire."

"What'll we do without grandchildren to watch—and meals to cook?"

"I'll have time to make some home-made flies," Michael said. "We can go for perch in the flats."

Claire picked up a few stones and held them on her palm for him to see. "Yes, there is that. Found some quartz."

"I see," he said, taking a few from her. "We'll put them in your garden." The sunlight shone on the pink surface of the quartz as he turned the rocks over.

"I see a few more up ahead. Wish we'd brought a bucket."

"Let's check the dinghy while we're here. There might be one in there."

As they approached the wooden dock, she pointed. "I see a few logs washed up on the beach."

"We can pull them in, so people won't run into them with their boats."

"Good idea. We'll use this line." He stooped and grabbed it from the small boat.

They picked their way around upturned kayaks and small pieces of driftwood, waves slapping the odd-shaped logs.

Michael reached them first. He knelt in knee-deep water to fasten the line on the log. "Oh, hell," he said, "This is no log—it's a man tied to a log!"

"Oh my." She ran to him. "Is he alive?"

Michael touched the man's throat, holding his fingers against the carotid artery. "I feel a pulse. He's hurt badly. Help me untangle him. Looks like he was hanging on to the log for dear life."

"The poor man."

Together they eased him onto the sandy part of the beach.

Taking off his jacket, Michael placed it under the elderly man's head. "I'll get someone to help carry him up to the house. He's too heavy for us."

"Oh yes, go quickly," Claire said, smoothing the man's wet hair from his face. "He's got a nasty wound on his forehead. Look here."

"We need a doctor. Wait here," Michael said. "I'll get Jerry, next door, and we can make some kind of stretcher to take him up to the house."

"Bring a couple of blankets."

"Okay. I'll be right back."

The man moaned and opened his eyes. Mumbling incoherently, he tried to speak.

"Don't try to talk," she said. "You're going to be all right." She placed her sweater over him. "Rest. We're getting a doctor.

Soon the men returned and carried him to the Gudefin house. The doctor arrived shortly and, after his examination, told them the old man might experience some memory problems from the gash on his head. It would take time, but he would likely recover.

All the injured man kept muttering was the name Margaret.

CHAPTER 12

FROM DONEGAL TO BLACKROCK ISLAND
ONE YEAR LATER

Miles landed the helicopter on the island within a short time. The rain still thundered down, blown sideways by the gale. "Made it," he said to Laine, shutting down the engine.

"Enjoyed the ride," she said. "The area is beautiful."

"It is that. Let's go in. I'm sure Patricia and Eamon are excited to meet you."

They ducked against the torrential downpour to the front door of the lighthouse cottage. Shaking off raindrops, Miles introduced her to his caretakers.

"Come in and dry off by the fire," said Patricia. "Your supper will be ready soon. But first I'll show you to your room, Laine, then bring you a lovely cuppa tea."

"I'd like a martini instead," Laine said, following her down the hallway.

"That you'll have. I'll tell Miles," said Patricia.

The shutters slapped against the cottage wall as they entered her room. "Och, the shutters bangin' against the place are giving me a headache. I told Eamon to fasten 'em down this mornin', but he forgot with all he has to do. He'll have to fix 'em before we go to bed tonight, or there'll be no sleeping in this place."

Laine laughed. "Don't worry. I could sleep through anything. It's been a long day."

"Aye, lass, but not through this noise," she said in a light tone. "I'll be in the kitchen, if you need something. We'll be eatin' soon enough." Placing bath towels on the bed, she turned toward the door.

"I appreciate it. I'll be there after I wash up." Gazing out of her bedroom window, Laine watched the mass of dark clouds sweeping over the ocean.

Walking into the living room a few minutes later, she found Miles talking on his speakerphone. A voice said, "Miles, where in hell are you? I've been lookin' all over for you."

"I'm on the island, Dodd."

Miles paced the room, frowning, and running his hand through his thick, blond hair.

"Well you gotta get to the farm," said Dodd in an agitated voice.

"I can't get off the island in this storm. You know that. What's the problem?"

"Somethin' terrible is happened." His voice rose even louder. "You gotta get here quick, lad."

"Hey, take it easy. What do you mean, something terrible has happened? What is it?"

"Rex is dead."

Miles inhaled sharply. "*What?*"

"Rex is dead. Shot in the backfield on the farm. Found him there, we did."

"You're joking."

"I don't joke about a thing like that."

"Tell me, man. When the hell did this happen?"

Laine, on high alert, listened. Something was off.

"Look. Don't argue. I need you here to decide what to do about it. Don't be takin' your time, lad. Find a way to get here to the farm as soon as you can."

She saw the inquisitive look on Mile's face when he disconnected the call.

"We've got a bad problem at the farm. One of my best horses was shot."

"I couldn't help overhearing. That's awful." Laine set her drink down and went to him.

"Miles, what is that you say?" Eamon shouted as he ran into the room.

"Rex is dead."

"Not our Rex. I don't believe it! Who the hell would do that?"

"For the love of — " Patricia heard the news and scurried in right behind Eamon, blessing herself and wiping her hands on her apron.

"We don't know. Best horse I had on any track — worth millions. Sadly enough, I sold him to the sheik's broker yesterday. He was going to be picked up tomorrow. What a disaster," said Miles.

"Why would anyone want to shoot your horse?" Laine asked.

"Don't know. He was a marvelous horse and worth every penny," said Miles.

"Only a bloody fool would do something like that," said Eamon, waving his arms in the air in exasperation. Patricia nodded again and again, keeping quiet.

"It seems senseless," Laine said.

"Yes, it's mind boggling. I can't get off the island until the storm lets up. Maybe I can take the boat over to the mainland tonight. What do you think, Eamon?"

"You'd be daft to do that, lad, in this storm. Whatever it is, it'll keep till mornin'. It would be pure suicide."

"I've got to find out who did this." Miles swiveled around and faced him. "It can't wait until morning."

"Aye, but if you go tonight, you'll be dead too. There's a ragin' storm out there. You know it! Waves are over thirty feet high. Wind is blowin' enough to bend the trees over and touch the ground. You'd never make it in the boat—it'd be your death. Not tonight—wait till it dies down—can't last forever."

"I know you understand."

"I do, lad. You know I do." Eamon scratched his head. "We'll find a way. When it's safe."

The cellphone rang again. "Yes? What is it, Dodd?"

"Forgot to tell you. Sean was on watch last night. Hasn't shown up for work all day. He may have seen something. We're lookin' for him. Not like him to be comin' in late to work."

"He the new stable boy?"

"Been workin' with us six months now. Good lad."

"I'll deal with him later. Have you sent for Wilfrid and Tom?"

"Aye, police cousins of yours are on their way. Called vet, Bronson," said Dodd.

"Soon as the storm will let me off the island, I'll be there." Miles said in a strong voice. "I'll call you when I am on my way." Miles disconnected. "It's a damn northeaster tonight—just my luck."

"I'm so sorry," said Laine, going to him and gently squeezing his arm. "What can I do for you?"

"Nothing." Miles pulled away and leaned against the fireplace mantle. "I know it was not an accident, Eamon. Someone shot Rex to get back at me, just like the other horses."

"Aye," he said. "But who?"

"I have my suspicions. I'll call some people and find out what I can. Someone wants my horses dead. If there's one thing I can do 'tis fight back and try to find out what's going on."

"Aye," said Eamon, his hands balled into fists.

"Could be that damn sheik went off the grid—trying to get back at me for the last horse he bought, but it doesn't add up. I already sold him several excellent horses and he had no complaints. Just that one incident—"

"There was no 'milkshaking' coming from this house. Wouldn't put it past that slimy broker to try to get another horse from you for a rock-bottom price, like he did last time."

"You are right about that. I turned down an offer for another horse he wanted to buy last week—maybe he shot Rex to prove a point."

"Be careful," Eamon said. "Don't say another word. You're hurtin'—not thinkin' straight. Might be something else goin' on."

"Like what?"

"Nothin', just rumors. Play it out till we get the facts."

Laine tried to figure out what was happening. Right now, she didn't seem too sure about Bourke or Eamon. Needed to know more. She wanted to ask them about the "milkshaking" incident, but it would have to wait.

"What rumors? We don't have any proof on anything at this point," said Miles.

"Not yet," Eamon said in an angry voice. "But we will."

Laine liked Miles, but a gnawing feeling rose in her gut. She didn't trust him now that she heard all this talk. Things were not adding up. She'd find out more by listening, so she kept quiet.

An awkward silence filled the room. Miles seemed to remember she was there. "Let's have dinner. I'm sure you are hungry, Laine, after the long trip."

She shook her head. "I'm fine. It can wait, if you need to take care of this."

"No, it's up to the police now."

She could hear Max reminding her to "get the Intel." Maybe asking a few questions wouldn't hurt. "Do you have any enemies you can think of?"

"None that would want to shoot a poor, defenseless animal of mine."

"I see."

Eamon interrupted. "Worse than terrible. It's a monster who'd be shootin' a lovely horse worth a million dollars. Have to be daft."

"Let's not talk about it anymore until we have the facts," said Miles.

Laine nodded. "I understand. If there's anything I can do—"

"You can move forward and work on the lighthouse tomorrow. At least we'll make some progress on that."

"That sounds like a good idea. Sure."

She'd call Max with an update later that night. Miles seemed like a decent man, but she knew she was not a good judge of character when it came to men—look at what happened with John. She wouldn't be fooled again—if she could help it.

A little before midnight, after they had eaten, they sat in front of the fire, talking about the work they would do on the lighthouse in the morning.

Miles said, "I think it's time to turn in. You must be exhausted after the long day, Laine."

"Yes, I think I'll get some sleep. Thanks for the lovely dinner, Patricia."

"Aye, I'll be seeing you at breakfast, I will," said Patricia, getting up from her chair.

Miles stood and started for the door. "Eamon, let's fix the shutters. Seems the rain has let up. We could use a good night's sleep. The banging is driving me nuts."

"I'll be gettin' the tools. Start with this one here." He pointed to the front of the cottage as he left the room.

"When do you think you can leave the island?" said Laine. She rose and peered out the window.

"As soon as possible. If I go tonight, I'll arrange for Eamon to bring you to the farm on the mainland first thing tomorrow morning. You can meet the men who will be working on the lighthouse, before they take the boat over to the island."

"Sounds good. I am tired. I look forward to seeing everyone tomorrow. Hope it turns out well for you."

"Goodnight, then." Miles lifted his foul weather jacket from the peg on the wall and put it on. He went out the front door as Laine headed for her bedroom and Patricia went to her room off the kitchen.

When Laine got to her room, she dialed Max and left an updated message. She changed. The wind howled outside her window as she lay on the soft down bed. She wondered about seeing John, Miles' horse farm operation, and now—a dead horse. If her instincts were right—and they usually were—John was alive. It bothered her. She couldn't sleep.

Agitated, she yanked off the covers and got out of bed. Slipping on sweats, she opened the window. She heard the hum of the helicopter engine and the thumping of the rotor blades. Miles was leaving the island.

It was time to take a late night stroll and work out her feelings.

CHAPTER 13

CARRICK'S PUB
BLACKSOD

Jack's boat was tossed about in the heavy rain. It pitched and rolled in the rough waves of the Atlantic Ocean and he loved it. Steady winds blew hard against the hull, heeling it on its side and then righting itself by his expert hand. He spun the wheel to his advantage as the white spray flew over the bow. He was fishing, and nothing could be better — except money — and Marla.

It was ten-thirty according to his watch as he peeked at the luminous dial while keeping his line taut. His rod was secure in the cup holder of the leather harness he had strapped to his chest.

Nothing was biting or striking now. Time to stop fishing — he hated to quit, but he called it a day. While pulling in the line, he thought about Laine. How had she found him? She was going to ruin everything.

He stared at the dark, choppy water surrounding him. It triggered a recent memory. Yes, maybe he could use the same plan — to get rid of her.

After placing the rod inside the boat and unhooking the harness, he navigated the boat toward the harbor. "Dead ahead," he shouted, thinking of Laine and laughing at his own joke. "Yeah, dead a—head."

The red and green buoy lights at the entrance of Blacksod Harbor guided him to his slip beyond Carrick's Pub. The old wood curragh glided swiftly into the well. Stern lines were quickly secured around the pilings under the single dim light on the dock. It was covered with bugs and spider webs, making the light seem to flicker in the rain. The engine hummed in neutral until he turned it off. He fastened the bowlines with a simple loop on the cleat and hid the key on a hook underneath the seat. He would always have tomorrow to bob around in the sea…and fish.

The rain made a light popping sound on his foul-weather jacket while he sat in the boat thinking about the huge brown trout on ice in the cooler. It was a fine trout he'd caught that day. It gave him a good fight. In the end, he'd subdued the wild fish as it thrashed about on the boat deck by bashing it on the head several times with his "priest."

He laughed out loud when he remembered he used the brass-headed wooden tool to give "last rights" to the fish. He had stolen the eight-inch baton-like weapon from an old fisherman in Donegal a few months ago.

He treasured the killer weapon. The perfect blows he practiced on each of the fish meant less mess on his boat deck—he hated cleaning up fish scales when they splattered and shot off his cutting board.

His process was always the same. He would yank and twist the hook from the fish's mouth using long-nose pliers to free it, so he could use it again. He'd dip it in the ocean to clean the blood or guts off the hook's sharp points. Then he performed a small sacrifice by holding the fish upright on his cutting board. Its stomach rested on the scored wood surface. Holding it in one bare hand, he killed it with several sharp blows to the head. If he wasn't careful to spike its brain, guts flew all over.

He laughed at the sheer pleasure he derived from his technique, each perfect kill. A single blow could do the job and there would be less cleanup for him, but it wasn't as much fun as the multiple hits he delivered. He knew fish didn't feel pain. It was something he could care less about even if they did.

He thought about the lengthy time he took separating the skin from the bones in a few sharp slices. Sometimes their mouth worked open and shut even after he had wiped out their brain—he thought it was funny—thought they were silently talking to him. It didn't stop him.

He ran the blade smoothly under the head of the fish, swiping down the fish's side on top of the spine. He wanted all the bones removed, so he sliced it slowly down the full length of its belly, until the blade slid out just before the tip of the tail. The fillets were beautiful pieces of meat without the bothersome tiny bones that could ruin his meal.

Each time he practiced filleting a fish, he became more of an expert, cutting and slicing their bodies like a skilled surgeon during an operation.

The same ritual continued when he prepared each fish on the seasoned outdoor grill in his backyard. It was one he enjoyed. He thought about the fish he'd prepared yesterday evening.

Large fillets—sweet to the taste—perfectly deboned. First, he dipped them in a bowl of whipped raw eggs. Then both sides of the meat were pressed firmly into the crushed Ritz cracker and garlic mixture spread out on aluminum foil. The slippery meat clung to the crunchy coating with an appealing presentation.

Next, he melted the clarified butter on high heat in the large, black iron skillet he kept for just this type of cooking. When it sputtered, he placed the fillets in single file rows on top of the nutty-brown colored liquid. As it cooked, it gave off a pleasant aroma.

Within minutes, the sautéed fish turned golden brown on the underside and along the sides. Quickly, he flipped the pieces with a wide spatula to cook the other side. He topped off his conquests by adding a pinch of sea salt and freshly ground pepper before removing them from the pan and placing them on a plate. Juice squeezed from fresh lemons was drizzled over the top of the fillets to complete the final stage in the process of cooking the fish.

Finally, steaming hot husks of corn were lifted from the grill with long tongs. He set them on the picnic table and roughly peeled back the charred, damp husks. The vegetables were placed on a separate dish containing soft butter and Hungarian sea salt, ready for the taking.

He remembered how he tenderly fingered the slightly curled, golden-brown pieces of fish, placing them into his mouth. He took his time, crunching on huge bites of corn from the cob, dipping it lavishly back in the salty butter until it was gone. Emptying his scotch made him feel good. He felt fine thinking about the killing ritual—eating the fresh meat right after he took its life—and…of course, drinking scotch.

All this thinking about cooking and eating was making him hungry and thirsty. Maybe he should go back out and catch more fish. He thought of Marla and sensed a headache coming on. Something was bothering him, and it wasn't her. What was it that was giving him a headache? Now he remembered.

"Damn her," he swore under his breath when Laine's face flashed into his mind. He pulled a pint of Bushmills from under the seat and screwed off the top. He wasn't taking any chances. Just thinking about her made him angry. What if he did something about it? There was something that triggered a memory when he was out fishing. Yes, that thing he did once before on the lake in Michigan came back to him. A happy thought. Maybe he could do that thing again.

As he took a long swig, the liquor burned slowly and easily down his throat. He felt fine, except for the memory of his wife. *Why the hell was she in Donegal?* He took another long swig, emptying the bottle.

Laine came from money and had it all, he thought. It made him mad to think about it. He was nothing in her eyes. He came from nothing and was nothing until he met her—she was ruining all of it now. He'd talk to Marla about that thing he was thinking of doing. This time, he didn't have to do it alone. She'd help him. Yeah, she would enjoy it.

The rain let up a little, but it drenched his jeans and ran off his jacket in trailing beads of water. He shivered as the cold rain soaked him. Marla could warm him up later. He needed the warmth of the pub, as well.

Pulling out his cell, he punched in Marla's number. "It's me. Meet me at Carrick's Pub in half an hour, after you get your mother tucked in. We have a few things to discuss." He listened to her excuse. "Yeah, I know it's late, Marla, but we need to talk."

The current rocked the boat from side to side in the well while he nodded his head up and down, up and down, while she chattered on and on. "Honey, I'll see you in less than an hour. It's important. I have an idea about something we can do with Laine. Oh yeah, wear black."

She squawked in his ear.

He interrupted her. "Yeah, put on the black tennis shoes I bought you and the black slicker I like. It's really coming down out here. Don't let it bother you. It's gonna stop by the time you get here. I'll be waiting for you at Carrick's Pub. Yeah, it's a dump. So what? It's a good place to meet and have a drink."

He hung up, satisfied with the conversation. Rubbing the stubble on his chin, he gazed at the empty bottle and tossed it into the water. Reaching under the seat, he brought out a new one and twisted the cap off. This time, it went down smoothly. He took another gulp, swishing the liquor around his mouth. Before putting it away, he slugged down another shot of the gold liquid.

He felt better as his insides warmed. A smile crept across his lips. He felt fine. Marla had told him he was good at what he did. He believed her, and she knew just how good he was.

Throwing off the hood to his slicker, he lifted his face to the rain. He licked the salt from his lips, liking it. Stashing what was left of the whiskey under the seat, he tidied up loose lines in the stern. Oars were left in a haphazard heap on the sides of the deck. The last of his gear was stowed in the bow space.

The rain continued to slide down his face as he peered into the dark sky surrounding him. He smiled. As the idea took shape and a plan crept into his thoughts, he blinked into the wet blackness. He was a horse broker and a fisherman. He knew how to navigate a boat in any condition and at any time. Why he hadn't thought of it earlier puzzled him. He knew just how to do it. He had done it before.

Gripping the piling on the dock in front of him, he steadied himself as he stood up in the rocking skiff. His feet slipped a little on the wood plank seat when he stood on it to boost himself up and onto the dock. Taking his time, he hoisted himself out of the boat in one jump. The skiff sprang free from his feet as he found the dock under his legs.

Seeing the boat tug and pull randomly on the lines made him laugh. The old thing has a life of its own, he thought. Out loud he said what he thought. "Dead wood having life. Now that's a good one. Wait until I tell Marla. She'll think it's brilliant."

Murky harbor water reflected under a single harbor light when he gazed down into the well. He flattened himself on the dock, peering into the water. He liked looking into the blackness. The rain soaked the back of his jeans while his prone body took in the smell of fish around him. He could not see the sea trout between the kelp, but he knew they were there in the water. He watched for small fish lips to appear and suck in tiny breaths of air at the surface of the water. They did not disappoint him as they shot up quickly from the muddy, mucky bottom of the sea, while silt floated to the top around them. In an instant, they quietly disappeared as fast as they'd come.

Kelp poked out of the sea in cockeyed directions, waving its arms upward toward the surface. It grew high and stringy between the rocks here in the well and along the shore at the front of the slip—perfect hiding places for the fish.

Jack hesitated, knowing this. Thinking about fishing in the dark excited him. He *could* catch one more fish before Marla showed up. Maybe two or three. He still had bait in the cooler. He could sit here on the dock and fish for a short time.

The water spun in circles before his eyes like a whirlpool. His head throbbed and his stomach ached.

Laughter and an occasional rough voice came from the pub a short distance away. It aroused him. Made him thirsty. Naw, he thought, no more fishing tonight. He'd have a few drinks in the pub instead. Scrambling to his feet, he trudged down the weathered, creaking planks of the old dock to the shore.

As he went along, waves splashed over brown, red, and gray pebbles beneath his feet. Stones crunched as he walked toward the well-lighted entrance of the pub.

Fascinated by flickers of movement at the water's edge, he stopped and pointed his cell phone flashlight at them. Small silver and white-stomached minnows fought against the lapping waves and struggled to swim away from the gravelly shore. Floundering in the turbulence of the waves, they gave up swimming, flipping over and over on the wet sand, gasping for air. Crabs popped up from pebbly holes; they scurried aimlessly for new homes to dive into before the next wave struck them.

The crabs' sideways walk delighted him before he pushed his toe in circles over their small, fragile bodies. The act crushed them into the pebbles and shattered their exoskeleton. The few remaining slow ones, who did not make it to the safety of a new opening, met his shoe that ground them into little pieces. Bits of broken shells were the only reminder of their existence until the next wave hit and washed them out to sea.

He looked for more of the pea-size crustaceans to obliterate, but the voices from the pub pulled him from his play. He smiled and gave up his game.

Misty rain followed by a warm breeze blew in from the sea. He noticed it immediately. If there was one thing he knew, it was the sea. A moist, salty film covered his skin. He felt refreshed — alive.

His plan would work.

His journey was about to begin. He stopped for a minute, lit a cigarette, and danced in and out of the waves as the white crests dared to soak his shoes. His feet made a sucking sound on the wet, pebbly sand as he zigzagged in and out of the breaking waves. He liked the cool water playing tag with his feet — it felt good. He felt fine. He'd order another scotch while he waited for Marla. It made him feel good, thinking about it as he walked to the open door.

Stepping inside the pub, he felt relaxed. A blast of hot, humid, stale, smoky air filled his lungs. Glasses clinked in rhythmic beats as they slapped the wood bar needing refills. Beer and shot glasses, regardless of the fisherman's state. No one was refused in this place and that included large, male beer-drinkers of huge capacity.

"Hey, Jack, the usual?" asked the elderly waitress as he slid into a cracked leather booth in the corner of the smoky pub.

"Yeah, Aideen, two orders of bangers and mash. Rashers and a scotch. I'm starved."

"Thirsty, too. You'll have your drink first," she said in a loud voice, scratching on her pad of paper.

A few regulars tipped shots of whiskey at the bar. "Hey, Lafferty, too good for us tonight? We've got an extra stool over here."

There was a long moment of silence as heads turned toward him.

Jack heard the thump of music. Felt the beat. Loud. Louder. Daring him to do something. A little surprise welled inside him. He had the "priest" with him tonight. This was that kind of place.

But then he remembered Marla was meeting him. He shook his head, waved them off, and lit up a cigarette.

"Not tonight. Meeting someone." He wanted that drink. They were not good men—not at all brave. Wasted themselves and never caught any good fish. He had no use for them, except as the occasional extra hand to help him with fixing the roof of his farmhouse. There would be no trouble with him or with them tonight, he decided.

"Nobody you want us to know," said the unshaven man, slurring his words. "Bet on it."

"It's nothing like that, Charlie," he said, inhaling the cigarette, biting and chewing the skin on his lower lip. "I'm busy tonight."

"Yeah, Jack's too good for us," said the other man, spilling his drink down the front of his dirty t-shirt. "Can't sit with us cause you're too busy doing nothing." He puffed out his chest, raised both fists, wanting a fight.

"Don't make anything of it," Jack said, looking at his watch. "Hunt deer on my farm today?"

They slapped each other on the back and laughed as if he'd told a joke. "Not today. Callaghan brothers were at your place. We got called in to fix the stables at Ashford Castle, we did. Another day—you owe us, Jack." They turned back to their stories, ignoring him, ordering more drinks.

"Yeah, sure." He checked his watch again.

Aideen brought scotch. Slapped it down in front of him and left. News blared from the flat-screen television over the bar. Newscasters mouthed the weather forecast for the coming week. He sipped his drink, listening closely to the broadcast.

"It's almost eleven. Where the hell is she?" he said in a low voice to himself. A long, hard draw on his cigarette filled his lungs.

What seemed like half an hour later, in she walked, displaying those beautiful long legs, her blond, silky hair bouncing.

"This place is a dump. Why'd you ask me here?" Marla grumbled as she slid across from him in the old booth.

"Keep your voice down." He smelled her perfume. Expensive. "Been shopping?"

She kept her voice low. "Yes, but that's beside the point. So what's this all about? You said you have a plan? Something to do with your wife? This place stinks." She covered her mouth with a ringless hand, wrinkling her nose.

"Hold on," he said as the waitress placed the food in front of him. "Got any ketchup, Aideen?"

"Americans have to have your ketchup," the older woman said in a sharp voice. "Ruin a meal, you will." She stomped over to the bar and grabbed the plastic container. Dark, thick red sauce oozed out of the top and ran down the sides of the bottle in her hand. Danny grinned at her while he wiped the top of the counter with a dirty rag. She shoved the ketchup at the bartender. "Clean it." He did as she said with the dirty rag and handed it back to her.

Heading to the table, she asked Jack, "Anything else?" Hands on hips, round face beaming under thinning gray hair, she set the bottle on the table. Then frowning, she asked Marla, "Want something?"

"No." Marla turned her face away.

"Another scotch for me, Aideen. That's about it." He squirted a generous amount of ketchup on his bacon.

"That's disgusting." Leaving them to eat, she thumped away, back bent over.

"So tell me." Marla jabbed a fork into his mash.

"Has to be tonight," he said, taking his fork from her. Jamming his mouth full of potatoes, he said warily, as though he was expecting something, "Oh yeah, and another thing, before we get into that... Rodriguez, the Mexican boy I met in the bar the other night—the one I hired to spy on Bourke, and now Laine too. Remember? I told you about him. I met him at the bar at the racetrack the other day. You know after we..." He grinned, food showing in his mouth.

"Quiet. They'll hear you," Marla looked around. "So, what about it?" She grabbed his scotch and took a long swallow.

"Well, anyway, the boy reported they're going to start tomorrow, ripping apart the lighthouse tower on the island. My wife's decorating it or something. Damn crew is meeting her early in the morning on the island. Said she's staying in the cottage with the old couple. He's going to look for her daily schedule for me. She always keeps one."

"What are you talking about?" Marla shoved another bite of his mash into her mouth.

He went on without hearing her. "And another thing, the boy has a cousin who might be interested in me as a broker."

"No kidding. So what?"

"His cousin buys racehorses. Says he can fix me up with him—got *mucho pesetas*. Good, eh?" Jack kept chewing. Food shot out of his mouth and landed back on his plate.

"I can broker horses for him in Mexico. Make a lot of bucks on the side too."

"Jack, you brought me here to tell me that?" She frowned, put down the fork, watched Jack eat.

"No, Marla. Didn't you hear what I was just telling you? Laine is on the island. We've got to grab her tonight. That's why I told you to meet me pronto."

"You're nuts. You don't have a plan. How are you going to do that?"

"I have a plan. We go tonight. Use the tunnels you told me about on the property. We'll be out of luck if they block them up during the construction." He belched, kept chewing, and washed down the mash with scotch.

"Tonight! You're not serious. It's late." Marla stared at him. She flipped her blond hair over her shoulder. Pulling red lipstick from her pocketbook, she smeared it on full lips, making the left side higher than the right.

Jack didn't seem to notice.

"We can sneak into her room on the island. We can find out where she keeps her damn tea. Drug it with arsenic. She loves her tea. She carries that damn tea tin with her wherever she travels. Drove me crazy. I'll put a massive dose of poison in it. She'll drink it and that's it."

"Sounds iffy," she said. "It'll never work. We don't have time to wait for the poison to take effect. It could take weeks. What if she doesn't drink it? Then what?"

"We can go to plan B and still do Plan A if we need it, or scratch it altogether. We kidnap her tonight. We use chloroform to knock her out. I've got it in the boat—found an old bottle of it in the farmhouse. We'll take her, knock her out, and she won't know what hit her." He grinned and rubbed his hands together.

"You've been drinking way too much. Not tonight."

"Yep, we go tonight. It's not a problem. Right after we finish eating."

Marla stared at him and said nothing.

"Listen, we can drug her, give her arsenic—skip that—yeah it takes too long. The chloroform is quicker and faster. We gag her so she can't scream, drag her through the tunnels to the boat, and dump her in the ocean—the sharks can do the rest. It's simple."

"It's not simple. What if they hear us when we take her?"

"Naw. She can try to scream her head off, but I'll keep her quiet. Like I said, she'll be knocked out from the chloroform." He wiped a drip of ketchup off his chin with his hand, wiping it on his shirt. "It's a good plan."

"Jack, what if you gag her, tie her up, and leave her in one of the caves tonight? There's a small one at the end of the tunnel near the stone steps leading to the harbor cove. Finish the job tomorrow."

He hesitated, thinking.

"Take her out in the boat tomorrow night. We'll have more time to plan things. It'll give us more time."

"I already planned it," he said. He felt good inside—warm. He ignored Marla. "We're going tonight while it's dark. No moon because of the storm. And that's that." He scraped the last of his meal from his plate with his fork.

"I like my plan better, Jack," she said and reached for his free hand. "You're so smart, but the weather is bad tonight. It's raining. Tomorrow is a better time to do it."

"It's fine, Marla. Remember, the sooner this happens the sooner we can be together. We have to get rid of her tonight. She's in the way now. If we dump her in the sea tonight, they'll never know what happened to her. That's what you want, isn't it?"

Leaning toward him, she exposed a full inch of see-through lace on her camisole under her half-unbuttoned shirt. "Sure, Jack, but I need a minute to think about this. I'm surprised you planned it so fast. Come on. How about you leave her in the cave tonight? Come back tomorrow night and dispose of her?"

His eyes never left her chest. "No, we dump her tonight like I said. I'm getting tired of telling you. We have to act fast. By the time they realize she's gone, we'll own her land. And everything else she has. It will be all ours. Laine and I are still technically married, you know. Or did you forget?" His boozy eyes met hers.

"Don't remind me," she said in a hard voice. "I get it. Let's go over it again. You are—"

"*We* are taking her, Marla. *Us—you and me.* After I drug her and gag her, *we* are taking her to the *boat. You and me* are gonna dump her in the ocean. Remember? I explained it to you already. Aren't you listening? I need you to show me how to get into that tower from the tunnels. What's wrong with you?"

"Nothing. *You* are going to put her in the cave and go back tomorrow night with the boat."

"Nope."

"Yes, think about it. Tonight, you park the boat on the backside of the island. Take the forest path to the harbor cove. The path leads directly to the entrance of the main tunnels. You can't miss it. You'll end up on the ledge that's just above the harbor cove. That's the entrance to the tunnels. It will take you underground on the property that leads to the lighthouse tower. You'll come to a hatch in the tunnel floor. It opens into the chimney of the fireplace. You can access the tower room from the hatch, and it also gives you access to the cottage. It's simple, I can draw you a map. You'll be fine on your own."

"No, this a two person job. We—meaning *us*—go together. Nab her and carry her out through the tunnels. Okay…to the *cave.* Done deal. We go back tomorrow night and give her sinking lessons."

"Sounds good," she said. "What do you mean *we*? You keep saying *we*." She sipped his scotch, leaving a red lipstick mark on the glass.

"I need you to lead me through the tunnels to the tower room. It will cut down on time. I would get lost. I know it. After we nab her, I can use the chloroform to knock her out, but I need you to help. The plan will work. Don't worry." He swiped the sleeve of his shirt across his mouth.

"It's better if you go alone this time."

"This is a two-man job. You can be the lookout after I drug her. I can carry her, but I need you to show me through the tunnels. You know them. I've never been there."

"I don't know, Jack. I have to get home — to my mother. You know she is not well." She rested her elbows on the table, hesitated when she saw his expression. "Yeah, okay, okay. I'll call my mother. Tell her I'll be late. This better work, Jack."

"Call her now. It's happening. We're definitely leaving." He signaled for the waitress.

"Give me a minute," she left the table and entered the ladies room. After several minutes, she returned to the booth. "Let's get going. I can't be gone all night."

"Yeah, it's time. We'll be rich and the land will be all ours. We'll have money from the horses too. I got another deal going with Rodriguez, that Mexican boy. I'll tell you about that later. Lots of money — he knows a lot of heavy investors in the racetrack business in Mexico — the country."

"You just told me that. I don't think you..."

"Yeah, well...didn't know if you heard me, so I repeated it to let it sink in. Are you hearing me?" He downed his drink.

"Yes, I heard you for the third time — counting the other day."

"Very funny," he said and smiled. Leaving the booth, he said in a low tone, "We're going to be living the high life, Marla. Might as well start now." He threw a hundred dollar bill on the table.

"I'll be right there." Marla took her time following him. She remained at the table, adjusting her lipstick, while Jack exited the pub. She stole a glance around the bar, grabbed the tip, and stuffed it into her handbag. A five-dollar bill was left in its place as she struggled into her black leather jacket and sauntered out of the pub.

Aideen saw Marla make the switch with her tip. Jack would hear about it the next time he was in the bar. A few minutes later she took a smoking break outside the pub; she sat hunched over on the wood bench next to the door.

The cool night air and the smell of fish from the sea reminded her of her father. He'd been a fisherman his whole life; his job was backbreaking. It was all he ever knew and was good at it, until the sea took his life when she was sixteen.

She remembered her father coming into Carrick's Pub after fishing. He would sit with her while her mother worked the tables as a waitress. She got her first job there and stayed after both her parents passed. All the fishermen went to Carrick's Pub. It was the best place to be then, and it was no different now. Fishermen told their stories in true Irish fashion, boasting about their exploits at sea. Usually, fistfights would follow and chairs would be smashed against the walls of the pub. Men and sometimes women had to prove a point after a few too many jars. Arm wrestling, laughter, and singing filled the rooms.

As a young child of a fisherman, Aideen remembered watching her father go out in the very same boats that were leaving the harbor now under her watchful eye. When her father came home from a day's fishing, she was happy. He worked with good men who knew their fishing business and had respect for the sea. Good memories, she thought.

Looking down the shore she saw the dim light by Jack's well. It gave her a clear view of what they were doing. They were leaving the harbor in his boat in the dark, without running lights. The curragh zipped past her post and headed out of the harbor into the rough sea. It quickly disappeared from view in the sea of green under a moonless sky.

She sat in silence, smoking, thinking about what she was seeing. The tiny orange dot glowed brightly at the end of her cigarette. It was the only thing identifying her presence in the darkness.

She wondered where Jack and Marla were headed.

CHAPTER 14

BLACKROCK ISLAND

It was just seconds after midnight when Jack and Marla sped out of the harbor and bee-lined to Blackrock Island in the curragh. Light rain and dark clouds hovered overhead.

Entering the inlet on the western shore of the island, they could see the cottage lights. The lighthouse tower beacon glowed a yellowish white above the black rock cliffs.

Marla shifted on the plank seat. "Jack, I didn't bargain for this. How much longer? It's cold out here and I'm soaked."

"We're here, Babe." Jack turned off the engine. The boat glided onto the pebbly shore, scraping its bottom on the rocks. Swinging his legs over the side, he slipped into the dark water. "Grab the anchor. Hand it to me." Grunting with effort, she did as he asked, and he wedged it into the rocky beach.

"How am I going to get out, Jack? It's slippery." She wrapped her arms around herself. "I can wait here while you go and get her."

"You'll be fine. Do what I did. Slide over the bow. I'll catch you."

"Ouch, that hurts!" she cried as her stomach caught on the bow cleat.

"Quiet! They'll hear you. Lift yourself off the cleat, Marla. I've got you." He grabbed both of her legs, pushed her up over the cleat and lowered her into the knee-deep water.

"My shoes are ruined! I just bought these today. Oh my God, the water is freezing!"

"I told you to wear your sneakers, so why didn't you? Okay, okay, I'll get you some new ones," he said in a strong voice. Grabbing her hand, he pulled her onto the shore. "Come on. You're okay."

"No, I hurt myself. Look—my blouse is ripped! My shoes are soaked. This is nuts."

"I'll get you a new shirt too. We've got to get goin'. Stop complaining."

She rubbed her stomach. "Let's get this over with. I gotta get home—to Mom."

"Yeah, yeah, yeah." He set off, picking a path along the rocky shoreline. Marla followed, tripping along in her heels.

After a short time trudging along the rocky beach, they made their way to the point. They could see Miles's yacht docked in the cove. Coming closer, they could see the stone stairs looming out of the rock cliffs. The entrance to the tunnels was at the top of the stairs on the ledge.

In the shadow of the stern of the yacht, Jack motioned Marla to a halt. "Wait here. I'll be right back."

"No way, Jack, I'm going with you. The steps are over there." She pointed ahead to the right. "They'll lead us to the tunnels."

"Yeah, okay let's get goin'." He stopped and put his face close to her.

"You reek of scotch, Jack. Get out of my face. Move it or I'm leaving." Her strong arms pushed him out of the way. "I haven't been here since I was a kid, so I have to make sure it's the right place. I'll lead."

"Fine," he said and dropped behind her, watching her hips sway as she walked, heels clicking on the rocky surface of the cove.

"This is definitely it," she said as they began the climb up the steep steps.

"We don't have all day. Can't you go any faster?"

"This is the best I can do." Marla was breathing hard when they reached the top ledge. She shined her light over the rocks, while Jack leaned against them, watching her. "The entrance is here somewhere." She moved her gaze left to right, up and down. Then she stuck her index finger toward the sky. "Got it." She hesitated, flipping her blond hair out of her face. "I'm really not dressed for this. I might trip on my shoes. I'll wait here."

A narrow black hole stretched a long way in front of them.

"Come on, Marla. You'll be fine. We've got to do this tonight, so I can collect the money and own the land when she dies. Remember?" He poked her in the back to get her moving.

"Stop it!" Her feet slid on the wet, uneven stones and she fell. "Jack, what's wrong with you? That hurt!"

"Jittery, I guess. Didn't mean to knock you down, Marla. Here, take my hand." He beamed the light on her and then in her face.

"Get the light out of my eyes, you imbecile. I can't see." Marla pulled herself up with the help of Jack's hand. "That's it. I've had enough." She turned and tried to go around him, back the way they came.

Jack caught her in an embrace and kissed her hard. "Didn't mean it, Marla. It was an accident. Show me how to get to the lighthouse. Come on. Will you do that for us, Marla? I'll buy you whatever you want tomorrow — when we get back to the mainland. Anything." He held her tightly.

"Well, all right, but stop shoving me. And remember, Jack, you said 'anything.'" She saw Jack watching her, smiling.

"Yeah, I did. Can we go now?" He gave her a short peck on the cheek.

"Follow me." Her shoes squished and squeaked as she walked ahead.

The tunnel was dark; water seeped from mossy crevices. It smelled dank and rotten. They wound their way through the curves and forks, lights dancing in a circle above and around them. Marla played with the light and found the old path to the lighthouse tunnel. Several huge X's, painted in white, marked the walls leading the way. At the fork, the color changed to red, yellow, or blue. Each fork had a different color.

"I think it's the red path."

"I hope you're right."

"Jack, shine your light next to mine—right ahead of us. To the left."

A flurry of bats flew straight at them.

"Oh my God!" she shouted. "Changed my mind—I'm out of here." She turned and ran smack into him, knocking both of them to the floor. A thick mass of bats soared near their heads. "I've had it." She pulled her arms from around her head, shoving herself off him. "I hate bats."

"Hold on. They're gone. We scared 'em, that's all, Marla." He held out his arms to help her up. "Really, they are not here anymore."

"Neither am I," she said, limping away from him.

"Slow down, will ya? We've got to get rid of Laine *tonight*. We're already here. Give it a few more minutes." He gripped her by the waist, pulling her back to him. He turned her toward him and kissed her. "For us."

"No, no, no. We need a new plan. Something else— this place gives me the creeps. It wasn't like this when we were kids."

"Yeah, back then you were fearless. Listen. The tower might be closer than you think."

"Tomorrow is close enough for me."

"Yes, we can come back tomorrow—like you said—make another plan, but let's do *this part* tonight. I have to know how to set it up. Just a little longer. Show me the way."

"Fine, but then we're out of here. Promise me, Jack, only a quick look—then it's adios. Better not be any more bats!"

They made good time watching for movements ahead. The light danced back and forth around the cave-like tunnel.

"Take your time. It's hard to see. Don't worry, I'll protect you."

"Yeah, right. That I'd like to see—like you did a minute ago."

"Well, I wasn't prepared. I'm prepared now. Prepared to get rid of Laine, too."

"I'm hearing a lot of talk. It stinks in here. What's that smell?" She peered ahead of her. He shined the flashlight on the ceiling, revealing an endless dark space ahead. Nothing looked familiar. "Sick! It smells awful."

"Yeah, it smells like something died." He shut his mouth when he saw her expression. "Bad air. This place doesn't get a lot of fresh air." He bit back his words. He was only making it worse.

Marla's face turned into a frown like he had never seen. I'm in trouble, he thought; better make up something good. "Hey, Marla, we can go to the racetrack when we get back. Bet on a few horses. I've got an inside tip from the Mexican boy, Rodriguez, on a winner. Wanna do that?"

"Maybe…I have to concentrate, it's tricky in here. *What is that smell?*"

Jack relaxed. Let her think. He kept his mouth shut.

Finally, after a few minutes, Marla stopped walking. She said in a small voice, "I think we're lost. This doesn't seem right—it's taking too long,"

She was talking to herself—not him. He got a bad feeling about it. He needed a drink.

"I remember going down the middle fork — following the red paint. We used to have a song about it. She sang, 'Red, red ...' something or other. Can't remember — oh, well. Or was it yellow — to the right, let's fight, fight, fight?"

"Take your time. What the hell we gonna do, Marla?"

"Who knows?" She shrugged.

"Sick," he said, covering his nose with his hand, laughing. "Something definitely died in here."

"You're not funny. I hate this plan of yours. Come on, I think the smell is better this way." She hurried ahead of him. "Yeah, it's not so bad now — almost gone."

"Yep, it's gone. Maybe rat met rat back there."

"Shut up about it!"

"Okay, okay, I was just making a joke. Lighten up."

Marla led them down several more paths turning left, winding up and down the wet, slippery rocks. Finally, after several minutes, they passed a huge wooden door on their right. A horizontal iron bar secured it to the wall.

"Hey, this is the kitchen. We're almost at the tower — a few more minutes. I know this place after all."

Jack put his finger to his lips. "Quiet! I hear people talking." Jack grabbed her arm.

"You're right. It's the door to the kitchen pantry inside the cottage. I do remember it. I hear them. Let's get away from the door before they hear us," she whispered.

"Come on, we're not far from the map room. I recognize this area. Are you coming?" She shined the light in his face, laughed at his look. "How do you like it?"

"Hey, I can't see, Marla. Knock it off." He blocked the light with his hand. Sweat beaded on his forehead. He felt bad — thought about another scotch.

"This way."

When they reached the end of the tunnel, Marla pointed at the floor.

"There's the hatch to the map room. I told you about it, remember? It's inside the tower fireplace. She shined her flashlight on the hatch embedded in the rocky floor of the tunnel. "Open it. It's on hinges. I know it's heavy, so be careful. Miles and I had to lift it together when we were kids."

"You did this with Miles?" He rubbed his chin.

"Yeah, it was a long time ago. Fun playing in these tunnels — hide and seek, you know. A lot of people used them back then, and we never saw any rats."

"Yeah, well…it's hard to see in here," said Jack, not liking what he heard. He scowled and looked around. "I don't see any hatch."

"You're stepping on it. What's the matter with you? We're here — I told you — above the fireplace in the lighthouse tower."

"How do you know for sure?" Jack saw Marla's mouth drop open.

"Are you kidding? I know these tunnels like the back of my hand," she said, knowing she sounded defensive. "Look. It's right there! Get off it." She played her light back and forth, revealing a stone slab. "Open it."

"Open it where?" Jack scratched his head. "All looks the same to me."

"What's gotten into you? Too much scotch, I suspect! Right there at the end of my light — the iron ring is there, too." She shoved his head down to look at it. "It's our way in. But don't fall down inside it once you flip it open."

"Oh, *that* hatch." He pushed her hand away. He felt nauseous. "Yeah, I thought it was some sort of door we would go through, like a kitchen door. So what do I do again?"

"Are you serious? Flip the damn thing open. It's heavy."

"Looks heavy."

"That's what I said, *heavy*. Come on, I'm cold. Hurry up, will you?"

"Quiet, Marla, I'm only gonna be a minute." He tugged at the rusty ring, but it didn't budge. "How'd you get this thing open, anyway?" He tugged harder, fingers cramping. The hatch creaked. "Hey, it moved." Sweat ran down the sides of his shirt, soaking it.

"This is ridiculous. I don't know why I had to come, if you can't even get the thing open. You dragged me here for nothing, Jack."

"Hold on, will ya?" He groaned. It moved a few more inches. "The hinges are rusty." He squatted on the floor. Straddling the slab between his legs, he yanked on the ring. It opened a few inches. Gripping either side of the thick hatch, in the middle, he pulled as hard as he could. It gave way and fell backward on his lap, pinning him under it. "Holy frickin' crap! You've gotta be kidding me!" He choked out a scream.

Shoving it slowly off his lap, gasping for air, he scooted backward against the tunnel wall. The hatch cover slammed down on the floor, opening the view into the fireplace.

Curled up in a ball, Jack held his hands between his legs, breathing heavily. "I wanna die, Marla. You should've told me it was *that heavy*." He rolled onto his knees; his eyes were squeezed shut and saliva dripped from his nose. Rising slowly, he bent at the waist with one hand on the wall, sucking in air.

"Get over it. You weren't listening. Let's get this done. And *stop* complaining. Why it had to be tonight is still a mystery to me."

He said in a raspy, hard voice, "*Tonight*? Are you for real? Guess you just missed what happened to me. You know damn well I had to know the layout so we can kidnap Laine. You have no feelings."

"That's not true." She figured she better change her attitude. "You okay?" She reached for his hand, brought it to her lips. "You did it. I knew you could." Marla rubbed her arms, looking through the large opening into the fireplace below.

"Yeah, I did." Jack felt better. Sweat rolled off his nose. He flattened himself on his stomach and peered into the map room.

"Dark in there," he said. "Hold on." His voice became a whisper. "A light went on in the room. "Shhhhh—I hear somebody. Turn off your light."

Marla knelt next to him. "See anyone?" Jack put his hand over Marla's mouth to silence her."

"I hear talking. *It's Laine! My wife!*" he whispered, putting a finger to his lips. They scooted away from the opening and listened.

Laine's voice filtered up to the tunnel. "I'm going to look over a few things now…yes, I know it's late. I'll call you tomorrow. Night."

Jack jabbed his elbow at Marla. "We can nab her. I think she's alone down there."

"How?" Marla said in a whisper. "We don't have anything with us."

"Let me think." He leaned into the space and could see his wife standing near the open window with her back to him. He scrambled back into the tunnel. "I've got it."

CHAPTER 15

BLACKROCK ISLAND

L aine thought she heard someone call her name and leaned out the tower window and looked down. No one below. "Smells putrid in here," she said, clearing her throat and pulling back inside the room. She wiped the ash smudged on her sweatshirt as she turned from the window. "That does it. Now I've ruined my clothes in this ancient place. It's filthy. Needs a good cleaning. Tomorrow won't come soon enough." She turned off the light and descended the spiral stairway to take a shower.

Jack peeked out of the fireplace when the room darkened. "Think she's gone. I'll check." He turned on the flashlight and waved it about the room. Empty.

"Yeah, thanks to you and your loud mouth," she mouthed down to him from the opening.

"I wanted to grab her. Finish what we came to do. There's still time."

"Next time. Let's go."

"She's definitely gone," he said to Marla, watching him from the open hatch in the fireplace ceiling.

"Good, let's get out of here. Come on."

"Wait a minute." He stepped out of the fireplace into the room. Brushing aside cobwebs, he wiped one from his mouth. He spied a mug on the refectory table, lifted it and sniffed. It was still warm and looked full. "Typical. Hmmm, Laine's favorite tea, but she didn't drink it." He put the mug down. "Too bad I don't have any arsenic with me."

"You've seen enough. Let's go while we still can."

"Hold on." He ran across the room, taking the spiral stairs downward two at a time. At the bottom, he found himself in the room leading out of the tower. There was a second small door that led into the cottage. He cracked it open, hinges squeaking. Down the hall to the right, a light glowed from a doorway. He hesitated then started to go toward it, but stopped when he heard Laine talking to someone.

Out of here, he thought, and slid along the wall, back the way he'd come. The door creaked when he closed it. He took off running up the spiral staircase. Taking the steps two at a time, he reached the map room. In the next instant, he was scrambling up the footholds into the tunnel. He said in an anxious voice, "Let's get out of here. Hurry. She might have heard me."

Marla stood shivering. "What are you talking about?"

"Laine might have heard me. I followed her into the cottage. She was talking to someone, but she didn't see me. Hold the light." He groaned and secured the hatch. "Let's go. Quick, Marla."

"Tell me you really didn't follow her." Marla took off in a run, flashlight leading the way, Jack following.

"Well, it wasn't you that was following her, was it?" He gestured with a slash of his arm. "Let's get something straight. I'm here to kill her. Correct that...*we're* here to kill her."

Marla was silent.

Darting down the passageway, they wound through the long, dark tunnels, tripping on the uneven stones. Finally, they reached the door to the kitchen pantry.

"Stop," Marla whispered. "I hear voices in there."

"No, keep going."

"Quiet, they'll hear you."

"Will you shut up? I am trying to hear what they're saying." Jack pressed his ear close to the crack in the wooden frame. "A woman is saying they're leaving early in the morning. They are going to Bourke's farm. A man is talking now."

"Can you make out what he's saying?" Marla crept next to him.

"He's saying 'round six. Miles is already gone."

They exchanged glances.

Marla motioned to leave, pointing toward the tunnel exit.

"Hold on a minute. Wait a sec. Let's see what else they say."

Marla put her head to the door and listened.

A woman's voice: "I'll be makin' the lunch in the morning for the crew what's comin'."

"Aye, I'll be pickin' them up on the mainland around eight. Laine wants to come, too, so she can see Miles's stables and meet the men. Be leaving early, I will, luv. Better check the boat and lock up now."

"I'll be goin' to bed. Morning will come soon enough," the woman said.

"Be back in a tick," the man said.

"You do that."

Marla and John watched the light go out in the crack around the door.

"We gotta get outta here, quick," Jack said to Marla and shoved her forward.

"Don't push me, Jack. What's the rush?"

"Didn't you hear him? He's going down to check his boat. He might see our boat—just our luck. Nothing but trouble is coming. Which way do we go, Marla? Make it fast."

"Don't get your jeans in a twist, Jack. I know this tunnel like the back of my hand."

Jack gave her another shove. "Yeah, I bet you do. Hey, I've got something to tell you. Did I ever tell you about that older guy I met from Donegal? Norbert something or other? Now there's a story."

"Tell me later."

He ignored her. "He couldn't swim. I figured out a way to knock him overboard and he drowned. That's how I got the land."

This got Marla's attention. She stopped and turned toward him.

"Go on." He spun her back around and jabbed a finger in her back to keep her going.

"That hurt," she complained. "Stop it. I'm listening. That's all I do is listen!"

"Yeah, right."

"So what happened?" Marla's flashlight played on the walls, making figure eights in front of her.

"You'd have been proud of me. It just reminded me of the story you told me about your father and how he drowned at sea—you made that happen right? We are the same, aren't we?"

Marla cut him off. "I hear the ocean, Jack. We're almost there."

"Good." Sweat rolled down his sides, soaking his shirt.

They took the stairs down to the inlet, raced to the curragh and climbed into it. Jack revved the engine and they headed out to sea. Once they were out of sight from the shore, he took up his story. "So like I said, we think the same. I flipped the old man overboard. You made the hole in your father's boat. If you hadn't done that, he would still be alive, don't you think?"

Marla turned to him and frowned, then nodded her head.

Jack went on, not noticing, while he steered the curragh. "It was a riot. Was it the same for you when you found out your dad was lost at sea?"

She wrapped her arms around herself, shivering. "I guess so."

"Yeah—that Norbert fellow *was* an old fool, now that I think about it."

She listened, saying nothing.

He smiled at her when she looked into his face. He knew she liked it by the way she stared at him, saying nothing. "You want me to tell you how I escaped?"

She nodded.

"The water near the shore was shallow, but it was hard to walk because it was rough. I could see ripples in the sand and fish feeding off the bottom. It was beautiful— colorful rocks—black, orange, gray. I jumped them, like stepping stones in a Bond movie. Got to the marshy shore, and sank up to my knees in the muck. It smelled like dead fish. Thought I was a goner, but I managed to crawl out of it and head into the woods."

Jack jammed the throttle forward. The boat slashed through the waves, pounding the bow up and down in the waves.

"Slow it down!" Spray drenched her, hair hanging limp, mascara running down her face.

"Can't. Got to keep ahead of them, so they don't see us. Hang on." He sped on, shouting over the roar of the engine. "I hotwired an old Ford truck from some hunting shack I found on the island—might have been an Indian's junker. Lots of 'em on that island—Indians that is. And here we are—you and me, thanks to my quick thinking. No more John Rafferty."

"There's no one by that name now." She hunched over and gripped the seat with both hands while he wheeled the boat through the choppy waves.

"It was exciting. Wish you could have been there with me. What a bastard your father was to you and your mother. Bet you wished I was there with you that night— the night you helped him to drown." Jack smiled down on her in the dark night.

"Yeah, right. We're a lot alike." Marla smiled as the boat raced toward Blacksod Harbor.

CHAPTER 16

BOURKE FARM - LUCRE
BLACKSOD

Midmorning. Gray clouds brushed over Bourke's farmland. Hundreds of thoroughbred horses grazed in the lush green fields adjacent to the stables, penned in by rows of limestone walls. Beyond the stables, oats and wheat bent their tops in the wind, snapping them against the ground. Above the crops, narrow-winged merlins circled overhead while eyes above their sharp, curved beaks surveyed the ground below, looking for dragonflies.

Miles stood at the edge of his green pastures behind the stables and glared at the body of his dead racehorse. He overheard his police cousins interrogate the two men who had shot it. Dressed in camouflage hunting gear, they slouched on bales of hay and mumbled their responses. Miles's men stood close, cradling rifles in the crooks of their arms.

"What's your name and where are you from?" asked Wilfrid of the older, bearded man.

"Joe Callahan, I am. This here's me younger brother Steve. We're from Limerick," he said in a clipped Irish accent.

"Where exactly were you hunting?"

"I told you. We was given permission to hunt there—right over there." He pointed to Miles's land.

"Place is not yours to hunt. It's Bourke's private property," Wilfrid said.

Joe looked at his shoddy boots and shook his head. The younger brother shrugged and sat in silence.

Miles walked over and stood in front of them. "You had no right to be on my land. Why the hell did you shoot my horse?"

"We didn't mean to do it," mumbled Steve. "It was an accident. We dinna know it was a horse. We was huntin' deer—only deer. Like Joe is tellin' 'em. We had permission to be on the land."

"No, you didn't have permission to be on my property. Accident, my arse. It's trespassing. Now you've murdered my horse and I want to know why." Miles moved in close to them.

The sullen hunters nodded again and again, taken aback by his tone. They looked away from Miles and over at the property.

"We'll take it from here," said Wilfrid. "Tom, handcuff them."

"Then what?" Miles's face reddened.

"We'll book them at the station. Then the judge will want to talk to them and most likely give them a hefty fine. Maybe jail time. We wanted you to have the chance to question them yourself—face-to-face—before we take them in."

"Right." Miles raised his fists at them. "What the hell's wrong with you? Can't you tell the *difference* between a horse and a deer?"

The hunters studied the ground. They said nothing.

"That horse was worth millions. Your negligence is going to cause all sorts of trouble for me." Miles stepped away and ran his hand through his hair. "Oh hell... Get these jerks out of my sight."

"Miles, we have it handled," said Tom, motioning them to the police car. "Let's go."

Dodd stepped forward with his gun. "We lads can be takin' care of 'em, we will."

Wilfrid said, "No, Dodd, we'll be stayin' within the law. We're taking it from here. Donna worry, Miles, it'll never happen again. Be sure of that." The police escorted the hunters past the horse. They directed their gaze away from the dead animal.

At the police car, the officers pushed the heads of the hunters down before they got into the backseat. The gravel flew from their tires as they drove off to Donegal Town.

Miles said to Dodd, "Damn it. I have to call that crazy sheik and let him know his horse has been murdered. I also have to call that slimy broker he works through and tell him I have a replacement horse. Swore I'd never work with that broker again. Now—I have no choice. This is a disaster."

"Aye, that it is."

Within moments, Miles spotted Laine and Eamon coming up the dirt road toward him and Dodd. "Hold up, will you? I don't want you to see this."

Eamon waved and they stopped by the stables to wait for Miles.

"For God's sake, Conner, cover Rex with something," said Miles, pointing to the horse.

"Aye, Boss." Connor ran to the nearby truck, retrieved a tarp, and covered the horse's body.

"I've called the vet. Won't be long till he gets here. Make it official, he will," said Dodd.

"Good man. Wait here for him. I'm going to tell Eamon and Laine what's happening. I'll check with you later this afternoon."

"Aye. I'll report back to you as soon as he gets here."

"Right." Miles left him and met the others at the stables.

Connor had gone ahead of Miles to tell Eamon what happened to Rex. "Callahan brothers from Limerick shot Rex dead. Dint know it was a horse. Thought he was a deer. Said they were huntin' on the neighbor's land next door with permission from a bloke named Jack."

Eamon looked at Laine and Conner, "'Tis a sad day for Miles, it is. Raised that horse since he was born."

"Connor," Miles asked, "what was the man's name again?"

"Callin' him Jack, the hunters did. Said he was an American drinkin' in Carrick's Pub. Said he was living in the Sullivan house."

"Are you sure they said the *Sullivan house?*" asked Miles. Conner pointed to the fields bordering Miles's land. "Told 'em the place is there, they did."

"It's Sullivan property all right. No one has lived there for at least a year. They had no right to be on that land. Or mine."

Laine's head came up. She heard it—*Sullivan* property. Laine listened as tempers flared.

Connor said, "Aye, the blokes traded work for huntin', they did. Fixed the yank's thatch roof on the Sullivan house, mowed the grass, and picked up a bit. Complained a lot about that. Said it was as tall as a man. Let go, it was."

"A lot of nerve letting out land to hunt on that's not his." Miles's face reflected his rage. "I'll look into this more. If you hear anything else, let me know."

"Aye, if you're finished I best be gettin' to Rex."

"Hold up a minute. Did the police get their address in Limerick?"

"Aye, Tom and Wilfrid put it on paper, so they said."

"Good." Miles turned back to look in the direction of his horse, frowning. "Let me know when you've buried him on the farm. Same place all the other horses are buried — under the pine trees. Have Dodd call me when it's done."

"I'll let him know," said Conner. He hurried off down the road.

"Trespassing it was. Nasty blokes, if ye be askin' me." Eamon grumbled. He rubbed his hands together, and kicked the dirt. "I can take Laine to meet the crew. Will you be waitin' here?"

"No, Eamon, you go to the island with the men. I have plans for Laine."

Laine put her hand on his arm. "I can go back to the island with the crew, Miles. You have things to do."

"It's all in good hands. We'll catch up with the crew this afternoon. It's not easy, but we'll get through it." He gave her hand a squeeze while his eyes never left hers.

"It's never easy." She removed her hand. For a moment, she felt a rush of excitement flow through her as he looked at her. She hadn't felt anything for anyone in a long time.

What's happening to me?

"Go on, Eamon, the crew will meet Laine later today. I'll bring her," said Miles.

"I'm off." Eamon headed down the road to inform the men.

"I was going to surprise you, Laine, but now that's ruined. I'd like to take you to your property that is next door to mine. That is ... if you want to. Would you like to see it?"

"My property? I don't own any property in Ireland."

"You mean you *thought* you didn't own any. Your family owns more property than anyone else on the west coast of Ireland. I thought you knew before now."

"Really, you have to be mistaken."

They stared at each other for a long, uncomfortable moment.

"Come with me. I'll show you." He gave her a smile.

"Fine." *Sullivan land—now this was a new one.* She climbed into the Jeep and they bumped down the dirt road leading out of his farm. Thinking back, she realized she didn't know much about her family history. Her parents would have told her if she had relatives in Ireland. Wouldn't they?

"It's not far. You'll get to see the coast."

"It will be nice to see the ocean from the ground." She gazed over at him. He had a ramrod-straight posture and a take-charge demeanor. For all his troubles, he was thinking of her. She drew another quick glance at him.

"I'd like to think we could have a drink and watch the sunset on the island tonight."

"So would I." His attention was knotting her insides.

"We're going to take a shortcut called the Fairies Walk to the Sullivan property. I think you'll enjoy it."

"I'm sure I will. What I've seen of the country is beautiful."

They made their way down the rutted dirt road. Fearnogs—alders—and fuinseog—ash—trees, canopied by thick foliage made of ivy, formed a green tunnel surrounding the road. The wind was cool and the shadows deep.

Miles said, "The *Druid's Circle* is in the grove ahead." He motioned to it as they neared the circle of stones. "It reminds me a little of Stonehenge in England."

"I would like to see it." Laine remembered Stonehenge in England and this structure did remind her of it. "It's a strange place."

"It is. We used to play here as children. Scare each other with stories about ghosts and witches. The fifteen stones surrounding the central boulder was an altar at one time. An altar for witches—bad witches. Irish legend, that it is." He laughed.

"I like it. Do you know the history?" She surveyed the tall, gray stones jutting upward toward the sky. Brown leaves covered the ground under bare trees.

"Not really. What you are looking at are animal skulls wedged on tree limbs looking out on the road. Never really liked this place."

"It's a splendid place and so near to your horse farm."

"If you like dead things, I suppose it is. Not my taste."

"Speaking of that, I am sorry about your horse. How will Rex's death affect your business? I know it is none of my business, but this place made me think of it." She wanted to draw Miles out to find out more information. Max would want the details.

"I don't want to burden you with it, but suffice to say, someone wants to ruin me — and my business."

"Horse racing and breeding is a cut-throat business."

"Yes, and I am going to find out who is out to get me." His face turned hard. He put the car in park, so she could see the skulls.

"There's a well over there with steps leading up to it — under the trees." She looked across the road from where they stood, away from the *Druid's Circle*. "Strange, the trees are green and lush over there — but not here. I see brambles too."

"That's the *Wishing Steps* and the *Wishing Well*. They're part of the legend that surrounds this place. It may be of interest to you. I have a book back at the lighthouse. You can read it, if you want to."

"Sure, I'd like that."

"Time to go."

The air from the sea filtered through the trees as they drove on. The fragmented rays of the sun shone white against the shadows. Laine pictured the Atlantic Ocean, the cool green-blue of the water, and whitecaps breaking on the surface of the waves. She felt good — despite the situation on the farm.

"It is peaceful here," she said.

"Yes. You are in the Belmullet Peninsula. The sea breeze is refreshing." At the curve, he slowed down. "You'll see the ocean around the next bend."

"I love the ocean." It was hard to focus on her mission — her objective — but she had to stay on track. She reminded herself to remember what happened — what's going on now. Keep asking him for information, she told herself.

"This is all Sullivan land. The whole coastline's yours."

"I can't believe it."

"Believe it. It's been Sullivan property for generations. I've done the research. It's yours, all right."

"That's pretty farfetched, since I don't have any relatives here."

"So you say."

The spruce and oak trees pressed in on them, smelling of summer. As they passed an overgrown cemetery, Laine put up her hand. "Can we stop there? I'd like to look at the headstones. See if you're putting me on." She gave him a smile — knew he was putting her on.

"Certainly, but don't say I didn't tell you." He pulled to the side of the road. It was overgrown with tall grass and weeds. "This *is* the Sullivan cemetery — a private cemetery on the Sullivan property."

"I don't believe you." She slid from the Jeep into the grass and wildflowers.

"Believe it. You sure are a tough one to convince." He turned off the engine and followed her through an unhinged rusty gate lying in the weeds.

"Oh, you're right. It says Sullivan. Unbelievable." She stared at the huge Celtic cross mounted on a marble pedestal in the center of the cemetery. "I *could* be related to some of these people, but I highly doubt it."

"You are." Miles laughed. "All of them."

Laine looked at Miles watching her roam the area. "Not a chance." Could I have relatives here? she thought. Why don't I know about them?

She examined tombstones tilted over and others straight. Lilies and iris bloomed in scattered patches. Birds pecked at the ground and took flight as they approached.

"They all say 'Sullivan.' I don't understand."

"This *is* your land. I've been trying to tell you—your family has been here for years. I thought you knew."

"How would I know? No one ever told me."

"I'm telling you. I looked up the family history. Our grandparents were friends. They lived here—your grandparents, that is—in the main house where we are going. I assumed when I wrote my email letter inviting you here to work for me, you knew the connection and about the land. About your family."

"Well, I didn't." She frowned, thinking back to Max's comment about her ancestors—he knew it all along. Why didn't he tell her? She was angry and he was going to hear about it. "This comes as a shock, Miles. It'll take me a while to digest it."

"I'm sure it will." He took her arm to lead her back to the Jeep, but she held back.

"Give me a few more minutes," she said in a low voice, thinking of killing Max. He had set her up with Miles. Knew about this property and used it for bait. She would have a lot to say to him tonight, but nothing to give him on this "milkshaking" issue.

Miles walked close to her while she wandered through the overgrown grass to a headstone with fresh flowers on it. Stopping in front of it, she read, "Norbert Sullivan 1935 to —. Who is Norbert Sullivan? Seems he is still alive. Someone put fresh flowers here."

"Norbert's your uncle. But—he disappeared about a year ago when he went to America. No one has heard from him since. Margaret must have put the forget-me-nots there. He lived in the house we are going to see."

"Margaret?" Laine asked with a lifted eyebrow.

"Margaret Hogan. They've been friends or, should I say, companions—for years. She owns the title company in Donegal. You'll be seeing her soon, I expect. I told her you were coming to Ireland. Have you seen enough?"

"Yes, but I would like to see the house you mentioned."

"Let's go." They exited the gate. He opened the Jeep door for her and she climbed inside.

"This is very strange. My parents immigrated to the States before I was born. They're both buried in Detroit. They never said a word about owning any property here or having any relatives in Ireland."

"That is odd. Maybe we can shed some light on this mystery when we visit Margaret in town."

"I'd like that." It stopped her for a moment. She might have family she did not know about here. Max would know—damn him. She had a lot of questions for him and he better have answers.

They left the cemetery, bumping along the road. The sun shined through gaps in the trees. The sky was cloudless, such a change from the storms the day before.

"Is it far?" she said in a light voice.

"Around the next bend. Patricia will have to tell you about the Fairy's Walk and the Banshee—legends we have."

"What's that?"

"Not what, but who—a feminine spirit— a banshee is a woman of the fairy mounds. I'll let her tell you about it." He laughed at the look on her face.

"I'd like that." The place was becoming more interesting by the moment, she thought.

Laine gazed into the deep woods. Listening to frogs croak from the stream that ran along the road made her smile. It was nothing like New York.

They pulled up to a white stucco home with a red door, green shutters, and a thatched roof. A profusion of primroses, sea holly, and harebell bordered each side of a winding pathway to the door. Wild flowers peeked above the long grass in a nearby field.

"It's exquisite but isolated," she said, looking around.

"And in good shape. Norbert kept it up."

Laine surveyed the house, the sky and the land. Skylarks warbled in the trees. The breeze blew warm, salty, sea air from the ocean. Waves crashed on the nearby shore.

"This is Norbert's house, but he actually lived in town." He paused a moment, frowning. "Jack could be the man who rents this place, if the hunters are right. I don't think it's possible. Norbert didn't like strangers on his property. I'm not sure I believe them."

"Right."

Miles tried the door. "It's open. Let's have a look. Hello, anyone here?"

Silence.

They entered into a large family room with a high, beamed ceiling. The smell of burned peat emanated from the open-hearth fireplace. A dark wood table surrounded by ladder-back chairs stood off to one side. Antique plates filled the hutch near the table. Tapestry-covered armchairs were arranged in front of the fireplace.

"Nice place. It is definitely being used." He picked up a newspaper from the table. "Yesterday's news."

"Maybe we should leave."

"Now that we're here, let's look around a little more."

"All right. When was the last time you were here?"

"Not since I was a child."

Miles walked into the bright kitchen and opened the refrigerator. "It's full of food." He opened a container of milk and smelled it. "Fresh."

Walking to the sink, she said, "A lot of dirty dishes."

Miles opened a cupboard. "Someone likes his liquor. There's enough Bushmill's Scotch here for a coronation. Expensive year." He shut the cupboard door.

"Scotch?" she said. Bad memories of John and his drinking returned to her. She shoved them aside.

"Yes." He opened a few more cupboards without commenting on them.

"I'd like to see the second floor." She returned to the main room and at the far end of it, climbed stairs to the loft. "There's an office up here with lots of information on local horse dealers, horse sales, saddlery and tackle — enough *EQ Life* magazines to paper a wall. Ashtrays are full of cigarette butts — packages of Camel cigarettes on the floor. It stinks."

"Mess down here, too. First-floor bedroom appears to be a man's room. Bed's unmade, men's dirty clothes all over the floor. Someone is definitely living here."

Laine came down the stairs and went to Miles in the bedroom. "Needs someone to pick up after him."

On top of a dresser was a blue lanyard with keys at the end. She picked it up, examined it, puzzled. *Couldn't be,* she thought. "Take a look at this. I had one like this on my sailboat in Michigan. The name's worn off. Do you recognize it?"

"None that I've ever seen. We use roped key buoys here in Ireland — in case you drop them in the water." He fingered the lanyard and set it back on the dresser. "Another coincidence?"

"Yes. I must be cracking up," she laughed. She had a funny feeling in her stomach.

"Doubt that. You might want to see the bathroom off the front room. I'm not sure what else there is to explore."

"Guess so." She went to it. "It's actually clean."

There was an ashtray with cigarette butts, a comb, toothbrush and toothpaste on the counter. She opened a drawer and slammed it shut.

Stop it! Corduroy Cologne by Zirh International — the same cologne John wore. This was all too much like him. She began to doubt herself, until she saw him in her mind — in the square, smiling, with the other woman. Tonight, she would ask Max to find out about this house and who was living in it. There was no doubt in her mind. It was all too familiar.

"Ready?"

"Let's go. I've seen more than enough." She rubbed her arm by habit.

"Before I forget, we can start construction on the tower today, if you're up for it. Patricia is giving the workers something to eat as we speak."

"Sounds good."

They were about to leave when they heard a door slam and an engine sputter from outside the house.

Miles ran to the front door. "Hey, you there. I want to talk to you. Hold up!"

A dark blue truck raced down the gravel road and vanished around the curve.

"Who was that?" She stood close to him, peering out.

He grabbed her hand and led her out of the house. "I don't know, but we weren't alone."

CHAPTER 17

MCGINTY'S PUB
BLACKSOD

When Jack sped out of the Sullivan driveway, dust flew from the tires of his truck. Taking the back roads to Blacksod Harbor, he would avoid running into Laine and Miles. The ocean cleared his head and gave him time to think. In a short time, he was fishing.

The fish weren't biting. The sun was past noon. Hours of trolling for salmon brought him no relief. He still felt bad. The water was rough. Several large waves hit the small boat broadside. He spun the wheel to avoid crossing his fishing lines, but one of the lines got tangled in the propeller. He'd have to cut it.

Taking the knife from his fishing vest, he tested it on a loose cord. It was razor sharp. "At least one thing is in order." He got up to cut the line, lost his footing, and landed on his side on the gas tank. The knife shot out of his hand and flew into the water.

"Damn it! Damn it! Damn it!" He righted himself. The Shakespeare pole in the rod holder was curved over as far as the motor on the side of the boat, ready to snap. He grabbed pliers on the deck and twisted the line until it broke. He grabbed the pole and placed it on the deck. Now he had to figure out how to free the line from the prop so he wouldn't sheer a pin when he headed into the harbor. He wrapped a line around his waist, stooped halfway over the stern, and pulled the line that was wound around the propeller.

It came free in his hands. "Great!" He shouted and slipped back into the safety of the boat as it pitched and rolled.

"Gotta have a drink." He stood at the wheel and downed what was left of the bottle of scotch then tossed it into the ocean. He sneered as the glass bottle mocked him by not sinking right way. It bobbed up and down on the rough waves. Finally, it filled with water and disappeared.

"It is all pointless. I've had enough fishing." He brought in the lines and placed the rods on the inside walls of the boat. Tackle was placed in the fishing box and shoved under the seat.

Soon he entered the harbor. When he pulled into the slip, the bow crashed into the dock between the pilings. The current was strong and threw the boat toward the rocks at the front of the well. Jumping up, he grabbed the pike pole, lifted the stern lines from the hooks, and secured them on the cleats. Next, he grabbed the bowlines and fastened them.

"I've had it." He flipped the bumpers over the side. Before he climbed out, he placed the key on the hook under the seat. He walked over to the fisherman in the well a few slips over from him.

"Bad wind and current for dockin' the boat. Been fishin', have you?" Kieran Breen bent over his net. "Working on me snap-nets, I am. On your way to be havin' a pull at McGinty's pub? Or Carrick's?"

"A pint sounds good at McGinty's. Come along?"

"Grand, but not just now. Be wantin' a Jameson or two when I'm done with this."

"Mending your nets by hand?"

"That I do."

"The fish aren't biting. I got skunked. Did you fish today?"

"Took the Yanks out fly-fishing on Lough Corrib this morning. Said I was the best guide they ever had—what do they know? Caught fourteen or fifteen kelts but no fresh salmon. Damn Yanks jabbering the whole time. No offense."

"None taken. Get any brown trout?' Jack lit a cigarette.

"Aye, one Breac Donn, the biggest one I've caught this summer. Lovely, it was. Goin' out at six tomorrow morning, if you want to go." Kieran straightened his back and grinned.

"Got to broker a horse for a guy. Another time."

"Say, I hear they got horses doin' flaps. They were racin' on Geesala beach this mornin'. Sell any horses for the race?"

"Could have, but no. I'm working a deal. Bigger than those sand runners." Jack flipped his cigarette butt into the water. Circles pooled around it.

"Aye." Kieran studied the net in his large, rough hands. "Hear they got swimmers off the lighthouse doing a relay for the Blacksod Point Challenge Triathlon. They'll be takin' up miles of ocean as fast as we are chattin' about it. New York lads are swimming all day long between the buoys out there. Daft, if you ask me. They could be fishin'."

"New Yorkers? You don't say." He lit another cigarette and tossed the match. It hissed when it hit the water.

"Three hundred Triathlon lads swimmin' in the roughest part of the ocean during the race, so they say. Get up good speed and manage to survive in Blacksod Bay. Bit of pain 'tis for us fisherman. We got to watch out for 'em. The buoys are rigged with safety rations and rest stations, if they be needin' it." He rubbed his hand over the gray stubble on his chin.

"That ocean is a real challenge. Where are they?" He hadn't seen the swimmers when he came into the harbor.

"Settin' up for the race a mile out from the Blacksod Lighthouse. Did you see the startin' line markers on the water out there? Practicing, they are."

"I came in from the north. Must have missed them. What's all this about?"

"Forgot for a second you're a Yank. Event happens every year. Our lighthouse is in the Guinness Book of Records, lad." Without breaking his concentration, he wove a knot while talking. "Blacksod is the most westerly point of Ireland before you reach America. We have one of the only two square lighthouses in the world, they say."

"I see." He yawned.

"The challenge starts here today."

"What does that have to do with anything?"

"I'm gettin' to it." The netting was pulled tight between his teeth; his hands pinched off the loose ends where he was making the knots.

Jack inhaled, waiting, not liking the story. To divert his attention he focused on the dark water, looking for fish. Tall yellowish-green kelp tangled around the rocks in the murky water.

"Irish lighthouse keeper Ted Sweeny sent the original weather forecast and Churchill delayed the D-day landin' for a whole day in 1944. They was tellin' him what storms was comin' in across Ireland. They say it changed the course of the Second World War, it did. Neutral, we was — Ireland, that is."

"Good to know. I'm feelin' a bit thirsty. Think I'll head up for a pint."

"Aye, I'll be joining you for a jar after mendin' the last net." He pulled another rope in place, tightening the knot.

Jack walked down the beach, staring at the greenish-white foaming waves that lapped the sand at water's edge. Dark triangles of water spilled out from under the curl of the waves and faded on the next wave. Peering down at his feet, he saw small fish flip over on their stomachs in the shallow areas, floundering in circles. "You'll never make it to the sea swimming like that."

He laughed at them.

He approached McGinty's pub, avoiding Carrick's from the night before. Sweat poured from his back, soaking his shirt. He noticed the small, colorful shacks in the distance, lined up like dominos, peering out on the ocean. Maybe I can own one of those, he thought.

Traditional music emanated from the pub. The moment he stepped inside, cigarette smoke fogged the air around him. The smell of yeasty beer and fried fish made him thirsty but not hungry. An older fisherman sat in the corner, smoking a pipe. Several stern-faced men huddled on stools at the bar, their cigars contributing to the white haze clouding the room.

Taking a seat at a booth, he ordered a shot of Bushmill's Scotch. Changing his mind, he said to the bartender, "Make it a double. And no. I don't want anything to eat."

"Down in the luck?"

"No fish, that's all." He downed the drink. The bartender refilled the glass without asking.

He felt fine. The drink warmed him. He toyed with an idea: time to buy another horse from Miles Bourke and sell it to the sheik. Make some money.

He ordered another drink.

CHAPTER 18

DONEGAL AUCTIONS

Stumbling from McGinty's after several hours at the bar, Jack folded himself into his pickup and called Marla on the drive to Donegal Auctions. Weaving back and forth across the dividing line on the road, he said, "Bourke's showing horses today—I'm gonna buy another one for the sheik. He just doesn't know it yet. Wanna meet me there?"

Jack frowned. "I told you. I can buy a horse there without a middleman. I am the middleman—what am I thinking?" He laughed at his own joke, feeling good.

She said nothing.

"Where are you, anyway? Sounds like a horn blasting in the background?" He was wandering all over the road. "What?" He shook his head. "Your mother's television? Turn it down. I can't hear you with all that noise. Better yet, I'll call you later. I'm here." He parked the truck and went to the sales area.

Horse buyers and breeders lined up against the metal rail of the horse auction block. The shouting and bidding for thoroughbred racehorses had started, and he had to squeeze into a place. Seeing men and women crowded on tiered bleachers watching the show made him laugh. Suckers, every last one of them. They talked over each other, outbid each other, and listened to cell phones, knowing nothing about horses like he did.

The place was alive—men arguing over prices, women crying at the loss of their horses, young boys and girls standing around talking or shoveling after them. In the center ring, men paraded horses in a circle in front of the crowd.

I'm here for the prize—the best horse, he thought. He watched and waited for the one he wanted. Concentrating, he studied his price sheet, making calculations. Miles Bourke's top selling horses were next.

The highbrow auctioneer rattled off the next horse," Duke, brother of Rex…"

Jack heard, "Blah, blah, blah." He already knew Rex's specifications. He'd sold it to the sheik a few days ago, but things had gone wrong. Very wrong. A few hours ago, the bartender at McGinty's Pub told him the Callahan brothers shot Bourke's horse Rex on his farm. What were the hunters thinking? They ought to be shot themselves—damn fools.

He studied the sheet and realized he'd have to find a replacement for Rex if he expected to keep the money. I need a winner, he thought. He looked at each horse, underlined several specifications, and scribbled notes on a pad.

Looking up, he had a jolt. Duke was in the parade ring, but he could have sworn he was Rex. He heard the auctioneer talking about breeding. "A direct blood line to Rex— Duke is…"

That's it! I can substitute Duke for Rex! They look exactly alike. Sheik Tariq would never know the difference; he's never even seen Rex. He pictured Kamal—a complete idiot for a sheik's broker. I'll cut him out. Deliver Duke myself. Yeah, it's perfect.

"Who'll give me one million to start the bidding for Duke?" asked the auctioneer.

A few men held up their hands.

Jack cut in and shouted, "Two million!"

The men looked shocked and stopped bidding. Jack smiled at them.

"Going once, going twice, three times? Sold!" The auctioneer smacked the gavel on the podium and stopped the bidding. After a short pause, he went on with the next horse, but Jack wasn't listening. He had his prize — his substitute.

An old man walked up to him. "I'm Dodd, head man from Bourke's Farm. What time would it be good for us to be deliverin' this fine horse to you?"

"Never. I'm taking it with me in half an hour. Load Duke in my trailer next to the paddock. Door is open. I've got a few things to wrap up." He put his fingers together, making the money sign.

"We'll be doin' the delivery to the sheik for you. It's part of the sellin' and the buyin' contract, it is."

"Let me tell you something, old man," Jack spat at him. "You won't be delivering anything. This horse is not *Rex*, but he'll have to do. You got my last horse shot! What if somebody put a gun to your head? You gonna go back for more? No, I'll take him myself, so there's no screw up."

"Are you daft? You dint have a horse named Rex. 'Twas Sheik Tariq's horse. Don't know where you gettin' your information from, but it's a lie. Shootin' was an accident, it was. What do you know about it?" Dodd squinted his eyes at Jack.

Jack realized he'd said too much. "Lucky guess. I hear things. But it doesn't change anything. I bought that horse, and I'm taking it with me."

"Where are you from?" Dodd clenched and unclenched his fists. "Sound like an American."

"No place you've been." He laughed in his face.

"That so? Ah well, we'll be happy to be deliverin' Duke to the stable tomorrow afternoon."

"No, like I said, I'll see you at my trailer in half an hour. Don't be late." Jack walked off.

As he moved away from the old man through the crowd of people, he thought, Duke is a gold mine—same bloodline as Rex—even looks like him. I have to tell Marla I can skim a million off the top of this sale—maybe even the next one too. Kamal, the sheik's handler, is such a simpleton, he will never know the difference.

Jack left the auction area and sauntered over to the post bar past the stables. He needed a drink. He'd have a scotch there to celebrate, before he drove back to the Blacksod Pub. After a few too many drinks, he forgot all about his horse trailer parked in the lot. Drinking and toasting himself was his new objective.

He felt fine.

CHAPTER 19

BLACKSOD TO BLACKROCK ISLAND

While Jack drove down the road to Blacksod Pub, without his horse, Miles and Laine left the Sullivan property and flew to the island. Sunrays weaved yellowish-white finger trails over green waves as tailwinds pushed them through the sky. A short time later, they arrived and walked the path to the cottage.

"Afternoon to ye both," said Patricia, watering the creeping buttercups, ragged robins and cuckoo wildflowers near the front door. "Be havin' your lunch, we will, but your crew's waitin' to talk to you both now that you're here. They're at the lighthouse." She tipped the green can, sprinkling water on pink and white geraniums in the window boxes.

"Beautiful flowers," said Laine.

"That they are. I'll be takin' some inside from the garden out back. These are for the lookin'. Lunch will be ready half past the hour."

"We won't be late." Miles winked at Laine and drew closer to her.

"Shall we go meet the men?" She smiled back at him and walked ahead.

The sound of buzzing and cutting came from busy construction crews setting up the scaffolds around the lighthouse. Ruddy-faced workmen with tool belts swinging at their waists gripped circular saws and cut slender planks of wood. The sun beat down on their backs and sweat rolled from their faces.

Eamon approached them as they neared. A burly man by his side eyed them suspiciously. "This is your foreman; name's Murray. Meet Ms. Sullivan."

"The pleasure is all mine."

Laine watched the large man bow to her and sweep the cap from his thick brown hair. "Nice to meet you, Murray. Call me Laine. We'll go over the plans, so we can get started on the tower." Laine shook his strong, calloused hand. He held on longer than she expected. Trouble, she thought, and broke the grip.

"Laine, my days workin' with you will be a pleasure, they will." His green eyes burrowed into hers.

"How far along are you?"

"Thirty-five this year, single and available. You?"

Miles laughed at the big man. "How far along on the lighthouse, Murray? Concentrate on the job. Ms. Sullivan will be here all summer, working with you and the men."

He poked Laine gently with his elbow. "You'll have to watch out for him. He's up to no good."

"Oh, that. Thought you meant something else, lass." Murray grinned and looked her up and down. "We've finished settin' up the scaffoldin' on the east side of the tower. Now we're workin' on the west side. Cracks in the exterior need patchin' and repairin', they do. We'll be workin' on tearin' out the lighthouse window. It shows a fine view of the ocean."

"Good. It needs to be replaced. The map room is a mess. It needs cleaning out then a good scrub before we plaster and paint it."

"Aye, the Mexican lad Rodriquez is sweepin' it up. We're needin' an expert to be cleanin' the fireplace. We'll frame the window in there later this afternoon. The lad will be cleanin' the extra debris here around the scaffoldin'."

"Oh, good. Think I'll take a look."

He was a charmer; she wanted to steer clear of him.

She wondered when she would have some reliable information for Max. She guessed she'd have to warm up to Miles, get him talking, but keep it professional.

The men followed her up the winding stairs into the map room, where the Mexican boy Rodriguez was sweeping around the fireplace. She observed he was wearing a baseball cap with a bonefish on it, pulled low on his forehead—hard to see his face. Her training kicked in: What was he hiding?

"Hello, Rodriguez. I am Laine Sullivan, your new boss. Like to fish?" She pointed at his cap.

"No speak English," the boy said. His black eyes fixed on her for a moment, and then he turned away, sweeping dirt and old papers into a dustpan. Particles of dust floated through the air as rubbish fell into a cardboard box.

Miles said, "Knows enough English to get by but really very little. Eamon met him in a harbor pub and learned he was looking for work. He hired him a few days ago to do odd jobs. Guess he helped out on one of the boats in town until they didn't need him anymore."

"He's no trouble," Eamon said to her. "A good worker, he is. He'll be takin' the old magazines and books in boxes down to the boat to take to the mainland for shreddin'. Nothin' worth savin'."

He sat on the oak chair at the end of the refectory table, nestled his cap on his knee and smiled big between his ruddy cheeks. "What about the old newspapers? Want those shipped out too?"

"Burn them in the trash cans on the west side of the island, but I want the other debris removed by boat," said Miles. "What do you want to do with this room, Laine?"

"Still a long way to go after the place is swept clean. Remove the window today and replace it. Get the fireplace cleaned out. Run new electric lines for the lights. Patch and plaster the cracks in the ceiling and the walls — a lot to do before we paint. We'll sand and stain the floors last. What else?" Her eyes surveyed the room. "Pick out rugs, furniture, and paintings."

Eamon watched the boy sweep. "Aye, it'll be a right place to entertain when you finish."

"I fancy you'll be dressin' up for entertainin' a party here?" said Murray.

"Sure. Why not?" She turned her back on him and walked over to Miles. "I ordered the wrought-iron chandelier we talked about, matching sconces and a hand-carved mahogany bar. An estate was restored along the coast not far from here. It will make a big difference in the room."

"What estate?"

"Have to check. I don't remember."

"I most likely know them. Let me know when you find out."

"Sure." She thumbed a quick note on her cell phone to remind herself.

Murray went over to the boy and gave him a shove in the back. "Finish up and carry the boxes down to the docks? Understand?"

He shrugged his shoulders and slumped on a wood crate, tapping his feet on the floor. He stared at Eamon, ignoring Murray.

Murray said, "I'll be showin' him wot to do with the rest of the garbage. Come over here." He pointed to a box and motioned for him to pick it up. The boy did not move off the crate and stared at the floor under the low-brimmed cap.

"I'll handle this, Murray. You've got better things to do than pick on this young lad." Eamon jumped up from the chair and went to the boy. He motioned to the boxes in the corner and pointed down the stairs. The boy nodded, after putting down the broom and dustpan.

"Thanks, Eamon." Laine coughed. "Murray, can you open the other window, please? It is getting stuffy in here. We've got to get started."

"Anything for a pretty lady." He shoved the window to the top of the frame. Glass shattered and flew on the floor. "Don't know me own strength—old window it was. Before you go, boy, clean this up."

He took two strides over to Rodriguez, grabbed the broom and pushed it into his hands. He directed him to the glass pieces. The boy slowly stood up and stared at him before starting to sweep up the glass fragments on the floor.

"Leave him be, Murray. I told you I'd take care of tellin' him wot to do around the place." Eamon stood between the boy and Murray, offering support.

"Thank you, Rodriguez," Miles said to the boy. "You report to Eamon from now on."

Murray scowled and crossed his arms on his chest.

Laine caught the boy looking from Miles to her. She smiled at him, but he ignored her and went back to sweeping. Something was off. She felt it but could not quite place what it was. She would have to think about it—later. Now she had more important things to do.

"It's getting close to lunch. We ought to go down... finish up here later," said Miles.

Eamon nodded. "The crew's been workin' hard all morning. Got to be hungry. Aye, tidy up after we leave. We'll be callin' it quits for the day at half five, so I can take 'em back to the mainland."

"Sounds good. We are on schedule, so we'll continue our discussion later." She went to the refectory table and searched among the blueprints.

The dark-skinned boy stiffened and stopped pushing a pile of glass into a cardboard box. He pulled out a pack of cigarettes, lit a match and watched her from the corner of his eye.

"There's no smoking in here," said Miles. He stood with hands clasped behind his back as he examined the Maggie McClellan painting of the horse farm and stables above the fireplace. "We need to have this artwork cleaned. It's filthy."

Laine checked her clipboard. "Yes, it is on the list. Maggie is actually a friend of mine. She'll work on it as soon as we ship it to her. Before we go, do you mind taking it off the wall? We can take it down with us."

"Give me a hand, Murray." They lifted the massive oil painting from the wall, carried it over to the doorway and leaned it against the door.

The Mexican boy lit his cigarette.

Eamon snatched it from him, tossed it on the floor and crushed it with his boot. "That'll be enough," he said to him and then to the others. "No worries about him. Doesn't know all the rules yet."

"What pub did you meet him in the other night?" asked Miles.

"Murray and I were havin' a jar at McGinty's Pub. We was lookin' for an odd job man and I hired him without references. Been a good worker, he has. Only been with us a few days, right, Murray?"

"Aye," he said, frowning. He looked at Rodriguez and moved close to him. Laine caught little of the conversation, but Murray had his back to her and spoke quietly to the boy. "Didn't know I was a listenin' to you talkin' to that Yank in the pub, did you, lad? Watchin' you, I am. Don't be takin' the deal and hookin' up with that dirty bloke. Not in your best interest. I know you're gettin' some of this. I heard you talkin' a bit of English. I know you're understandin' a bit of what we're sayin'. You don't fool me, you don't."

The boy's face turned red. He slipped quickly behind Eamon.

Giving up the conversation with the boy, Murray directed his attention to Laine. "Where do you want the old window frame? Take me a while to get the rest of it out of the wall after lunch, it will. It's been here a couple hundred years." He scratched his chin and grinned. "It's gonna be quite a job. But, we'll be startin' again after the feast Patricia is fixin' for us, we will."

"That would be nice. What do you think, Miles? Pull it all out or try to fix it?"

Miles ran his hand over the wood. "It's rotted. Replace it."

"Good," Laine retrieved her blueprints and photographs from the refectory table. Her schedule fell off the table onto the floor, unnoticed. "I'm starved. Let's do this later."

The boy was sweeping the rest of the glass into the box and stayed far away from Murray. He maneuvered himself by the table, grabbed Laine's schedule from the floor and jammed it in his pants under his shirt. He picked up a box and made his way down the steps ahead of the group.

"I'm goin' to tell the rest of the lads outside 'tis time to eat," said Eamon. "Me wife had me fixin' the shutters all mornin', pickin' up the mess in the yard and bringin' her top soil for the flower boxes. I need a rest now and a good supper. I'll be tellin' the crew to meet you in the cottage. Come on, Murray. Rodriguez?"

"Let's go, Laine. I bet you are starved. It's been quite a day, and it's only one o'clock." Miles paused for a moment in front of her. She saw he wanted to ask her something, but changed his mind. Instead, he took her arm and led her to the stairs. "The boy went ahead with a box. Funny, he did know what we wanted."

"Yes, I guess he did." She had an uneasy feeling in her stomach.

The yard looked orderly when they stepped outside. The sun felt warm on her skin. She opened her arms to the breeze sweeping in from the ocean as they walked toward the cottage.

"I'm going to take a minute and check the boat to see how it's riding. I can see it from the top of the cliff. Want to come?" asked Miles.

"Sure, but before we go, can we look at the window we're tearing out?"

"Be my guest," he said, walking close to her.

They rounded the wall of the tower and looked up at the space.

"A larger window there will let more light in. I think it will make a big difference in the feel of the room. Deliver what you want."

"Yes, I like the idea. We can see the sunset over the ocean from this side of the tower. Sunrise from the other."

"Yes, that's the plan." Miles picked up a few stray boards and placed them in the trash bin near the scaffolding.

"They've done a remarkable job in such a short time." Laine added a few pieces to the bin.

"They're a meticulous crew. I've worked with them for years. Murray is one of the best. A bit overbearing, if you know what I mean, but he gets the job done. The men respect him, and the ladies...we'll leave that for another day." He laughed at her look and took her hand.

She pulled away, picked up a few nails and placed them in his hand. He looked into her eyes and put them in his pocket.

"He's harmless," said Laine.

"That's what you think."

"Hold on a minute. I want to step back a few yards and see what the window looks like from over there by the trees." She paced a few steps, turned and gazed upward, then nodded. "Looks good to me."

"Are we done?"

Within moments, they were looking down the cliff at the boats in the cove. He put his arm around her shoulder. She didn't move. It felt strong.

"There's Rodriquez talking with some man I don't know. Looks like he carried the box of trash down to the dock. What's he doing?"

"It's very strange," Laine eyed the boy with suspicion. Something about the man was familiar to her. Oh no—not again! John.

Her insides churned. She dashed away from Miles and ran toward the stone steps. This time he would not get away from her. She would find out the truth. "I'll be right back."

"Hey, where are you going?"

"I have a bad feeling about this." Laine flew down the stairs.

"I'm coming with you."

Her insides tightened, while she looked at the tall, thin man under the brimmed fishing hat. He took a roll of bills from his pants pocket, peeled several from it and jammed the money into the boy's hand. The boy quickly shoved it in the pocket of his jeans and looked around. Seeing Laine and Miles bearing down on them, he shouted to the man, who quickly ran to the boat and jumped in.

"Hey, you there. Hold up! I want to talk to you." Miles passed Laine on the steps.

She saw the boy hesitate. The man yelled to the boy. "Get in."

He untied the line, scrambled inside and shoved the curragh away from the dock. They sped away from the cove at top speed.

"Come back here!" Miles shouted, bounding down the steps to the landing at the bottom.

The boat kept heading out to sea.

Miles, hands on hips, huffed. "I don't like this at all. Rodriguez heard me. What the hell were they up to? Who the hell was that man?"

"They wanted to get out of here in a hurry. That's for sure."

She remembered the way the man cocked his head as he ran—it was John. She was sure of it. But what was he doing with the boy and why was he avoiding her?

"Are you okay? You seem distant."

"I'm fine. I'm sure that man heard you—Rodriguez, too. This is all wrong. I am trying to piece it together."

"Odd, very odd."

"If Patricia wasn't fixing a meal, we'd go after them. There will be time for it later. I'm going to find out who that was and get to the bottom of it. I'm going to put in a call to the harbor and see exactly who that is with Rodriquez. When they show up in Blacksod Harbor, they'll have a waiting party."

Miles pulled out his cell and called Tommy at the police station. He left a message as they headed up the steps to the top of the cliff. "Let's go eat."

"Good idea." Laine grabbed her cell phone and made a note to herself to remember what she saw. She had to tell Max that John was definitely on the island. It was all strangely familiar, yet terrifying. What game was John playing now? How was Miles involved in all of this?

She watched them disappear into a small dot on the horizon. She kept to herself the idea it was John. She would have to contact Max and see what he could find out. She had the description of the curragh and she knew the name of the Mexican boy. It might help them discover the connection. But what was it? Nothing made sense.

She was no closer to the truth than when she began. Why did John fake his death and lie to her? She was getting angry, very angry, and she would use every skill she had to get to the bottom of it.

She was no fool. He was not going to make her one anymore.

CHAPTER 20

BLACKROCK ISLAND

Just before midnight the next day on the island, Jack and Marla tucked the curragh under a rock ledge at the mouth of the inlet, around the corner from the cove. A sliver of moon hovered overhead in a starless sky.

Jack pierced Marla with a stern look. "Laine is going no place except with us tonight." He slung the cloth tarp over his shoulder and began walking.

"Okay, I heard you. Use your penlight to find the path so they won't see us coming."

"What do you think I'm doing?"

"Forget it."

"Want to start complaining already?"

"No, let's get this over with tonight and stop fooling around."

"No kidding. Did you think this was some kind of game we are playing?"

"Can't you be nice? I'm here... and helping you."

"Yeah. I'm just antsy, that's all. Don't worry. It will be over soon, and we can go on a vacation."

"Like I didn't know that."

They stumbled up the path leading to the tunnels and reached the small cave a short distance from the opening. Wind swooped down from a hole in the center of the cavern above their heads, a cool breeze. Directly below the hole was a fire pit filled with half-burned wood and ashes.

Marla shivered and hugged herself. "It's freezin' in here. Make a fire in this pit, will you?"

"We can't make a fire; they'll see the smoke, dummy. Once we get moving, you'll warm up. You're going with me to get Laine."

"What? I said I would come here and wait in the cave for you, remember?"

"We went over all this at the bar." He patted his pocket, checking for the small bottle of poison she had given him. "It's here," he said, smiling. "Let's go. I can't wait to put this stuff in that stupid tea tin she carries around with her. She'll be dead within days. Won't know what hit her. Good idea, don't you think?"

Marla sat on the stone slab and shook her head. "You're going by yourself. Get this over real quick. I said I'd help you with the boat. I didn't bargain for climbing through those tunnels again. Last time was enough for me. You know the layout and you don't need me to lead you."

"No way, Babe, you have to show me the way. I did it only once—you know that."

"You're a smart man. You can figure it out." Marla stood and aimed her light around the cave. Bats fluttered from crevices and soared out of the cracks. She ducked, hands protecting her head, and screamed. "All right, all right. I'm going. Let's get outta here. Move it!"

"Good girl. I'll go first." He pointed his light at the exit.

"I thought you said you didn't know the way."

"You can be my guide from behind. If I go first, I can protect you."

"Hmmm. Fine. Take a right at the first fork." She crossed her arms over her chest and looked around for more bats.

"Got it." His Topsiders shuffled on the wet, rocky floor as they maneuvered their way through the tunnels.

"Should have worn boots without heels. I didn't expect this tonight—I don't know what makes me follow your dumb ideas."

"Place is slippery. You could get hurt in here. Watch it."

"Good time to think of it. Like you even care if I get hurt." Marla poked him in the back.

"What?"

"Nothing," she laughed and poked him again.

"Quit it."

"See how *you* like it?" She grabbed him from behind and hugged him through the tarp.

"Yeah, I get it. Just cut it out. I'm trying to remember the way."

They inched their way through the winding tunnel. At the first bend the walls closed in and narrowed. Jack smacked his head on a low-hanging rock and dropped his penlight. It blinked out.

"Damn!" His fingers swept the ground in search of it. Something scuttled across his hand. "What the hell?" When he jumped up, he hit his head on the rock again.

"Ouch, that hurt!" He felt his head to discover a small lump had formed on his forehead. Blood trickled down his cheek. "Where's that stupid light? I can't find it."

"You okay?" Marla focused her beam on his face.

"Get that out of my eyes!"

"Okay, just looking." She swept the beam along the ground. "There it is. You're stepping on it."

He stooped to retrieve it and the tarp wrapped around his neck. Flipping the switch on his light, he found it did not work. "It's broken, damn it. And this thing is driving me crazy." He shoved the tarp back over his shoulder.

"Typical," Marla muttered.

"What did you say?"

"Nothing." She stifled a laugh.

"Marla, knock it off. I've got enough problems." He wiped the blood off his cheek and stared at his bloody hand. "What the hell. I'm injured."

"You sure are. It's just a scratch. Let me..."

"Don't touch me." He knocked her hand away from his face. "It hurts like a son of a bitch. Let's get this over with. I can't wait to get out of here."

"Me too."

A few moments later, Jack stopped and fumbled around in his jacket pockets.

"What'd you stop for?" Marla played her light around the dark, wet rocks. "We've got to keep going."

"I need a cigarette."

"Now? You don't have time. The kitchen entrance door is at least another few minutes up ahead. You have to get in there to put arsenic in her tea like we talked about. I'm not going to stand around in here freezing and watching you smoke. Let's go." Marla rubbed her arms to get warm.

"We've got time." He slapped his pockets for his pack of Marlboros. His hands shook as he lit five matches before one caught. He dropped them on the ground.

"What's the matter with you?"

"Nothing." He threw the empty match cover in the air after holding the last match to the end of his cigarette. Inhaling deeply, he leaned against the wet wall of the tunnel. "This place is disgusting. How could you ever play in here as a kid? Weren't you scared to death?"

"No, I liked it. It was fun. The dark is my friend. It calms me."

Rodents scurried over their feet in the beam of Marla's light.

"Rats! Marla, those are rats! Rats the size of small dogs! Maybe you're right. We can think of a new plan instead of poisoning her. We could kidnap her from her bedroom tonight—forget it. Nab her at the shopping mall or something. Let's go—let's get out of this place. This is getting weirder by the minute."

"Okay, okay. Keep your shirt on." She flashed her light around the cavern. "They're gone." Marla watched him sweat. "Big tough Jack. As kids, we used to try and trap the rats. Played a little game with them after that. Drowned each big rat down at the dock...or at least I did." Marla smiled at him.

"Yeah, you liked the dark as a kid. Right. Not. You're full of it. You're just making this stuff up to make me look like an idiot." Jack took a last puff and crushed the cigarette beneath his boot. "Shut up, Marla, I've heard enough of your crazy stories for one day. Which way now?"

Marla righted herself and played with the light. "I was putting you on. Testing you. See what you'd do. Straight ahead. Keep going...and pick up the pace."

"Yeah, right. You're a big tease. Gimme that." He took her light.

"No, Jack, give it back. I need it."

"Live and learn, baby." He shot the light back and forth along the dark hole, lighting the way further into the tunnel ahead of him. It widened and smoothed out past a fork to the right. On their left was an alcove he had not noticed before. A candle was melted into a hole in the rock. They crept along, stumbling through the dark passages toward the kitchen.

"How much farther, Marla? We have to be close."

"Ahead on the right. Look for the wooden door."

"Here it is. Help me lift this bar across it off the hinges."

They lifted it and set it on the rocky floor.

"Don't be long when you get into the kitchen. They might hear you if you make too much noise."

"It'll only take a minute." He inched through the doorway into the kitchen pantry. Ahead of him was another door that led into the kitchen. He eased it open. It squeaked. His eyes darted around the room while he waited. Silence — no one was there, so he stepped inside. Marla poked her head around the corner and peered after him. He waved her back and put his finger to his mouth.

He paused for his eyes to adjust. A dim light from the hallway helped him to find his way around the room. He looked for the Earl Gray tea tin. "There it is. I knew it! Laine still drinks the damn stuff." Fishing the bottle of poison from his pocket, he unscrewed the cap of the arsenic Marla had given him. Tapping a generous amount into the tea tin, he smiled. Next, he screwed the lid back on and shook the can several times. When he finished, he made certain all was in place. He scanned the floor for any footprints he might have left. He did not see any, so he slipped out of the kitchen into the pantry and then into the tunnel. They hoisted the board onto the iron slats, bolting the door shut.

"Let's get out of here." Sweat rolled down his face and mixed with the dried blood.

"Did you do it?" Marla whispered.

"Piece of cake. Go ahead and get the boat ready."

"What do you mean 'go ahead and get the boat ready'?"

"What's the problem?"

"What are you going to do? You'll get lost without me to show you the way out."

"Nope," he grinned. "I'll find my way back. Maybe Laine will show me out."

She laughed. "Get outta here."

"Go on, Marla. I'll wait until I hear her come into the kitchen. You know we talked about it."

"Then what?"

"Then I grab her. Simple as that."

"No, that's not the plan. You're grabbing her in the tower, dummy, not the kitchen. Poison takes days to kill her—make her really sick. You can't nab her in the kitchen—too many people will hear. I thought you knew that." Marla kissed him on the cheek. "The poison is our backup plan."

"Marla, you're giving me a headache. Yeah, I know that. She's always up before dawn drinking her damn tea and then she goes to work. The Rodriguez kid gave me her schedule. She'll go to the tower to start her work for the day. I saw her daily planner." He glanced at his watch. "It's almost time. Get going. I'll meet you at the boat as soon as I can. I'll bring her with me." He gave her a peck on the cheek.

Marla laughed. "Okay. I'll meet you back at the boat. Don't forget to gag her after you conk her on the head and knock her out."

"Are you crazy? Think I'm some kind of...? Forget it. She won't know what hit her. Just like we planned. Then we dump her in the ocean, and the sharks will do the rest."

"Right. Drowned just like Norbert."

"Yeah." He smiled at her back.

Behind the kitchen door Jack heard pans rattling. "Quiet," he shushed her and ran into the dark tunnel ahead, toward the tower, with the flashlight bouncing off the walls.

"Oh no! I can't see. I don't have a light. Oh, yes I do." She fumbled for her cell phone and turned on the flashlight. She had only a little battery power left and was delighted it worked in the tunnel. As planned, she exited the tunnel and ran down the path to the boat. She climbed in and got everything ready—just like they'd planned. Jack's foul weather jacket always kept her warm so she slipped it on. Hiding behind a clump of trees, she waited for him to return. If he did not return in an hour, she would go to their plan B.

CHAPTER 21

BLACKROCK ISLAND

While Jack charged through the tunnels, Marla hid in the trees, waiting. At the same time, Laine woke to good smells emanating from the cottage kitchen. Glancing at the clock, Laine saw it was 6:30 a.m. Rising, she walked to the window. It's beautiful, she thought.

Her view of the ocean revealed rolling waves lapping along the shore at the bottom of the black rock cliffs. Sunrays of orange and bright yellow bathed the ocean in a warm glow. She felt fine.

She tore herself away from the peacefulness of the new morning sun, dressed and made her way to the kitchen for her routine cup of Earl Gray tea and Patricia's homemade breakfast.

"Good morning, Patricia. You're up early. What smells so good?"

"Mornin' to you. There's brown soda bread comin' out of the oven. You'll have a cuppa tea, won't you?"

"I will." Laine reached for the tea tin she had left on the counter the night before. "I always bring my own tea with me when I travel." She held up the canister of *Earl Gray.*

"It's my favorite. I don't think you can get it in Ireland." She tapped the leaves into a teaspoon strainer while the kettle boiled. "Want some?"

"No, thanks. I had me own black tea earlier." Patricia ticked off on her fingers then began setting nine places at the long oak table. "We'll be havin' a bite to eat when the crew gets here this mornin'. Miles and Eamon went by boat to fetch 'em." Smiling, she wiped her hands on her yellowed apron. "You'll be workin' with them today, you will."

"Yes, it is all so exciting. I'll eat with them when they get here." Laine dipped the tea strainer into the hot water in her mug. "Right now, I'm going to the tower to get a few things done. I'll be back shortly." She snapped open the tea strainer, dumped the wet leaves into the waste bin and set the strainer in the sink. "If they get here soon, please ask Miles to come and get me."

"Aye." Patricia pulled a large black skillet from the cupboard. "We'll be startin' our day off right, we will. Got the fry-up ready, I do."

Laine looked quizzical. "What on earth is a 'fry-up,' Patricia?"

"Rashers—that's bacon to you. Sausages. Fried eggs. White puddin'. Toast. Sliced potato and fried tomato."

"Wow! That's some breakfast."

"'Tis a real Irish breakfast. Those lads will be workin' hard, so we feed 'em good." She slowly stirred the pudding in the pot.

"Sounds great." Laine waved as she left. "Okay then, see you later."

She carried the steaming mug of tea down the hall and up the tower stairs to the map room. She placed it on the round table by her briefcase. Even though the sun came in through the window, the room remained shadowy, dark and dim. She turned on the light, needing it to fill the space with warmth.

"What to do first?" Laine muttered aloud. She unrolled the blueprints. "Looks like the window today. Knock it out to rebuild it twice the size. Let some light into this creepy place." She walked to the window that looked out over the Atlantic Ocean. "What a beautiful sight."

Waves bounced and rolled as green foamy crests curled over the peaks of jagged water. Ebony storm petrels soared above the waves and flew toward the black rock cliffs. She heard the high-pitched singing of distant birds.

Miles has a lovely place, she thought. He was on her mind a lot.

What am I going to do about it? I have to find out what's going on at the racetrack and how he is involved. Involved — that was the key word. Do I have feelings for him? I must have the start of something — I can't stop thinking about him.

Stop it, she told herself and went back to her work.

She examined her designs on the table. "We'll get this place looking cheerful in no time." As she reached for her briefcase, her mug of tea crashed to the floor.

"Oh, no, what a mess!" She glanced around the room and looked for Rodriguez's broom and dustpan. It was gone. "Where is a mop when I need one? Patricia has one. I have to clean this up." She ran from the room and skipped down the staircase to the cottage.

CHAPTER 22

BLACKROCK ISLAND

Jack hid in the tunnel, put his ear to the hatch opening and listened for Laine in the map room. It was quiet. The poison was working, he decided. He scrambled down the footholds embedded in the chimney walls and landed at the bottom. The room was empty. *Empty!* He nicked his shin on the grate when he stepped from the fireplace and tripped over the andirons. Tumbling into the room, he landed in a puddle of water.

Slapping the seat of his wet pants, he sneered, "What the hell is *this?*" He clamped his mouth shut, fearful she might have heard all the commotion. Where the hell is she? I know I heard her. He patted his pants again.

Spying broken fragments of a mug on the floor, he looked around the room. "Damn it, she spilled her tea. Now what am I gonna do? Guess it's time to get the hell out of here. The crew will be here shortly and Marla is going to rip me a new one."

He kicked a piece of the mug aside and tracked through the tea puddled across the floor as he entered the opening of the fireplace. Grabbing the niches in the rocks, he inched his way up the secret entrance, back into the tunnel. Slamming the hatch shut, he flipped on the penlight and started his journey back to the boat. He ran, stumbled and tripped on the uneven tunnel floor, while his flashlight lit the way. He had to stay ahead of Miles and his crew or they might see him.

His only thought now was to get off the island. He knew from the boy that a crew would be coming early that morning. He was almost out of time.

At the first fork, he took a left. Nothing looked familiar. "Not again." He rubbed his bruised head.

It took him a few minutes to realize what he had done. He backtracked. There were three choices at the fork: left, right and center. Choosing center, he proceeded to run down the tunnel with many twists and turns. The ceiling dipped and the tunnel began to narrow as he ran smack into a rock jutting out from above him.

"Shee-it!" He yelled when he fell. "Son of a bitch. Damn place." He touched the gash on his forehead while he pushed up from the ground and crouched down. "Now what do I do? I should have listened to Marla and left when we saw the rats. *Rats!*" He ran bent over in the wet, slippery stone passageway. Water dripped from overhead, signaling he was in the wrong part of the tunnel.

"Now, I've done it," he mumbled. "I am completely lost. It smells of stinky, stale air in here. What if I can't find my way out? What if I am eaten up by the rats?"

His mind unraveled and he whipped around to go back the way he came. Black shadows played tricks on him. Don't scream, he told himself. They are only shadows on the walls—not evil spirits. Feeling nauseated, he bent over and gagged as he weaved in and out of the narrow tunnels.

I have to have a smoke, he thought. The match glowed yellow against the dark walls of the tunnel as he lit the cigarette and inhaled. That's better.

Can't hear the ocean, he thought. I must have taken another wrong turn. What if there are more rats in this part of the tunnel? I could die in here and no one would know, except Marla. Would she really care?

Sweat beaded on his forehead and stained the armpits of his shirt. His back was soaking wet and a dull ache throbbed in his forehead. He smelled wet, damp, stale sewer water, and he pitched his cigarette butt on the ground.

"Time to go. I don't care if they hear me or not," he mumbled and shined the flashlight down the endless black hole.

Backtracking again, he hoped he'd find the way out. He returned to the spot where the three tunnels merged. This time he took the fork to the right.

"This looks familiar," he shouted. His breathing was labored. The light picked up his discarded matches on the ground. He listened and heard the waves. "Hallelujah, I did it!" He shut his mouth as fast as he opened it.

The smell of sea salt was in the air—the ocean—the end of the tunnel. Running to it, he saw the sea and flew down the stone steps to the cove and on to the beach. His shirt and pants were wet by the time he got to the curragh. Marla hunched into his foul-weather jacket, waiting for him in the bow. She was applying red lipstick. Very red.

"We gotta get out of here!" Jack pushed the boat into the water, jumped in and fell half on Marla's lap.

"Ouch, what the hell are you doing? That hurt! Where's Laine?" She stared at him.

"We're leaving."

"Get off me. You're getting blood all over my jacket. Your jacket. Look at you—your pants are soaked. *What happened?* Where is she?" She straightened herself, while he scrambled over her to get to the console and his seat. He fumbled for the key and jammed it in the ignition.

"The deal is off. Don't ask me any questions. Just don't."

"What's going on?" she screeched, gripping her seat as they sped out into the rough water.

"Not now. I told you, don't ask me anything. Miles's crew will be landing on top of us any minute."

She looked around. "I don't see anyone."

His face turned hard as he jammed the throttle forward to its maximum speed. Marla was thrown about in her seat. The hull smashed through the waves while the spray shot over the bow and drenched them.

"Stop it. You're going to kill us. Slow down!"

He ignored her and steered the boat through the pounding water.

"Talk to me. You brought me all the way over here for nothing? What the hell happened?" A huge wave hit them broadside. Marla crashed to the deck. Tears poured down her face as she inched herself back onto the seat.

"We have to come back. She wasn't there."

"Are you kidding? I thought you had her schedule." She wiped the stinging salt water from her eyes. Black mascara streamed down her cheeks. That and the fresh red lipstick smeared across her cheek made her look like a clown.

"Just shut up. I've had enough. She was there but then she wasn't. That's all I can tell you. We have to come back."

"No way. I'm seasick. I'm not used to being bounced around like a corkscrew. My back hurts. Slow it down!"

"Tough. Get used to it. I'm doing this for our own good. Can't you see that?"

Marla was silent. She watched him grip the wheel, ride the waves and force the boat to take the pounding.

The curragh leapt like a dolphin toward the mainland. Spray from the ocean continued to soak them relentlessly, while the boat pitched and rolled. Continuously, the bow slammed into the waves. The hull shuddered. It threatened to break into pieces as it plowed through the rough, dark sea.

After a while, Marla shouted, "We're gonna sink! Look at all the water down here."

"Bail it out. We're not gonna sink." He felt his irritation rising. Didn't this woman understand anything? He spun the wheel to starboard and then to port, leaving a zigzag trail behind them.

She grabbed the bucket, but it flew out of her hand into the ocean. Her hair hung limp around her face.

"Damn it. Now we don't have a bucket."

"I didn't mean to do it."

"Forget it. Get down! Miles's boat is coming straight at us. Exactly what I wanted to avoid."

"What're we going to do?"

"Nothing. Pull your hood over your face—quick. Flatten yourself on the deck."

"I can't. I'm sick. There's too much water." She tried to squeeze herself into a small ball in her seat.

"Do it! He'll see you." He jammed his hat low on his head, pulled up his hood and crouched low behind the wheel.

"Great plan."

"What did you say?" He angled the boat away from Miles by steering north.

"Nothing."

"I heard that. Yeah, it was a great plan until it got screwed up."

"You'll think of something."

"Yeah, I will." Jack fixed his eyes on the lighthouse tower at Blacksod Harbor. It was then he saw the Olympic swimmers ahead, stroking through the rough water. Skiffs ran alongside the swimmers; spotters shined high beams of light on them and illuminated their way to the next buoy. Their muscled arms stroked through the water like fans spinning on a hot day. They wore black dive suits that kept them afloat in the water. Nothing was going to stop them from finishing their trial workout. Nothing, he thought.

Jack admired that. He felt he was one of them. Going forward in his boat. Moving fast in the waves and guiding his curragh against all odds — against Miles. Against Laine — yes, against *her* — that was the goal.

Men rode Waverunners and towed sled-like boards behind them to rescue tired swimmers. Rescue them — not let them drown like he was going to do to Laine.

"How can they swim in these waves?" Marla asked.

"I heard they're strong from working out. It takes years to get in shape. They train in swimming pools that blast tons of water against them while they swim against it. Yesterday, team leaders put out extra buoys to guide them in the competition. The finish line buoy is close to Blacksod Harbor."

"What are you talking about?"

"Nothing, Marla. Nothing. Nothing for you to worry about."

A new plan formed in his mind while he watched the swimmers.

"I've got an idea. Next time we're going to stash Laine in your favorite cave. The one you and Miles hid in when you were kids."

"What? The cave with the bats?"

"Yep, she'll love it."

"Whatever you want. I'm cold. Are we there yet?"

"All you do is whine." She is getting on my nerves, he thought.

She gave him a hard stare. "I'm not whining. I'm just cold."

"Whatever you say."

Clouds covered the sun as they made their way to Blacksod Harbor.

CHAPTER 23

BLACKROCK ISLAND

As Jack and Marla sped away from the island, Laine ran from the tower to the mudroom in the cottage. She went inside to look for cleaning supplies to mop up her spilled tea and cracked mug. She dug through buckets, rags, and other paraphernalia.

"Ah, here's one." She produced a stringy mop. On second thought, she added the broom and placed the dustpan in a plastic bucket. On her way out, Murray, coming in, blocked her path.

"You're a lovely lass this time of day. I see you be needin' a helpin' hand."

"No thanks, Murray, I can take care of it myself. Will you please step aside?"

She tried to go around him, but he didn't budge. He grabbed the mop and broom from her hands as the other supplies clattered to the floor.

She nudged him out of the way, stooping to pick them up.

"I didn't mean for this to happen. I'd like to be takin' these for you. Least I can do." Above a wide smile, his eyes never left her. He stepped back and cleared a path for her.

She scooted past him while grabbing the cleaning supplies from his hands. Miles opened the door as she was going out, with Murray close behind her.

"Good morning. Is there a problem?" He focused his eyes on Murray then at her.

"No problem. I broke a cup in the tower. Murray offered to help."

Murray laughed. "Likes me, she does—any man can see that, he can."

"You're full of yourself. I think Patricia's waiting breakfast for all of us."

"Well, then, it will have to be later, Miss Sullivan—the helpin' you clean up. Lovely lass, she is, Miles. Won't you be agreein' with me?" He gave her a wink.

"Yes, she is. Go inside and get some breakfast, man." Miles smacked a friendly pat on his back.

"That I will. Didn't want to leave Miss Sullivan in her troubled state, did I now? She'd be needin' a *man* to help her with the job. I'd be that man." Flexing the muscles on his arms, he smiled at her.

"I have a hunch you were not thinking about cleaning up. I know you too well."

"That you do, Miles. Especially when there's a lovely lass as this needin' my help, she does." He squared his massive shoulders, turned and waked away.

Miles took the supplies from her. "Watch out for him, Laine. He's got his heart set on you."

"He's a handful, but harmless. A big flirt and not afraid to say his feelings—that's for sure. It's refreshing, in a way."

"Don't know about that. Usually gets what he wants from the women. He has a reputation for having a string of ladies in every town. I wouldn't let your guard down around him—unless you want to, that is."

"Hadn't thought about it in that way. Something to think about." She said it in a teasing voice and laughed when she saw the look on his face, liking it. "I need to pick up the mess in the map room. It's not a big job, but I should really..."

"Can't it wait until after breakfast? Is there something bothering you? It's not like you to be in such a hurry to clean up, especially before we eat."

"Yes, but we can talk later. I've got a few things I want to run by you."

"How about talking now?"

"There have been a lot of coincidences since I got here that don't add up, but I'll make it short."

"Go on."

"First, I thought I saw my husband in town. Next, you showed me the Sullivan land that I didn't know I owned, then poor Rex was shot, and finally, there was the voice in the tower."

His head shot up. "What voice?

As quickly as she could, she related her experience from earlier that morning. "Someone definitely called out my name, but no one was there. I checked."

"I'll have the men look into it. We'll get to the bottom of this. Donna worry." He took the supplies from her and set them on the ground.

"I have an odd feeling I am being watched. I know it sounds silly, but someone is trying to scare me." I want to draw him into my confidence, she thought. Then he might confide in me and tell me what's going on with the horses at the racetrack.

"That would make a difference. That old tower gives off some queer noises."

"You're right, it does, but then again there are some strange things going on around here."

"It seems so." Miles put his arm around her shoulder.

"I know it."

She stood there with him and looked at the ocean. It reminded her of her last assignment. She had the same bad feeling in Cuba—right before she was abducted. When she'd talked to Max that morning, he'd told her to trust her instincts. Watch your back—don't trust anyone—not even Miles.

But she'd just confided in him.

What was she doing? She pulled away from him. A second later, she reached behind her back to locate the small pistol hidden under her shirt. She needed to feel it there—comfort herself—remind herself that she could use it if she had to...if she got in trouble.

"Is there more?" He was watching her struggle with her thoughts.

"Not that I can think of now. Let's enjoy the 'frying up.' It's all so silly."

"It's important to you, I can see. I am glad we talked this over." With a kind look on his face, he took her hand and led her inside and to the kitchen.

"I'm glad we talked about it too."

She felt fine.

CHAPTER 24

BLACKROCK ISLAND

After Miles, Laine and the crew finished breakfast, they returned to the map room. The construction crew set to work under Murray's direction on the exterior of the tower while she and Miles remained inside.

"Miles, I want to go over the blueprints with you."

"Good idea. At least show me what you would like to do today."

"Have you looked at the information I sent you?"

"You mentioned making the place brighter. I like the idea." He inched toward her, watching her work, fingering the edge of the first page of the blueprint.

"Really? No discussion."

"Do you ask all your clients what they think of your blueprint ideas?"

She laughed. "Never."

"There's always a fear when restoring an historical lighthouse. I leave you to it. I've nothing to add to what you've proposed. There had to be a change."

"It will look original. I have taken that into consideration."

"Glad to hear it. I want to ask you something." He took her hand. "It's about…"

A clattering and scraping noise came from outside the open window. Then a loud crash. They searched each other's face, puzzled.

"What was that?" She dropped his hand. Rushing to the open window, she peered down. "Oh, no, the scaffold collapsed!"

Miles let his surprise show before he leaped into action. "Follow me. It's not safe." He guided her down the winding staircase to the yard.

At the base of the lighthouse, stern-faced men were hurriedly pitching boards away from the area below the east window.

"Anyone hurt?" asked Miles, quickly scanning the rubble. He picked up a piece of a metal pole and set it off to the side.

"Aye 'tis Murray. Hurry lads, the weight will crush 'im to death." Eamon crossed himself then lifted a board out of the way.

Jumping in, Miles grabbed the end of a board with another man. "We'll get you out, Murray. Don't worry. Hang in there — just hang in there."

"Aye, lad, we're almost to you," Eamon yelled into the pile of wood.

"Oh no, his legs are bent backward!" Laine pointed to the unnatural angle of his limbs.

Miles and the men doubled their efforts to clear the way. Lifting and sweating in the sun, they worked rapidly to carve a hole in the death tomb.

Laine paced on the perimeter of the rescuers. If they don't get him out of there soon, he'll bleed to death, she thought. It triggered a memory of something that happened in Cuba. She could still feel and hear the reverberations from the bomb blast. Pushing the thought from her mind, she got ready to perform first aid. She would have to make a tourniquet for his legs to stop the bleeding.

"Take off your shirt," she said to a young man near her.

"What? Me shirt?" He arched his eyebrows.

"Yes, I need it." Her look had him ripping it off in an instant. Handing it to her, he ran back to help the men.

Miles elbowed his way through board after board to get to him.

"Poor bloke." Eamon lifted the end of a large board that had fallen on Murray's torso. Sean took the other end; together they lifted it from his body.

Murray groaned.

"For the love of…he's alive!" shouted Eamon.

"Hold on, Murray. We've got you. Hold on!" Miles cradled Murray's head in his arms.

Laine saw his facial muscles soften as Miles talked quietly to him. This was a Miles she didn't know, but was glad she was privy to it now. Murray was deathly pale; she knew she was going to blow her cover if she was not careful. I can help him, she thought. I have to help him. She made her decision.

"Take it easy, Murray, we'll get you to the hospital," said Miles.

"Murray, no worries." Eamon spoke close to his ear. "Hang in there, lad."

"Let me see him. I'm trained in this kind of thing." Miles's surprised look gave her pause, but she dismissed it. She ripped the shirt she'd just taken from a worker into long stripes and tied tourniquets on both legs above the knees. Miles and the men looked on, fascinated. Taking the wounded man's wrist and applying pressure, she noted her watch.

"He's got a pulse. But barely." She felt his arm. "It's broken. I need something to stop the bleeding. Miles, give me your shirt. There's not enough of this other one."

He gave it to her.

She ripped it. Wrapping the strip around his arm helped to apply pressure to stop the bleeding. "He needs medical attention now — we have to get him to the hospital. Do you have a stretcher we can put him on to evacuate him?"

At Miles's direction, they raced to get it.

"Let's get moving. We have no time to waste. Can we take the helicopter?" asked Laine.

"Yes, I'll get it ready. Come quickly, men. Do what she tells you."

The crew did as he instructed. They carefully covered Murray with a tarp and lifted him onto the stretcher per Laine's instructions. As they carried him across the lawn toward the helicopter, the wind from the rotors tore at them. Dirt flew in the air surrounding them as they loaded him into the chopper. In a few seconds, they were airborne, heading to the hospital on the mainland.

CHAPTER 25

As they flew toward Donegal Airport, Miles expertly controlled the cyclic stick, tilting it forward and back to alter the rotors. He maintained his speed and manipulated the collective and the foot pedals to keep the helicopter level.

"Stay awake, big guy. We're almost there," Laine said to Murray.

A slight grin curled from the corner of his mouth.

She examined him with her eyes. He fought hard to stay awake to look at her. His eyes, reduced to pinpoints, showed her he was in shock. Blood soaked his chest where his right arm was cocked in an awkward angle. She shifted the tarp to keep him warm. His eyes closed.

"Murray, wake up. I need you to stay awake."

Squinting, he forced his eyes open and mumbled, "Tell Miles danger is a comin'. Jack and the boy are up to no good." He drifted off.

She placed her hand on his cheek. "We're almost there. Stay with me."

He moaned.

"Murray, you're one tough man. Keep your eyes open — look at me. Try to stay awake. We're almost there."

He stirred, whispering. "Rex's murder—Miles needs to know. Eamon, get Eamon." Breathing hard, he tried to focus on her.

"He wants you," she shouted to Eamon over the thumping of the rotors. She puzzled over Murray's comments. It didn't add up.

Eamon put his ear to Murray's lips. "Sayin' Donahue's Pub. Ach, bad horse business, drugs—Jack and the Mexican boy."

Murray grabbed his sleeve with his good hand. "Rodrig..."

"Hard to be understandin' him. But somethin' about Rodriguez and drugs."

This caught Laine's attention.

"I've information," Murray said. A surge of pain went through him and he groaned, squeezing his eyes shut.

"Hang in there. Time to tell us later, lad," said Eamon.

Laine nodded to him. "Don't worry. We'll give Miles your message. We're almost there."

Bouncing through the sky, the helicopter swooped low as they neared the landing pad.

Miles shouted back to them. "I'll ride with Murray to the hospital. The ambulance is waiting. We have clearance to land."

Eamon grinned at Murray. "Got the helicopter ride you been waitin' for—a bit different than you expected, lad. We're a landin', now. Get you fixed up quick, we will."

Murray mumbled in a raspy voice, "Aye." He struggled to talk, but the words failed him as another wave of pain knifed through his body.

"Take deep breaths and try to relax," said Laine, reaching for his good hand. "I know it's bad."

Watching her, he took a few breaths.

Eamon cut in. "Hear you had quite the time with the lasses in Donahue Pub last eve." Wiping the sweat from his forehead with his shirtsleeve, he nodded at Laine. "We'll be waitin' to hear about it. Hold on there, lad. 'Tis a bugger, it is, but we'll be gettin' you fixed up soon."

Miles stared down at the injured man. "Yes, we all can't wait to hear what you were up to. You're my favorite foreman. Hear the ladies were standing in line. No one is taking my foreman's spot. I'm counting on you to get better. I need you to do that for me, Murray—I know you can do it. We will be at the hospital with you. I will personally check up on you."

Murray struggled again, cracked a small smile and bit on his lower lip, fighting back the pain sweeping through his body. She could see he was slipping out of consciousness.

"We're here. Hold on."

A short time later in Donegal Hospital's waiting room, Eamon went for coffee. Laine listened to Miles on the cell phone with his police cousin Tom.

"The scaffolding let go on the lighthouse tower. Murray was critically injured, so we flew him to the hospital in Donegal."

Laine watched his face tighten as he pressed the cell phone to his ear.

"Rodriguez, the Mexican boy, did not show up for work this afternoon."

He listened, frowning.

"Yes, he helped the men secure the bolts on the scaffolding yesterday. Never picked up his paycheck, which is very odd. He and Murray did not get along. I saw the boy take off in a boat with some man who paid him money down by my dock. I don't know the man, but they were heading toward Blacksod Harbor at full speed. I'll tell you the rest later. Let me know what you find out." He hung up.

Laine was watching him. "Want to talk about it?" She saw the dark look on his face. Clearly, it was sabotage, according to what she'd just heard. Miles had told the policeman the same thing.

"There's not much to say, but the police are on the lookout for Rodriquez and the man we saw. I called Dodd at the farm to get an update, but the farm workers haven't seen them. He said Rodriguez cleared out his bunk — took all his things. He won't be coming back. That's for sure."

"Who would want to do this to Murray and to you?"

"Don't know, but I am going to find out. Wilfrid and Tom, my cousins — the garda — that's what we call our police — are making it their top priority. You met them at the stables the day Rex was shot. They are good at what they do. Whatever it is, they'll get to the bottom of it."

"Yes, I remember them. While we were flying over, Murray tried to tell us what he heard in Donahue's Pub." She told him what he'd said. "He might have overheard something that could be helpful."

She decided she would ask the men a few questions when they got back to the island — dig a little deeper. Murray's incident and his statement about the drugs might help them. Have to call Max right away, she thought.

"Yes, you could be right. When he's able, I'll talk to him. The only time the crew was not together was at breakfast. The man gave Rodriguez money, so it could have been a payoff to loosen the scaffolding and hurt Murray. It adds up."

"Payoff?" she asked, not wanting to give herself away. She had seen it too. The boy was involved in something with the man. She had to find the connection.

"Yes, money. It is too coincidental. Murray is injured — that boy could have tampered with the scaffolding. Who knows? Murray would never have left anything loose or unsecured on the site. I know his work — been the best foreman for years — conscientious to a fault. It was deliberate, all right, but I haven't figured out why."

"Who would want to hurt you or your men?" Laine asked in a soft tone, drawing suspicion away from herself.

"None that I can think of — unless, of course, Sheik Tariq's broker has a problem with Rex's death. I told him we would replace Rex with his brother — same quality — the horses looked exactly alike. He was irate and threatened to sue me. He finally settled for Duke at half price. He shouldn't have been out of sorts. He got the best deal."

"Seems like more than fair," said Laine, memorizing what he was telling her.

"And, well, yes, there was another incident a few months ago. We sold a horse to the same broker who sold that one to the sheik, too. The horse collapsed and died on the racetrack at the Kentucky Derby."

"What happened?"

"The vet called it a 'milkshaking' incident. It's horrible. It's hard to believe the broker would do such a thing to seek revenge for the death of that horse—unless of course, he caused it just to make me look bad. It crossed my mind, but to what gain? He already made his money from the sale."

Laine thought for a moment before answering. "I don't know how he thinks. It does seem strange. What's 'milkshaking'?"

"It's murder in a shot. The horse is injected with a solution in the nostrils to make it run faster. The protein-like substance speeds up the metabolism. It literally ran itself to death in the race. It's completely illegal. What a fiasco. The poor horse suffered tremendously. The sheik tried to blame me, a ludicrous charge."

"It sounds awful. Now that you've refreshed my memory, I know I read something about it in the news in the States. You were exonerated from all of the allegations, right? I'd like to know more about what happened, if you want to tell me."

He can give me the information first hand, she thought. I might get a break after all. Max will be pleased. Giving Miles her full attention, she waited for him to answer.

"Yes, I was not at fault, but it nearly ruined my business. The sheik is still buying from me, so I guess we'll see how it goes in the future. I sold Duke to his broker at the auction. It's a good sign we are still in business. I have several excellent horses, but Rex was the best. Duke is my second best horse. While we were bringing Murray to the hospital, Dodd took care of the sale."

"It sounds promising."

"I agree. There was some kind of mix up at the auction after the sale. We informed the broker we were delivering the horse to the sheik's stables, but he didn't want that. That's how we do things per our contract. He told Dodd he was taking the horse himself. Dodd said he'd have to wait until tomorrow. The contract would have to be changed, if he wanted to take the horse himself. The broker screamed and cursed at him in the paddock. Said the sheik would be so mad he'd buy up all my land and turn it into a chicken farm. He was out of control. Just because he has a lot of money does not give him the right to put down and belittle other people."

"Definitely out of control."

"It's a liability issue for us. After making a scene about it, the broker never showed up at his trailer to pick up the horse. Dodd waited for over an hour. Finally, he gave up and took Duke back to the farm."

"So what happens now?"

"We rescheduled with the sheik's man. I usually don't do it that way, but in this case we are making allowances."

"I wonder why the broker didn't want to follow protocol."

"Not sure. Dodd says he is a very odd American man. Thinks he got drunk at the racetrack bar and forgot to pick up the horse. Crazy business."

"He's American?" She was getting at the heart of the matter. Keep him talking, she thought. "Forgot to pick up his horse? Sounds like a whack job to me."

He laughed at her comment, arching his eyebrows. "Yes, it was odd. A few hours ago, the sheik's headman, Kamal, actually picked Duke up in Sheik Tariq's private horse trailer. It was arranged for tomorrow with the broker, but the sheik wanted him today."

"Guess they weren't taking any chances this time."

"You could be right. From what I heard, the horse trailer was something else. The men were flabbergasted when it rolled up to the stables all shining and white with Sheik Tariq's name painted on the sides in solid gold letters surrounded by diamonds."

"That would have been fun to see." Smiling, she leaned in toward him.

"There's more. There was a line of armored cars guarding the front and back of the trailer. Armed guards in bulletproof vests came in military vehicles to protect the horse. A lot of security for one horse. It seems unnecessary. The horse is insured. Funny thing—sending the sheik's headman and not the broker cuts out the broker fee. Not sure how the sheik is going to handle it."

"It's odd the sheik wanted to cut out the broker. I'm sure he is furious."

"It's surprising. I would think so."

"The broker must have done something extremely bad to bring this on himself." Armed guards to protect the horse were over the top, she thought. Even by Miles's own admission, the last horse he sold the sheik died a brutal death at the Kentucky Derby, but why all the security? The whole thing smelled.

"He and the sheik must have had it out, since there was no broker's commission in the revised contract Kamal brought with him today. Dodd said he was clear that, going forward, there is no broker or anyone in place, for that matter."

She listened, thinking about it. I have to check in with Max and tell him what I just heard. Things here are escalating. The sheik changed the process for picking up and paying for his horses. What is really going on? Who is this broker?

"It's out of the ordinary, from what you are telling me," she said.

"Not at all what we do. We've never had a problem before — hate to have one now. I've never done business like this. Oddly enough, sending his own man, Kamal, was unprecedented."

"How have you always done it?"

"There was always a broker. He used this broker to buy the last two horses and Rex."

"Men picking up a horse in a golden carriage sounds a little like Cinderella." She laughed to relieve the tension. "Wish I could have been there. It does seem odd, given it's the way you've done business in the past. Surely, the sheik knows that."

"Possibly the broker wasn't working out, so he let him go. What's his name again? I had Dodd deal with him, so I don't' recall it." He rubbed his chin, thinking. "Oh well, I'm not even going to try to get it straight. When we get back to the farm, I'll show you the surveillance camera tapes, if you'd like to see them. Keep it interesting while you are here." Turning to her, he smiled and put his hand on her arm.

"Yes, I would." She felt his hand on her arm. The lightness of his touch was electrifying. Feeling like this was new to her. "Do you have tapes of the American that bought your horses?"

"I do. We have tapes of everyone who buys our horses. It's a precautionary measure. A lot of politics are involved. Big money in horses, especially on the international scene. With the trouble at the Kentucky Derby, I should be happy the sheik and his friends are still buying from me. There's a lot of money-laundering floating around the racetrack, and I don't want to get involved in it. I run a clean business, so I like to keep the clients I have. I know each of them personally — even the sheik." He pulled his hand from her arm and ran his fingers through his hair, smoothing it out.

"Do you know anything about money-laundering in the States?" She missed his warm hand on her arm. What's going on with me? she wondered while trying to focus on what he was saying.

"No, but I am wrapped up in a legal battle there."

She felt uneasy.

"As I told you, I sold the sheik a horse that someone drugged or injected before the race. I had nothing to do with it. It is being investigated. The sheik is demanding the White House get involved in the problem."

"The President?"

"Afraid so. The sheik is demanding compensation for the loss of his horse on U.S. soil—besides wanting to sue me here in Ireland. Saudi royals and their friends may pull out of the racing business altogether. They are thinking of setting up their own private races. A lot of money is tied up in this business. It'll hurt the sport and make the U.S. look foolish. On a personal level, it could ruin me."

"I had no idea. This is huge. I hope the sheik is happy with Duke as a replacement for Rex."

"That's what I am hoping. It's not a good situation. I meet with him next week on the island to smooth things out. He entered Rex in one of the richest turf races there is. It's the Prix de L'Arc de Triomphe at the Longchamp Racecourse in France next month. He was a Group 1 horse and had the best chance of winning the purse. It's 865,000 Euros this year. I don't have another champion like him—Duke doesn't even qualify for a 2,400 meters race. That's going to be another problem. The entrance fees are steep."

"Got my attention. Someone had a motive for killing your horse. This changes everything."

"That's how I feel about it myself. I explained the problem to Kamal—told him Rex was accidentally shot. He was extremely agitated. Told me not to worry the sheik about it. He said not to upset him at all. He'd handle it. I told him Duke is the same bloodline, even looks like him. I said I planned to discuss it with Sheik Tariq when I see him. Kamal asked me not to say anything yet. That was strange too. Of course, I will tell him. You can meet him if you would like to."

"Yes, that would be nice," she said. "They say not to worry, but you have a lot to worry about."

"Too many worries."

"You have your work cut out for you."

"I want to keep the channels open with the sheik. We're as close as you can be as business partners. The problem has to be solved."

"I understand." She wanted to keep him talking. He was giving her information she did not have. Max would be elated. She could not wait until tonight to call him. This was the link she was searching for to help them move forward.

"I am not sure what the sheik had in store for Rex, but I think it was bigger than we all imagined. He was a winner— there is no doubt about that. Duke will be too, in his own way. Like I said, they have the same breeding."

"Hopefully, you'll be able to give him what he wants in Duke."

Miles hesitated before speaking. "Another odd circumstance just crossed my mind. Kamal told Dodd he would contact the broker himself—tell him he was transporting Duke. I've wracked my brain for anything that might be off, but I am coming up empty. It's as if he did not want me speaking to the broker again."

"A lot of odd things going on around here. Eamon and I heard Murray say you were to beware of a man named Jack who was in Carrick's pub. He said Donahue's but Eamon said it was Carrick's place where he hired the boy."

"You say, Murray said the man's name was Jack—the one he had trouble with?"

"Yes, we heard him clearly. It seems I've brought you bad luck ever since I've arrived. There are too many accidents—or whatever you want to call them." She did not want him to think she was too involved in what was happening around them, so she didn't ask another question. That name, Jack, kept coming up—here again today. She wondered what connection he had with Miles.

"I have no idea what's going on. I don't know a Jack. I didn't recognize the man in the cove either—now that I think of it. Another unknown. Now that I look back, I should have gone after him and Rodriguez. Find out what they were doing on the island. My police cousins said they did not come into the harbor that day. They had to land some place along the shore. Another mystery."

"Did you recognize the boat?"

"No—curraghs are common around here. No telling where it came from. There was no name on it I could see. I'd recognize the man's shape, if I saw him again. Could you?"

"I didn't really get a good look at him." She lied easily. Felt bad. The man resembled John.

"Hot coffee." Eamon entered the glassed-in waiting room with their cups. Setting the cardboard box on the small table, he handed one to each of them and sat on a plastic chair opposite the two of them.

They picked up their coffee and offered their thanks. She flipped through magazines while Eamon nodded off. Miles spoke on his cell phone.

"Laine, you were an expert with Murray—back there on the island," said Miles.

It caught her off guard and she choked on her coffee. After a couple of coughs, she managed: "Thanks."

"A bit of a surprise how easily you took over. I can tell you've done it before. It may have saved Murray's life. We're grateful to you." He smiled at her then sipped out of the Styrofoam cup.

"I guess I am quick on my feet." Her cell phone rang. Checking the caller ID, she did not answer it, knowing it was Max. "My office. I'll call back later." She muted the ringtone then slipped it into her pocket.

"Do you have any formal medical training?"

"No, not formal." She hated lying to him, but she had to maintain her cover. "None, really. I volunteered with the Red Cross for a short time." She stared at his strong face, liking it. "Nothing special."

Miles's forehead creased. "Special enough. You many have saved Murray's life."

"If you'll excuse me, I need to go to the ladies room." Inside it, she checked the stalls. Empty. I have to relay this information to Max as quickly as I can. She punched the number into her phone and quickly relayed the details about the broker, problems at Miles's farm, the "milkshaking" incident, and the meeting with Sheik Tariq next week on the island. She added the drugs, Rodriguez's situation and his meeting with the man she thought was John. She hung up knowing he would follow up on all her intelligence.

When Laine returned to the waiting room, the doctor was updating Miles and Eamon on Murray's progress. It saved Laine from answering any more questions from Miles.

CHAPTER 26

KOOLMOORE STABLES

The sun was high in the cloudless sky when Kamal directed his man to drive the sheik's horse trailer into Bourke's farm.

"Pull in backward over by the barn doors," Kamal told the driver, a short man with a strange dark face, pointed nose, and his head marred by wrinkles and scars.

Farmhands stared at the line of armed guards as they filed out of the rear of the trailer, taking places on each side of the ramp; they waited for further instruction from Kamal.

"Wait here," Kamal told them. "I will bring the horse."

Within seconds, he entered the barn. Soon he returned with Dodd, Bourke's man, leading the horse at his heels.

Kamal snatched the reins from Dodd when they reached the horse trailer. He handed them to a guard.

"I will load him for you," said Dodd, stepping forward, grabbing the reins on the bit under the horse's chin.

"You're not needed anymore. I will take the horse to the sheik. Our business is finished here. Let go of him."

"I can put him in the trailer for you," said Dodd, eyeing the other man.

"No, my driver will do it."

"Whatever you say." Dodd let go of the reins and stepped away from the horse. The driver gripped the reins and walked him up the ramp and into the trailer. Within seconds, the man reappeared outside the trailer. Kamal nodded and waved off Dodd, who watched him from the barn with his men.

Kamal said to the guards, "Close it up."

They picked up the ramp and placed it inside the trailer. Quickly they climbed into the trailer and fastened the doors from the inside.

Within minutes, the horse trailer left the farm on its way to the sheik's Waterford estate several hours away.

Soon after they arrived, Kamal saw Sheik Tariq through the stable window as he pulled into the farmyard in his Silver Cloud Rolls Royce. Several military Jeeps paraded closely behind the car. Armed, well-muscled men circled the sheik as he stepped from his car.

Kamal wiped his sweaty hands on his robes and ran outside to greet him. This had better work, he thought. If he finds out this is Duke instead of Rex, I'm a dead man.

The air was crisp and threatened rain, but the men were oblivious to it. No one spoke. The sheik's billowing white robes spun around his body as he floated across the yard toward Kamal.

"Kamal? All went well with my horse?"

"Yes, yes, my brother. He is waiting for your inspection." Kamal cowered in front of him. Dropping to his knees, he pressed his head to the ground over and over.

"Quiet." The sheik said to him. He turned to his bodyguard. "Abdul, tell the guards to wait here and take up their positions."

Kamal got to his feet but continued to bow as he peeked at the men scurrying to their positions on either side of the stable doors. Standing at attention, they were alert behind dark Oakley sunglasses, machine guns cradled across their chests, watching and waiting for the unexpected. The rest of the team scurried to set up a perimeter along the white fences surrounding the yard.

Kamal peered out from a head wrapped in layers of white cloth while he quietly waited for the sheik to command him. He mistakenly looked up. Above a pointed beard, the sheik's beady black eyes fixed upon him. He lowered his eyes immediately.

He continued to bow, saying, "My brother, welcome. Assalamo Alaikum."

"Get up."

Kamal lifted himself on tiptoes to kiss the sheik on both of his cheeks. "Kaif hal ak," he said, offering peace to him.

The sheik stepped away from his air kiss. "I want to see my horse. Take me to Rex. I don't have all day."

His stern eyes made Kamal tremble. "Yes, my brother. I will take you to him." Shaking his turbaned head up and down, he backed away from him and headed to the stables, leading the sheik to his multi-million-dollar horse.

On entering the barn, they removed their sandals and placed them on the mat. Kamal watched the sheik take in the surroundings. His dark eyes examined the long white marble hallway that separated the horse stalls on the left and right. Multiple crystal chandeliers gleamed brightly from the ceiling.

Kamal trembled as the sheik noted the glossy mirror-like finish on each stall door, pausing to see his reflection — hesitating — continuing on to Rex's stall.

"Read the name of each horse to me," he commanded Kamal. The name of the horse was etched on a solid gold plate at the entrance to each of the stalls. Kamal read them. All except Rex.

"Spell it." Kamal spelled out the diamond letters one at a time. His voice cracked on the last letter.

"Bring him to me." The sheik waited, watching Kamal's every move.

"Bring him out," Kamal said to a young groomsman, who scurried inside the stall to lead the horse to the center of the hall.

"Excellent. I am waiting." The sheik stepped back to let the horse out. "You have done well." Kamal watched him finger the diamond letters again on Rex's stall door. Watched him take in the horse, smiling.

Kamal gripped his hands together to keep from shaking. I have to make him think it is Rex, he thought. He followed the horse between a line of stable hands dressed in white uniforms and turbans, each kneeling and bowing from his waist before the sheik. Per his instruction, they were bent with head over knees, and foreheads pressed onto the marble floor along the walls of the hall. No eyes were averted. No one talked.

"Kamal!" The sheik's voice boomed and bounced off the cold walls. "What is this?"

"What, my brother?" He wrapped his arms around his chest and took deep breaths.

"These men. Tell them to rise and go about their duties. Stop wasting time!"

Kamal took a deep breath, relieved yet still shaking. He leveled his voice. "Leave us! Be quick about your work. You heard your master." The men scattered.

Kamal watched the sheik's long strides take him down the plush red carpet floor to the horse. He ran ahead of him. "As you requested, I selected ropes made of gold twine to hold the horse in place." Kamal pointed to the roping design laced with purple threads tightly woven among long strands of golden material. The sheik stared hard at the ropes that held the horse to the clips fastened to the bit and then to the walls on opposite sides of the hall.

"Here he is, my brother," Kamal stammered. "Rex, a spectacular racehorse! He will win all of his races for you."

The sheik walked around the horse. Silent. He examined the horse's nose that was pushed through the loop of the nose twitch and the gold ropes that held him.

The groomsman held the reins of the feisty Arabian horse. He ran his hand up and down the horse's neck to quiet him. He tightened each of the gold ropes fastened to the opposite walls to restrict the horse's movements when the sheik stepped near him.

He studied the horse. Stared at Kamal. "You have inspected him? Is he healthy?" The sheik peered down at his underling, making him feel even smaller.

"Yes, my brother." His voice croaked out an answer. "Yes, he is a fine horse. I have inspected him over and over myself. Excellent horse. He will make good money for you on the racetrack—a winner." He backed away from the sheik, bowing, giving him more room for his inspection. He was shaking under his robes, watching the sheik's reaction. His breath came in gulps.

The sheik ran his hands down the horse's legs, along his flanks and over his forehead. Taking his time, he examined the pasterns and fetlocks and lifted each hoof. His practiced fingers probed the throat and jaw, curled down the lips and tugged up the eyelids. The horse's nostrils flared.

"Whoa, whoa," the groomsman said when the horse tapped his hoof on the ground.

The sheik gave Kamal a puzzled look. He pulled back the horse's lip again, silently reading the numbers tattooed inside. His face turned crimson with rage.

"Kamal, I did not buy this creature! Who is responsible for this deception?" Stamping his feet several times, he flung his arms wildly. His white robes whipped around him. Spit flew from his mouth. "Explain this to me, Kamal!"

The horse snorted, bucked and nearly kicked the groomsman.

"But...my brother...you picked out this horse yourself. It is Rex. Rex. You bought Rex from the broker Jack Lafferty at the auction. I picked him up today at Bourke's farm." He petted the horse, trying to stop the skittishness by talking softly to him. The horse bucked and kicked again. The sheik jumped back and closed the distance to Kamal.

The moment the last words left Kamal's lips, the sheik struck him across the face. Grabbing the man by the front of his robes, he lifted him off the ground and threw him on the floor like a ragdoll, near the horse's hooves. "Do not tell me this! What are the numbers branded in his mouth? Read them to me."

The horse reared, but the ropes at his head confined his movements. Kamal rolled quickly away from under him. The groomsman grabbed the reins to keep the horse in place while he continued to buck. His nostrils flared. Ears flattened against his head while he snorted and neighed.

Kamal rose, cowering before the horse, and pulled back the lip. He said, "5552140963, my brother."

"Read it again!" Grabbing Kamal by the throat, he gurgled out the numbers while the horse thrust its head around in a wild frenzy.

"Exactly. Rex has a '7' in his mouth—not a '9'—you blithering imbecile." Letting go of Kamal, he slammed him into the horse. The horse threw his head back, but the ropes kept him from rearing up on his hind legs. He bucked again, swung his hind legs to the left and then the right, knocking the groomsman to the ground. Kamal jumped back.

"Get this beast out of my sight!" The sheik waved his arms, inciting the horse even further. "Remove him from my sight. Dispose of him. Now!"

Kamal shouted at the groomsman. "Take him to the shed and dispose of him." He led the horse away. Kamal threw his hands up in the air and shrugged. He peered into the sheik's black eyes, swallowing him up.

"*You* are going to be disposed of today if I don't get results. I want to know what happened to Rex."

"Give me a chance to find the man, Jack, who did this, my brother. I will find him, my brother. I will kill him, my brother." He fell to his knees, bowing low, making himself small at the feet of the sheik. His forehead pressed into the marble. His body shook. He stiffened—waited for the strike. It came swiftly. The sheik stamped his foot onto Kamal's back; he felt his bones crack. He stifled a cry and covered his mouth.

"Find the horse I paid for by the end of the day, or it will be you who pays with your life."

"I w…," he mumbled, holding his side, tears running down his cheeks. "I will find him."

The sheik nodded to his bodyguard, pressed the heel of his bare foot into the man's face. "You do that." Releasing him, he swooped toward the door.

Kamal slowly stood on his feet. Blood seeped through his robes as he gripped his side. He watched the guard fasten the sheik's sandals before they exited the barn. He crept toward the door.

The sheik said, "I will expect you at my suite at 9:00 this evening. You will bring Rex to me."

"Yes, my brother. Yes, my brother." Kamal stumbled over the words as tears continued to run down his cheeks. He tried to bow, but the pain cut off his breath. Making an attempt, he bent at an awkward angle and almost passed out. His face tightened in pain and swelled as he mumbled his words. "I will do as you command, my brother. I will seek revenge for you this day. I will bring Rex to you."

"You will, or you will be with Allah today." His fisted hands shot toward the sky pointing toward the unknown.

Kamal nodded to his back, gasping for breath.

As the sheik left the stables, his white robes swung wildly around his muscular shape. Back straight and chin pointing upward under his long, black, bearded face, he swept to the sleek car, where a bodyguard held the door open for him.

Kamal listened and watched from just inside the barn. The sheik held out his hand and his man placed the cell phone in it. At the same time, the other guards quickly maneuvered into position to leave the yard. Soon, they filed into their respective vehicles, waiting for him to give the signal.

Before he folded his long body into the Rolls, the sheik's face twisted into a deep purple and red color while his voice carried to all who surrounded him. "Saheed, find the broker, Jack Lafferty. Make sure he understands I know he tried to deceive me. I paid three million for that horse. I will not be made a fool. Take care of him today. Do you understand?" He waited for the response. "Yes, and then...remove Kamal from my sight." He looked over at Kamal and hung up. Nodding to his bodyguard, he entered the car. His guard snapped the door shut.

Kamal knew it was a good day to die. He watched as the sheik and his entourage roared out of the farmyard. Gravel sprayed out from under the tires as the Rolls fishtailed down the winding narrow road between the white fences bordering the pastures. Hundreds of thoroughbred racehorses grazed in the lush green fields under an overcast sky.

CHAPTER 27

BLACKROCK ISLAND

On the flight to the island, orange and red sunrays bathed the helicopter in bright light while its shadow reflected the egg-shaped frame on the surface of the Atlantic. As they approached the landing pad, the hum of the engine alerted Patricia of their arrival. Laine watched her from the cockpit window as she hurried down the path to meet them at the tarmac. Within a short time, they exited the helicopter.

"How is Murray?" Patricia wrung her hands.

The grim look on Miles's face answered her. "He broke both legs and his right arm. If it wasn't for Laine's quick response, he might have died."

Patricia crossed herself. "Bless the poor lad." She crossed herself again and Eamon put his arm around her.

Laine walked a short distance ahead of the group down the path to the cottage. She listened to them talk about the day's events. She thought about Murray. What was he trying to tell her on the flight over to the hospital? It puzzled her.

The orange sunset faded into the horizon as they entered the cottage.

"I've got stew a warmin', while the soda bread's a finishin'. I've been worryin' myself sick this whole time thinking about Murray. Havin' a wee nip, so I am."

"Good for you. We're going to join you." Miles draped his brown leather jacket over the back of the chair.

"What can I do to help?" Laine asked.

Patricia made a scooting gesture with her arms. "I can manage this." She removed a platter of fruit from the refrigerator. Crackers came next, then fresh butter. "Have a glass of wine."

"I think I will." Laine poured her wine and took a sip. "If you don't mind, I want to freshen up before dinner, Patricia. Do I have time?"

"Go on with you. You've plenty of time. I'll bring you some clean towels when I get a minute."

Laine went to her bedroom. She dialed Max's number, but it went directly to voice mail. "Yellowbird reporting in. Urgent updates. I'll check back later." She hung up, plugged her cell charger into the outlet. She entered the bathroom to wash. A door creaked and footsteps in the hall told her Patricia was bringing fresh towels. She'd take a shower later. After a short time, she switched into jeans and a sweater. There were no towels on the bed. Strange, she thought.

Entering the kitchen, she watched Patricia stir the liquid in a pot on the stove. Listening to the men talk, she scooted next to Miles.

"It was no accident today. Murray's never been lax on the job. He checks and double-checks all his work. I wonder what the hell's going on." He bit into a sliced red apple wedge. "I've got the lads working on it. Tom and Wilfrid are like bloodhounds. If there is something to find, they'll find it."

"Aye, so they will," said Eamon.

"Poor lad." Patricia opened the refrigerator and removed a block of fresh Irish Cheddar. She lined up the stew bowls, ladled the mixture into each bowl and placed them in front of the waiting friends.

Laine poured herself another wine and looked at Miles. "He was lucky."

"Yes, it'll take some time, but he'll make it. What did he say again on the helicopter?"

"He mentioned Rex and that you are to beware of Jack. Something about Donegal Pub and Rodriquez. I'm not sure what he was talking about."

"It's strange. I'm not sure either."

She worried he would ask her again about her skills when she helped Murray. The doctor complimented her in front of Miles on the expertly wrapped tourniquets.

Eamon cut in, slurring his words. "Murray said it was important for you to know, Miles. He was repeatin' the same thing over and over. Couldn't say wot was wot cause the pain was so bad, but he was talking about Jack."

Laine nodded.

"Troubles a comin' he was sayin'."

"I wonder what kind of trouble. We've had enough of it lately."

"Eamon, will you take Murray's place—temporarily—until he comes back? I think he'd like that."

"Aye, I'll be havin' the honor. But only 'til he comes back."

"Done," said Miles. He turned and gazed at Laine. It seemed like he wanted to ask her something, but he hesitated. His look was soft, and he did not look away from her.

A warm feeling coursed over her entire body, comfortable with his look.

They sat in silence for several moments, staring at each other. Eamon moved to help Patricia with the cleaning up. The couple talked quietly at the kitchen sink.

"What is it, Laine?" said Miles.

"I don't believe in coincidences." She sipped her wine.

"I don't believe in coincidences either."

"Another accident? I'm not so sure."

"None of us could have foreseen or avoided it. Murray was conscientious. Something is radically wrong. In a few days, I will ask him what he knows about Jack and Rodriguez. It's his health that concerns me now."

"It's a horrible way to live—not to be in control of your life—especially your health."

"Yes, but people can change. Make life better." Miles drank the last of his whiskey.

"Is it possible?"

"It is."

"I'm not sure—takes time and energy. I thought I changed things after my husband's death." She was hoping to draw him out—the whiskey making him talkative.

"How?"

"I made better choices." I'm getting too personal, she thought.

"Want to talk about it?"

"For starters, I run my own business. I also run my father's architectural firm...with the help of key associates. I can't afford to get soft." Her voice turned hard, professional.

"What do you mean?"

"I have to stay on top of things. There's a lot to learn since my parents died," she said bitterly, catching her tone, softening it. "For starters, I didn't even know about the land—here—in Ireland."

"There is a lot for all of us to learn. One step at a time." He took her hand.

"Yes, I guess you're right." Laine was pleased to hear him speak so plainly. "I thought coming here to the island to work for you would give me peace of mind. I could start again. Begin again."

She let go of his hand. I feel something for him, but I have to stay focused on the job.

"I'll be here if you need to talk. We all have our secrets." His eyes never left hers.

"I don't know why, but I believe you." Inside herself she was not smiling at all. Max had warned her about getting close to any subject in her investigations. It was clear that she had to stop this kind of discussion. Step back from her feelings.

"I'm here to listen, if you want to talk."

"I think I'll have a shot of that whiskey, if you don't mind." She knew he was sincere. She could feel it. It was awkward for her to know it — to believe it. She resolved to push her feelings aside and concentrate on the job ahead.

"I'll get it for you," he said, smiling. "Ice?" She shook her head. He reached for a short glass, poured and handed it to her. "Slainte!" He tipped his glass with cheers to her.

"Thanks. To you too." She wished she knew what was going on. She needed a break.

"There's a lot to find out." Miles watched her closely, giving her time to think.

"A lot more than we know."

"It will all come out eventually."

"Yes, I suppose it will." She couldn't take her eyes away from his inviting look.

Patricia and Eamon were talking to each other as they rinsed and dried the dishes. The shutters slapped rhythmically against the outside walls of the cottage. A hard crack on the side of the cottage wall stopped all of them.

Patricia placed her hands over her ears. "The noise be bangin' my head in, Eamon. Thought you'd fixed 'em earlier today, luv."

"Aye, so I did." He placed the last plate in the cupboard. "The wind's a tearin' 'em loose from the hinges again. Another storm is a comin'. Be fixin' 'em — after the whiskey cake, luv."

"Canna you be doin' it now while we're waitin' for the cake to cool? I'll be doin' the icin' and you can be stoppin' the racket. Eat our cake in peace, we will."

Eamon frowned. "Aye." He headed for the kitchen door that led to the mudroom. "Donna worry. I'll be doing it now, luv."

Patricia smiled when the outside door slammed. "Miles, Laine, have another jar. The cake will be ready soon. Enjoy what's left of the day. Eamon will fix that racket, so we can rest tonight. It won't take him long."

"I'll check on him in a minute," said Miles, giving Laine a warm smile. "He may need a little help in this wind."

She smiled back at him. "I know I would."

The dark night was black against the windowpane. The wind howled as they quietly sipped their drinks. Laine tried to piece together the information Murray had given her on the helicopter. None of it made sense.

CHAPTER 28

BLACKROCK ISLAND

Outside the cottage, the light from the kitchen burned brightly against the darkness. Slap, slap, slap, the wind blew the shutters against the cottage. They groaned under the weight, hanging on a single hinge, lopsided, banging against the wall. Eamon shined the flashlight on hinges that had worked loose from the foundation. It would take only a minute or two to adjust them.

Odd, he thought, he had fixed them a few days ago.

The breeze felt good to him—he liked the outdoors.

He went into the mudroom for tools. Carrying the metal box outside, he stopped and studied the sky above the Atlantic. He knew storm petrels snuggled in their cliff nests for the evening. The birds were silent—no more exchanges of tweets or squawks. Dark clouds sailed past a full moon. He was at peace as he watched the wind bend the tops of the tall trees. It was nearing complete darkness, except for the light of the moon.

Living on the island gave him a sense of how life worked. He knew things—nature's force and the danger it presented. It made him feel alive.

Eamon pictured himself as a child with his father. He remembered stories his father told him of the bears, wolves, owls and snakes infusing the darkness on missions to search and destroy on the island. He told him they needed to hunt and prey on the smallest of creatures—taking their lives before theirs were taken. They slithered and crept boldly from their hiding places in the night. It was their means of survival, he remembered.

His father taught him to observe them—learn from them—use his instincts. He took his advice. He learned from the island—like his father.

The silence, except for the wind, filled him with pride. He felt good. Patricia would be wantin' to serve the cake. He had to fix the shutters. Enough daydreaming.

Curious, he thought as he pointed his light at the empty screw holes. He shined his beam on the ground, spotting several screws in the dirt. He felt someone watching him. His instincts kicked in but not in time. Something hard struck him in the back of his head, knocking him to the ground.

Dazed, he sprang up and shouted, "Bugger!" In a boxing stance, he lashed out, balled fists swinging wildly in the air. Coming full circle, he connected with a punch. He popped his fists in front of himself again, missing—hitting air. He couldn't make out the man in black who'd hit him. Covering his eye, the man swore at him and ran toward the cliff, disappearing down the steps.

"I'll kill you if I catch you around here again!" Eamon shouted after him, struggling to keep his balance. His vision clouded. He felt nauseous and his knees buckled as he pitched forward to the ground. He vomited on the hard earth. Now, as he crawled inside, the mudroom swam around him. He tried to focus. Hoisting himself up, he swayed back and forth, taking small steps toward the kitchen.

"Dirty bugger," he slurred. "Me head." The room went black as he collapsed on the floor.

What seemed like hours but, in fact, was only several minutes later, he blinked his eyes open, trying to get his bearings. He was facing down on a broom, but where? He recognized the mudroom. His mind was foggy as he lifted himself up. His head ached. He managed to stand and stumbled through the door into the kitchen — into the light. The brightness hurt his eyes. His legs wobbled as he fought to keep himself upright. He leaned against the doorjamb, breathing heavily.

Miles and Laine were deep in a conversation, but they stopped talking and stared at him.

"Miles, lad, I see two of ye. Me head is cracked." His legs slipped out from under him. Pitching face first onto the kitchen floor, he groaned as his cheek met the wood.

Patricia was cutting the cake, her back to him. She ran to his side. "Eamon! Eamon, there's blood running down your shirt! Back of your head is cracked!"

"Got hit from behind. Maybe a shutter tore loose." He moaned and squinted at the light.

"Hang in there," said Miles, helping him into a nearby chair.

Patricia pulled ice from the refrigerator, wrapped it in a towel and pressed on the wound to stop the bleeding. She said in a concerned voice. "Donna be worried."

Laine watched from her chair, resisting the urge to help. Not wanting to draw attention to herself, she listened quietly.

"I was goin' about fixin' the shutters when someone clobbered me on me noggin'. Close to dying I am. I'll be needin' a whiskey to help me heal me head." He gave Patricia a weak smile.

"We'll see about that, we will." Holding the ice to his head, she did not smile.

"I socked the bugger, I did. Got 'im good after he hit me. He'll be having a black eye, he will. But me poor head. Donna go after 'im, Miles. He went off down the cliff, he did. He's long gone by now."

"Did you recognize him?"

"No, but we'll be lockin' the doors tonight, we will."

"Eamon, you need a doctor," said Patricia.

He shook his head. "Nay. 'Tis only a scratch. Me head's hammerin' and a poundin' like a thunderstorm." He rubbed the back of his head. He fisted his hands and used them to push himself up from the table. He swayed from side to side, gave up and fell back into the chair.

Miles and Laine exchanged a look of concern.

"Can you describe him?" asked Miles.

"I told you, lad, don't ye listen?" Lines creased his forehead, eyes wrinkled in the corners. "Hit from behind, I was. Don't know who did it, but when I find him, I'll show him what for, I will. Stop your fussin', Patricia." She continued patting his head with the towel. "Another whiskey will fix me up. Keep me from dyin'."

Patricia smiled at him. "You've had enough for one night, luv."

Miles said, "Take a lot more than a tap on the head to make you stay down."

"Aye," said Eamon. "I'll take that bloke next time we meet, I will." He clenched his fists again, looked to see if Patricia was watching.

"I'll be right back." Miles went outside into the yard and came back with a large flashlight. "There's blood on this, Eamon. Your blood, I'd wager." He brought it up to his eyes, carefully inspecting it. "Appears to be a heavy-duty construction type flashlight. Someone was outside watching us. But why? And why did he strike you? That's what I want to know."

"Aye, me too. Hit me with it, he did." He tried to get up again but slumped back in the chair.

"Like you said, he is gone." Miles walked over to the kitchen door and locked it. "Do you think you can describe the man—what little you saw of him as he ran away?"

"He knocked me down from behind. All dressed in black with a hood over his head. Then he took off—after I hit 'im."

"Okay, we'll get to the bottom of it. Let's get some rest and we'll talk about this in the morning."

"I hope you'll be all right, Eamon," said Laine. It was another incident to report to Max—the violence was escalating. Someone was making their lives miserable—but who?

Everyone in the room was a target. If they wanted Eamon dead, he would have been killed. This, she was certain, was a warning.

"I'll notify Tom and Wilfrid. I want you to know we'll find out who did this, Eamon. Bring him to justice."

"We will, at that. We'll have none of it again. I'll be on the lookout."

Miles said, "I'll install alarms and sensors tomorrow. That'll put a stop to it."

There it was, Laine thought. Something was tickling the corner of her memory. Yes—the sense that someone lingered outside her door as she freshened up before dinner. Could whoever was out there have been the one? He could have loosened the shutters to get Eamon outside. Then a bonk on the head. Suitable warning. But of what?

Someone wants to hurt Miles and his friends. Miles was no pushover. He was going to take action.

CHAPTER 29

DONEGAL HARBOR

The next day, Miles met Laine in the kitchen, nibbling on a muffin. "Mornin' to you. Would you enjoy a boat ride into Donegal town today? We could have brunch and then go shopping for sconces for the lighthouse."

"Sounds good to me. I was just going to have a cup of tea. How about you?" She walked to her tea tin, but hesitated when she saw his look.

"Let's head out and catch the first rays of the sun. It's quite a spectacular scene. If you still want tea, we can have it on the yacht."

"It's a wonderful idea. I'll get my bag and meet you at the boat." She swept past him, smelling the sweet scent of his cologne. It made her think a little too much about where it might lead. She brushed aside her feeling and ran to her room.

The engine purred as they pulled out of the cove. The sun's bright yellow rays blanketed the water until low clouds swept over the ocean.

In a short time, they were seated in Donahue's Pub, waiting for their meal. The fishing charters cruised in and out of the harbor into Donegal Bay.

"You look like something's bothering you."

"Eamon's fine this morning, but I'm determined to find out who was on the island last night and why he bonked Eamon," said Miles, rubbing his chin, glancing out the window.

"Yes, I would like to know that too." Laine watched a man filleting fish on the dock below.

Miles reached for her hand. "Do you feel comfortable staying on the island? I can make arrangements for you to stay at the Abbey Hotel in town, if you think you would be more comfortable."

"I am fine on the island." She picked up her tea to avoid his grasp. "I don't scare easily, but thanks anyway."

"You are a special woman. I can see that."

"I can't believe it!" She put her hand up to silence him. "There's that woman who was with my husband the other day. Look, she's on the tour boat down there."

"Are you sure?" He focused on the scene below. "Oh, that's…"

Laine gave him a frantic look, threw her napkin on the table, stood up and grabbed her bag. "I'm going to talk to her. See what she knows."

"I'll go with you." He left money for the bill on the table and followed her out the door.

They hurried to the docks at the pier. Reaching the waterbus, Laine ran up the metal gangway with Miles close behind her. A chain link railing at the top prevented them from boarding the boat.

"Excuse me, can we have permission to come aboard?" Miles shouted to the two men on the stern.

"We've already boarded the passengers. The ship is full for this tour," said a crewman. The other man, who appeared to be the captain, peered at a chart without looking up.

"You'll have to wait for the 3:00 p.m. cruise." The crewman walked over to them. "We're busy getting ready to take out the tourboat. Captain donna have time now to be talkin' with ye."

"No, we're not going on the cruise," said Miles. "We just need to speak to the woman who was on the back deck a few minutes ago.

"It's important that I talk to her," said Laine.

"You mean Marla?" said the crewman, eyeing Laine suspiciously.

"Yes. I need to speak with her." Laine rattled the chain. The crewman looked over at the captain.

"Yes, it was Marla O'Brian," said Miles.

"Aye, the only woman crew aboard *Morrigan*. She tells passengers 'bout the ruins and the famine. On the next tour, you can hear all about it when we cruise along in Donegal Bay. What ye' be wantin' her for now?"

The captain walked over. "I'll take it from here, Sean. How can I help you?"

"I need to talk to Marla for a few minutes. If that's possible." Laine smiled her biggest smile at him. "May we please come aboard? It's very important that I speak with her."

He hesitated and returned the smile. "Aye, if it's that important, but for only a minute. We'll be leaving the dock soon." He turned to the crewman, "Sean, let them aboard."

"Aye." He unfastened the chain.

"Watch your step." The captain extended a hand to Laine and then to Miles.

"We appreciate it. I'm Miles Bourke. This is Laine Sullivan."

"Happy to make your acquaintance. Captain Padraig and my crewman Sean. I've heard of you. You're the racehorse breeder in Blacksod."

"One and the same," he nodded. "Fine waterbus you have here. Looks brand new."

"We upgraded a few years ago. Added a second floor."

"Hate to interrupt, but can I see her now while you two talk?" Laine asked.

"Sean can take you to the wheelhouse. We are leaving in five minutes, before the tide goes out."

"I won't be long." Miles and the captain went into the navigation room while Laine followed the crewman along the deck into the wheelhouse.

"Up them steps there. She'll be checkin' her microphone and settin' up for the talk. I have to get to my station. I'll be leavin' you here."

"Thanks." She climbed the narrow stairs.

Marla was plugging a microphone into the console. She flipped switches and spoke into it. "Testing. Testing – one, two, three."

"Hello," said Laine. "Can I talk to you for a minute?"

Marla whirled around. She took in a sharp breath at seeing Laine. "No, I'm busy. How'd you get up here anyway? It's only for the captain and crew?" She turned away.

"Captain Padraig said I could talk to you." Laine stared at her. Marla's fingers clicked the microphone button on and off, ignoring her. She is behaving badly, thought Laine. "You are Marla, aren't you?"

"Who wants to know?"

"I do." Laine stepped toward her, closing the distance between them. "I'm Laine Sullivan, John's wife."

"Who's John?" Marla asked, slamming the microphone down on the console. She put her back to Laine and flipped through a manual.

"Don't play innocent with me. I saw you with him in front of the church last Sunday. He's *my husband*. His name is John Rafferty. You were there with him." Laine felt the anger rise inside her. The woman was lying. She would pry the information out of her.

"I don't know no 'John Rafferty.' I've got work to do. So if you don't mind, you need to leave." She flipped pages and scribbled a few notes.

"I'll repeat myself. Miles and I saw you Sunday in Donegal Town Square. The two of you were arguing in front of St. Patrick's Church. I know what I saw."

"I don't know what you're talking about." Marla tossed the manual aside and her fingers drummed on the ship's wheel. "I haven't been to church since…hell, I don't know how long. I'm too busy with the cruises." She picked up her microphone again. Pushing in the button, she shouted, "One, two, three, testing. Embarkation point of emigrants to Canada and North America during the famine years is on starboard. Departure point of Coffin Ships on your right." Click, click, click sounded the microphone switch.

Laine saw the red nails and lips, long blond hair — definitely the woman with John. "What were you doing with my husband?"

"You're nuts, lady. Stop wasting my time. I'm working here. Are you deaf?" Marla pressed a button and the ship's horn blared long and sharp, drowning out Laine when she tried to speak. She pressed the button several times, holding it in longer and longer until the blast pierced their ears.

"Tell me where he is," Laine shouted above the horn's wailing. "I need to talk to him."

"You bitch. I've got work to do." Marla held down the button for another long blast. "Get out of my wheelhouse. I don't have time for this." She shoved Laine aside and took the stairs down to the door marked *Private Crew's Quarters*.

Laine followed, but the door slammed in her face. Her eyes narrowed into thin lines when she heard the door lock click. "I'm going to find out what you're hiding. Believe it. You have not seen the last of me! You're lying, Marla. One way or another I'll find him. Bet on it. I'll be seeing you again — real soon."

The door stayed closed.

Laine thought, I'll get Max to run her name — get whatever he can on her. She quickly returned to the stern of the boat to inform Miles they were leaving.

He was talking to the captain on the stern when she arrived. "Let's go."

"I'm ready. Thanks for the information, Captain. I'll follow up on it.

Laine was halfway down the ramp when Miles caught up to her. "You okay? You look angry."

"I am." Laine's face was tight. They stopped at the end of the pier. When she looked back at the waterbus, Marla was rubbing the captain's back and then kissing him.

"Miles, look at her! She's all over the captain. Last week it was my husband. Now it's him. She's something else. She pressed the damn horn button every time I tried to talk to her. I didn't learn a thing."

Miles stared at Marla. "She was wild when we were growing up. She had a mean streak in her." Taking Laine's arm, he led her away from the boat. "She drowned her cat. Sadly enough, she bragged about it to anyone who would listen. There's definitely something wrong with her. Stay away from her."

"So you've known her a long time?"

There was silence.

"Yes, much to my regret. Another thing you should know..."

Laine saw him struggle with the telling of it. He squared his shoulders and his face turned hard.

"Under mysterious circumstances, her father drowned in Donegal Bay. The police said his small boat had a hole drilled in the deck below the gas tank, hidden under tape. They thought Marla did it, but they couldn't prove it. She was only twelve at the time, but her father left them when she was two years old. She never quite got over it. It was no secret she hated him. She and her mother lived at her mother's parents' home while her father drank himself silly in the town pubs. Womanizer as well. It took a toll on her. You've seen what she is like in the short time you've been here."

"She lied to me about being with John."

"Not surprising. But it is better left alone when it comes to getting involved with her. Wish I could help you figure it out, but she is not one to tangle with."

"Yes, I see that. It is all very strange." She thought Max could pull up the police report on her. It was worse than she thought. "I guess we need to return to our original mission for coming off-island—pick up a few items for the lighthouse."

"Sure, if you still want to go."

"Maybe we should head back to the island."

"I've got another idea. Let's go to Margaret Hogan's real estate office while we are in town. We can find out if she knows anything about Marla. She knows all the town gossip."

"Good idea. Well then, I guess we could have lunch first, since I ruined our earlier meal."

"No worries. I was hoping you'd say that."

As they approached Donahue's Pub, Miles opened the restaurant door for her. The hostess led them to the same table by the window where they had sat earlier. The bright sun caressed the rolling waves at high noon on Donegal Bay. By the time the *Morrigan* waterbus cruised out of the harbor, they were served a glass of wine. On the top deck of the boat, passengers waved from their seats to the crowd on the wharf. Powerboats, curraghs and sailboats glided into the foamy greenish-yellow waves of Donegal Bay for a day at sea.

After a short time, the staff served spinach salad and grilled salmon, while Laine observed the activity on the pier. Traditional music played in the background.

"I don't believe what I'm seeing!" She jumped up from her chair to get a better view from the window. "Marla is not on the *Morrigan*."

"What are you saying?" asked Miles, watching her focus on the events in the harbor below.

"She and *John* just got into a dark blue Ford pickup truck in the pier parking lot. I knew it. John is alive! I wasn't mistaken. My husband is really alive! What is going on?"

Miles went to her, put his arm around her shoulder and held her to him.

CHAPTER 30

Marla watched Laine and Miles walk down the ramp. Her heart still thrashed in her chest. She drew in a sharp breath. "Oh God, Liam. That woman is so irritating. Showing up here when I have work to do."

"What's wrong, Marla?" the captain asked. "Who were those people?"

Marla could only shake her head. Finally, she sputtered, "I don't know. She got me so upset I feel sick."

"What did they want?"

She searched for a reply and put her hand to her forehead. "She mistook me for someone else. She was so offensive I told her to leave."

Liam drew her into the empty wheelhouse. He pulled her close to him and kissed her hard. "I'll be glad when today's cruise is over. We can go home and spend a little time together." He brushed her hair from her forehead. "We haven't made love in a *long* time. That last job took me away from me wife for too many months."

"True." She yanked herself away from him. "Liam, I can't go on the tour today."

"Why not?" He kissed her again. "Let's think about tonight."

She didn't respond.

"What's wrong?"

"I can't talk about it." She backed away.

"What's *wrong* with you? You saw the queue. The ship is full."

"Too bad, Liam. I don't feel well. I have a bad headache. I need to go home."

"Who's going to narrate?"

"You do it. You know it as well as I do."

"Marla, you *never* get headaches."

"I'll make it up to you tonight. I promise."

He picked up her hand, kissed the palm, then slowly let it drop. "Where's your wedding ring? His face was inches from hers. "Where is it?"

"It's on the kitchen counter at home. I was doing the dishes, and I forgot to put it back on."

"You've never done that before. What's going on here, Marla? Are you hiding something from me?"

"Absolutely not. How could you even think that?"

"I hope I'm wrong." He looked at his watch. "If you're going to, go. I got to get to work." He turned on his heel and headed for the wheelhouse. "I'll see you at home for dinner."

It sounded to Marla like a question. "Sure." She smoothed her hair, left the wheelhouse and stumbled down the ramp. She pushed her way through the crowd. In no time, she crossed the gravel parking lot where her car was parked under the trees on the far side of the lot.

"What are *you* doing here?" she exclaimed when she reached her car.

Jack sat behind the wheel of her car, smoking a cigarette. "Aren't you happy to see me?" His elbow rested on the open window.

"I have to move the car someplace else. I might get a ticket if I leave it here. Follow me to the shopping mall and I'll drop it off. We'll take your truck because I am out of gas."

"Well, I guess I better get going." He slid out, walked a few cars down and jumped into his truck. Marla pulled out of the space and roared past him in the lot.

"Get moving," she yelled to him.

Jack shoved the truck in reverse.

Within a short time they reached the crowded mall parking lot. After switching vehicles, they drove along the coast road. Jack noticed a black car a short distance behind them, but he ignored it.

"What's up?" Jack flipped his cigarette outside then turned up the music.

"Just drive. Slow down, will you? You'll kill both of us the way you are weaving all over the road. And turn down that damn radio. I have a splitting headache."

He shut off the radio. "You're in quite a mood."

"Yeah, I am."

"And why is that?" Jack glanced over at Marla, but she had her eyes closed while her head rested against the window. This is strange, he thought.

They drove in silence for a short time. Finally, Jack pulled into a roadside lookout facing the sea. He turned to Marla. "Okay, Babe. Start talking."

"You'll never believe who visited me on the ship today."

His face looked quizzical. "Who?"

"Your wife."

"What?" Unbuckling the seat belt, he turned toward her.

"She's looking for you. She saw us in Donegal Square last Sunday in front of the church."

"What'd you tell her?" He pushed his hands through his dark hair.

"I lied. I told her I didn't know you."

"Good." He gazed out the windshield, silent, for several minutes. "We've definitely got a problem. We'll have to get rid of her—for sure. Why don't you meet me at McGinty's at eleven tonight to discuss it. We'll figure out the best way to do it."

"Not tonight, Jack. I have plans."

"What plans?"

"Don't bug me. Take my word for it, I can't meet you tonight."

Jack gave her a suspicious look. "You got some other guy?"

"Oh, Jack, don't be dumb. We can meet tomorrow night. That'll be better."

Wrapping his arms around her over the console, he pressed his lips against hers, drawing her into a long kiss. "Okay, then let's meet at your place."

"No! We can't." She pushed away from him. "I've told you time and time again my mother is living with me. She's very sick. If we wake her up, I'll be up all night taking care of her. She needs her sleep. McGinty's is better. What time did you say? Eleven tonight? I'll be there."

"I need some air. Let's go for a walk." Jack opened the car door.

She knew he was angry by the way he frowned at her. After a moment, she joined him on the bench overlooking the sea. The wind whipped her blond hair. The ocean roared along the rocky coastline, washing up on the sandy beaches. Sea petrels flew in patterns over the waves near the shore. A few seals basked in the sun on the rocks below them.

It was peaceful until they heard the gun shot. The back slat of the bench they were sitting on splintered.

Marla screamed. Jack shoved her to the ground. Scanning the area, he saw a silhouette of a man holding a rifle, aiming at them from behind a tree a few yards away. Another shot rang past them, kicking up the dirt past the bench.

"Let's get out of here. When I say go, head for the trees. Ready?"

He grabbed her hand at her nod. "Run!"

Crouching low to the ground, they zigzagged in and out of the trees toward the truck.

CHAPTER 31

Kamal watched Jack and Marla race toward the Ford pickup after his shot deliberately missed them. I'll give them a good scare now, he decided. He laughed while they scrambled into the truck. Guess I could have fired at them in the harbor parking lot, he thought. No, this is a better place. They'll know I mean business.

Moving behind a large tree trunk, he focused his line of sight on Jack inside the truck. This should be easy, he thought. He tucked his rifle snuggly into his shoulder, lined up the crosshairs on what he thought to be a few inches from the back of Jack's head and placed his finger on the trigger. Taking careful aim not to kill him, he fired. The glass in the back window shattered, and the bullet zinged past his target and out the front window. Glass flew in all directions. He smiled when he heard the woman shriek.

"What the hell!" Jack screamed.

Kamal detected the fear in his quarry's voice. Liking it, he pulled the trigger again and again after lining up the sight on the right rear tire. He fired repeatedly but missed as the truck fishtailed on the gravel road.

"Think I wouldn't find out you cheated me, Jack?" he yelled. "I am going to get you, if I don't get my money. This is just a warning!"

Kamal fired another shot at their side view mirror. It shattered. "Aha! A direct hit." He laughed hysterically.

"It must be that crazy Arab. Damn you, Kamal!" Jack pulled away as the tires grabbed the pavement.

"Praise be to Allah." Kamal tucked the rifle under his arm and ran to his car. He slipped the Remington into its case then stashed it in the trunk. You can't run from me, he thought as he slipped behind the wheel. Slamming the stick shift forward, he tailed Jack's truck, keeping out of sight a short distance behind him.

The wind picked up and dark clouds rolled in over the rough waters of Donegal Bay. A light rain obscured his view and made it hard to follow him down the winding road into Donegal Town.

After Jack pulled up in front of the Abbey Hotel, Kamal pulled into a parking spot. He watched Jack drop Marla off at the front entrance. She glanced around, hurried in the front door as Jack drove to the parking lot across the street. Shortly thereafter, he went into the hotel.

Kamal made a choice. I am going to make sure Jack brings the money to me. Oh yes, this is foolproof on my part, he decided. Scanning the lane, he found it was empty, so he reached into the center console and removed a length of rope and his Glock. He snapped the gun clip in place and shoved both items into his jacket pocket. Locking the car, he walked the short distance to the hotel.

In the foyer guests milled about, some sipping tea, others reading newspapers in the plush leather chairs. Kamal tapped the bell several times on the check-in counter.

A young clerk appeared from a doorway. "May I help you, Sir?"

"I'm here to meet a friend. Jack Lafferty. Has he checked in yet?"

"He's already registered, Sir. I saw him enter the Eas Dun Bar a few moments ago, just there, Sir."

"May I have a room near his room?"

"We're fully booked, Sir. The summer festival is in full swing."

Kamal slid a hundred Euro note across the desk. "What room did you say he's in?"

The young clerk quickly pocketed the money. Checking the book, he said, "Oh. Yes, he's in suite 305. I see I can put you in the suite next door — suite 307. Is that all right?"

Yes."

"Our rate is 300 Euro for the night, Sir."

Kamal gave him cash and scribbled a name into the register. The clerk handed him his key.

"Thank you, Sir. Anything else, Sir?"

"Where did you say Mr. Lafferty is now?"

The clerk pointed across the foyer. "If you're hungry, I recommend the Killybegs's monkfish and the seafood chowder. They're really quite good."

Kamal headed toward the bar. The warm glow of the chandeliers made the room inviting. His eyes skirted the area. Jack, alone at a table in a corner, hunched over a tall drink. Kamal patted the pistol in his pocket. You will help me this day, he thought. The room was empty but for the waitress and the bartender. Jack did not see him until he was upon him.

"Hello, Jack. Mind if I sit down? We've got a few things to discuss."

"Yes, actually I do. I know it was you trying to kill us back there." Jack pushed his chair back to stand up.

Kamal yanked a black leather chair away from the table and sat. "Not so fast. Sit down. We have a few things to discuss. If I wanted to kill you and your girlfriend, I would have. We have a problem, Jack."

"What kind of problem?"

"A three and a half million dollar problem."

"What are you talking about?"

"Where's the money you skimmed off the top for Rex and the other horses? The horse you sold me doesn't even qualify for any of the races."

Jack shifted in his seat. "You have the horse. You picked him up yourself."

"The horse was not Rex. We both know that. I want the money."

Jack gulped his scotch before answering. "Not my problem now."

"Yes, it is." He leaned close to Jack's face. "The sheik wants his money by five o'clock today. Three and a half million dollars."

"I don't have it."

"Get it." His black eyes bored into Jack's as he smiled. "We don't tolerate carelessness."

"Look. I'll see what I can do. You've got to give me more time. I can get you *some* of the money by five, but not all of it."

"How much?"

"A million, I think. Yes, a million. I'm working on another deal."

"Not enough. We want it *all* by five or..." His voice trailed off. He looked around the room and leaned in close to him. "Or else."

"I'll see you here at five." Jack replied and signaled the waiter for another drink.

"You better have it all." He abruptly shoved back the chair, tipping it over. He swept across the room, catching Marla's elbow at the entrance to the bar. He swiftly steered her back into the foyer the way she came.

"Oww! That hurts," Marla squealed.

Kamal leaned close and whispered, "Shut up. I've a gun in my pocket pointed at you. I'll use it if I have to. We're leaving. Move it." He poked Marla's side with the barrel of the gun. "This way. We're going for a little ride."

Kamal rushed Marla out of the hotel before Jack realized they were gone. They circled to the back alley. The delivery door was open. When they entered, a maid was loading a laundry cart onto the freight elevator. She smiled a "hello" as they entered. He nudged Marla inside with the pocketed pistol. The maid looked at him with a curious expression then looked down at the laundry.

"Don't say a word," he whispered in Marla's ear. She nodded at him.

The maid gave Marla a long look, then exited on the second floor. Quickly, Kamal punched the close-door button. Soon, the elevator doors opened on the third floor. At suite 307, he dragged her by the arm into the bedroom.

"Sit." He pointed to the chair. "Pray to Allah your friend brings me the money by five o'clock today."

Sitting in the chair, she stared at him. "What are you going to do to me?"

He laughed. "Shut up." He pulled the rope from his pocket and tied her hands and feet to the chair. He took the pillowcase, tore a thin strip from it and gagged her.

Kamal gave her one last look before closing the door to the bedroom. Now I will take care of Jack, or he'll never see her again. Smiling, he left the suite. As he walked down the hall to the elevator, the same maid who was on the elevator with them on the way up pushed her cart out onto the third floor. She kept her head down and took no notice of him.

He would please the sheik today or he would soon be with Allah.

* * *

"Maid service." The older woman knocked loudly on the door to suite 307. "Maid service," she said again. No one answered. She remembered the man with the turban headdress and the blond woman getting off the elevator a short time ago. He had grabbed the blonde's arm and shoved her down the hall to the suite. A few minutes later, she saw him hurry out of the room, but the woman was not with him.

On the elevator she'd seen fear in the woman's eyes and it made her sick. After working in the hotel for many years, she knew something was wrong,

Swiping the room card in the lock, she hurried into the suite. The bedroom door was closed. "Hello? Anyone here?" Her eyes swept the room. Seeing the closed door to the bedroom, she ran to it and turned the handle.

"Oh, for the love…" The woman was gagged and tied to a chair. "I'll have you free in no time. Donna be worried." She stopped and stared at her. "Marla, is it you?"

Marla nodded her head.

"I just recognized you. 'Tis me, Brigid from St. Mary's school." She freed the gag from her mouth. She could see recognition in Marla's eyes. "What's going on?"

"We have to leave before he gets back. He kidnapped me." Marla gasped for breath. "Let's get out of here."

"Aye." Stooping low, Brigid forced the ropes from her legs and then her wrists. "That we will. Follow me."

The two women slipped into the hall. They made their way to the stairwell and ran to the basement laundry room.

"I have a car out back." Brigid pointed to the door.

"I'm right behind you." She pulled a dark blanket from a laundry bin and covered her head.

They flew out the door and hopped into the car. Brigid drove while Marla sank low in the front seat.

"Take me north of town but not on the main road. I don't want him to see us." She rubbed her arms where the ropes had bruised the flesh.

"Aye, wherever you want. Keep down, lass. I knew he was a bad one when I saw him on the elevator."

"He forced me to go with him."

"'Tis the way of it. I could see he was up to no good."

"I've got to find a place to hide. I know where to go, if you'll take me."

"That I will."

Marla gave her directions to her mother's house in the country. "Do you have a phone?"

"No, but we can be stoppin' down the road a bit, if you be needin' one."

"I can make the call later."

"It's no bother. I'll be callin' in sick meself for leavin' the hotel early. Got me a half day off now, I do. Thanks to you."

"Yes, I guess you can think of it that way." She patted the woman's leg. "You saved my life."

"Happy to help an old school mate, I am."

"It might have ended badly, if not for you."

"Best thing to do is stay out of town a few days. He was up to no good."

"Yes, you're right. He doesn't know you helped me, so you'll be safe."

"Aye, so you say."

Marla glanced over at her as they sped down the road away from Donegal Town.

CHAPTER 32

KOOLMOORE STABLES

On the mainland inside Koolmoore Stables, Kamal, on his knees, cowered before Sheik Tariq. "Forgive me, my brother."

"Forgive you? Your face offends me. A woman bested you! You let that broker Jack swindle me! Now both of them got away!" The sheik's eyes narrowed at him. "Tell me what it is you have to say."

"I tied her to a chair in the hotel. I gagged her—but..." His head touched the cold floor before the sheik. "I went back to the hotel to get her, but she was gone. Jack has disappeared. I cannot find them."

"Hotel? You were in a hotel with a woman? Infidel!" Sheik Tariq flew into a rage. His fists punished Kamal's face over and over again before the wounded man sank to the floor. "You let this happen?"

The guards watched. They did not move. Eyes alert, they said nothing but stood at attention.

"It's not what you think, my brother." He cautiously peered up at the sheik then bowed low. His head swam. The swelling from his left eye prevented him from seeing clearly. Blood trickled from his mouth like water. He awkwardly pressed his head to the floor, waiting for the next blow. It came as a hard kick to his ribs. His breath rushed out of his lungs as his ribs cracked. Falling onto his side, he groaned. With tremendous effort, he tried to right himself by rolling onto his knees. Gasping for breath at the feet of the sheik, he pleaded with him. He choked out the words. "Forgive me, my brother. The horse you bought was murdered. I thought I could get the money back for you."

"It's been two days since I've heard from you. Where *is* my money?" His hand drew back to strike him. "Tell me!"

Kamal cringed. The white robes in front of him rose up like a giant statue, making him feel small. He squeaked out the words. "I don't know. The woman escaped. I left her for a moment only. The maid freed her." The corner of his mouth turned up. "But I took care of the maid," he lied.

"Silence," roared the sheik. His raised hand struck Kamal again. "You told me the woman would lead you to the American broker, but that is not true. You said you would bring my horse to me. It's a lie. You say you were trying to recover the money. More lies. My horse is dead! There is no money! You failed me." He folded his arms across his chest and harrumphed. "Your fate is sealed."

Turning to his bodyguards, the sheik nodded. The men moved swiftly. Kamal felt the smooth marble under his body. His arms felt like they were being pulled from the sockets as he was dragged along the floor.

"Please, my brother, I beg you. Give me another chance." Kamal cried out while his long, bloody, white-robed body swept the smooth floor of the stables. Both of his eyes were swollen shut, so he could not see the sheik clearly. A jabbing pain shot through his body over and over. His side felt like a knife had pierced his lungs. He listened for a response.

"Praise Allah. There is nothing left here for you." After a few moments, the sheik spoke again. "Get him out of my sight."

Kamal knew he was going to his death. He had no fear. It was his fate. He had failed. He heard the horses whinny and stomp their hooves in the stalls. It would be the last time he would hear them.

"Shut them up. Where is the head man?"

Kamal listened while he was being pulled across the floor.

"There is no headman—now," said the boy.

"You are my new headman. Fetch my Arabian horse. The one Kamal purchased from Bourke. I'm going riding now. Don't make me wait!"

Kamal heard him stamp his feet. Sheik Tariq was enraged. Kamal had witnessed it many times, and he feared what would happen next.

The men shoved Kamal into the trunk of the limousine. It was hard and rough on his back. A shooting pain pierced his body when he was maneuvered into position inside the trunk. He could hardly breathe. He prayed silently to Allah to make his death swift.

He heard the boy tell the sheik the horse was ready. It seemed far off in his mind. Kamal cringed, knowing the sheik would punish the innocent horse for his mistakes.

"Give me the reins. I do not want to wait. You will do well for me, boy."

Kamal heard the cries of the horse. It whinnied loudly when it was struck by the leather riding crop. Instantly, horse hooves struck the ground in a rapid pounding of the earth. He knew the sheik was galloping away from the yard, plunging his heels into the stallion's belly. Hurting him. Making him run until he dropped.

He felt sick.

The trunk slammed shut, pitching him into total darkness. Tears seeped from his eyes. He was on his way to Allah.

CHAPTER 33

BLACKROCK ISLAND

It was after midnight when Marla and Jack hid the curragh behind a line of vegetation on Blackrock Island's beach.

"Wait here. We've got to make this fast," Jack said.

"Whatever you say. I can't keep doing this with you. We need money to disappear for a while and get Kamal off your back. Jerk almost killed you."

"Yeah, don't remind me. How he found out I swindled the sheik still puzzles me."

"He'll come after you again. Those people do not play around. Sure you can handle it?" She stretched her legs in the boat and leaned back in the seat. Pulling the zipper of her black jacket up to her neck, she yawned.

"Haven't I been handling it?" Jack's eyes narrowed at her. "I am handling it."

"Yeah, sure you are. Get going. I'm already sick of waiting."

"I'll be back — this time with Laine." He smiled at her.

"I'm ready to be done with this. If you are not here in an hour, we go to Plan...what?"

"Yeah, yeah, yeah, there's no other plan. We'll be done with this tonight. You'll see."

Marla gave him a sour look.

Taking the path through the forest, he stumbled over the rough ground. He could see the light shining from the lighthouse tower. It reminded him how easy it was to get to the cottage and hit the old man Eamon on the head. He laughed at the scene and played it over and over in his head as he flashed his small light on the trail. When he was above the rock ledge that led to the caves, he scrambled down the side of the cliff.

I hate these dank, dark tunnels, he decided. Marla's directions echoed in his head as he sped through them. "Take the first right," she told him. "Don't forget..." He blocked out her voice in his head.

After a short time, he reached the opening for the fireplace hatch. He was excited because for the first time he didn't get lost or smash his head on that damn rock. Marla will be proud of me. Wait until she sees Laine wrapped up like a mummy. He laughed.

"I know these tunnels as good as she does. Have to rub it in. She's getting on my nerves."

He stretched out uncomfortably on the jagged rock floor above the hatch and pressed his ear to the crack. He heard breaking glass and loud voices coming from the fireplace attached to the room below him.

He heard Laine say, "Oh, Miles, I'm so sorry."

Oh, Miles, I'm so sorry, he mocked her to himself. She would be sorry—soon—very sorry.

"Don't worry about it, Laine," said a man's loud voice. "It's only a glass. I have more glasses and wine. Don't do that. I'll clean it up."

"It's no bother."

Miserable bitch, he thought. She's caused me a lot of trouble. You're going to have more to worry about than spilling your fancy wine and breaking the glass, honey. The cold floor was giving him a headache. Sitting up, he lit a cigarette and inhaled.

How long am I going to have to wait here? This is ridiculous. He bent awkwardly to listen.

A woman's voice with a heavy Irish lilt shouted, "Here's another plate of starters for the both of ye. Eamon, me luv, set them on the table just there." He heard the scrape of chairs. "We'll be sittin' down to a lovely meal, we will."

What does she mean—starters—sitting down! Jack dropped his cigarette on his leg. It burned a hole in his jeans.

"Shee—ite!" He stifled a shout as the butt burned his skin. He knocked it off his leg. It flew in the air, hissed, and landed on the stone floor. His leg burned as he pulled the scorched material away from the singed flesh.

"Oww, that hurt," he mumbled and put his head back to the crack by the hatch cover.

A man's voice floated up to him. It was probably the one the bossy woman called Eamon.

"I've got me favorite crab cakes here for you. Made by me own wife, they are, and fresh caught from the sea. Patricia cooked 'em up lovely, she did."

Jack heard the sound of plates clattering. They are eating down there on top of that pile of junk, he thought. At this rate, I'm going to be here all night.

Something crawled across his face and he smacked it with his hand. "Damn thing bit me," he said in a low pain-filled voice. Realizing his mistake, he shut his mouth—they might have heard him. He waited. They were still talking. A welt rose on his cheek. It was itchy; he scratched it until it bled, swiped it with his hand, and rubbed it on his pants. Sitting on the hard floor made his legs feel numb. Lighting another cigarette, he inhaled deeply and waited.

"Patricia makes 'em the best there is," said the man.

Laine said, "Better tack that tarp back on the window, Miles, the rain's coming in."

Jack said in a low voice, under his breath, "Did she say rain? Marla's going to be a raving lunatic if she gets soaked. Damn it."

"Heard a nor'easter is forecasted. There'll be another storm tonight."

Jack heard hammering. Hmmm, the storm is going to make it easier for me to dump Laine. He smiled at the idea.

"That does it. The tarp will hold for now."

The loudmouth woman's Irish voice said, "I think we'd better finish eatin' in the cottage. It's gettin' dark and cold in here."

"You're the cook. Let's pack everything and head in," said Miles.

"Aye, a terrible storm's a brewin'," came in the other man's voice. "Come up from the cove half hour ago. Lines on the boats tore loose—fixed 'em good as new. The boats were bouncin' around like corkscrews."

Jack pressed his ear closer to the hatch. The man's speech was harder to understand, but he heard him all right. It was going to be a bad storm.

"Right," Miles said, "it's best if we go down to the cove again before we eat. We'll take another look."

"One broke free of its moorings—but I got it cleated. You donna want to go down those stone steps in this downpour, lad. They're slippery."

"There's only the platter and glasses. Eamon can carry 'em over to the cottage for me. Come on now. We'll eat and then you'll go."

"I'll be down in a minute," Laine said. "I'll grab my designs and finish them up in the house tonight. There's not enough light in here to see anything."

Jack's head came up and then went down to the crack again. She's staying behind. Good. I can grab her when she's alone.

Eamon said, "When I was doin' the fastening up at the cove, me eyes sighted a small curragh pulled up on the beach. It was past the point—hidin' it was. No one was lookin' after it."

Great, thought Jack. Just great. They saw the boat. Where the hell was Marla? Hope she hid someplace out of the rain.

Miles answered, "I'll get my rain jacket. Eamon, get yours. Let's check it out."

"Aye."

Jack scrambled to his feet. *Damn it, Marla! Why didn't you cover the boat with something?* He stood there, thinking. *How the hell can I grab Laine if they leave the tower and go down to the boat?*

He then heard Miles say, "Let's see if someone is on the island. A stranger won't be leaving without us knowing why he's here. You can be sure of it."

"I'll keep the supper heated on low in the cottage," said the woman with the lilt in her voice. "Take your time. Laine, do you need help?"

"No, thanks, Patricia. I can manage."

"I'll see you downstairs then," Patricia replied. Her voice faded away along with the footsteps.

Jack waited a moment and pressed his ear tightly against the hatch. Nothing. As quietly as he could, he pulled it open. He was careful not to drop it on his lap again. Laine had to be alone, gathering up her things.

Gradually, step-by-step, he lowered himself into the fireplace and peered into the room. *Yes, she was there with her back to him.* Everyone else had gone.

Humming a tune, she placed the plans in her briefcase. She swept up loose papers on the table, organized them, and slid them into the bag.

He watched her. Pulling the cloth from his pocket, he quickly poured a large amount of chloroform on it. The floor creaked as he swiftly ran toward her. In the next instant, his arms were wrapped around her neck from behind. Jamming the cloth over her nose and mouth, he held it tight to her face. She struggled and jabbed him with her elbows, but he dodged the move. She grunted, twisted, and kicked backward at him with her shoe. It connected with his shin, but his boot took the blow. She was good, but not good enough, he thought.

After a short time, he felt her go limp. She was heavy in his arms, and her legs bent at the knees. She was a dead weight. As he pressed the cloth tighter against her face, she slumped against him. She was unconscious, for sure. After waiting a few more seconds, he removed the cloth. He heard her shallow breathing. Hurry, he thought, before she comes to. Looking at her face, he admired her beauty. He always had thought she was a knockout.

"Such a shame it had to come to this, but I need your money, honey." He laughed. "Sheiks don't like to be cheated and Kamal's going to get me killed. Marla too. We have to have money to get the hell out of town. I'm sure you understand. So you see, darling, that's where you come in. It was always about the money, honey. I *need* all of your money just like you wrote it in your will. When you are dead, I inherit."

He laughed, soaked the cloth with a large dose of chloroform, and pressed it to her face. He waited and spoke to her. "That'll last for a few more minutes, anyway. It'll be nice to take a trip to Costa Rica. I've never been there. Marla hasn't either. You're going to make that happen for us. Time to go, Babe."

It took a few seconds to heft her over his shoulder. The fireplace was tight when he placed his foot in the foothold inside the rock wall of the fireplace. He scaled the wall. At the top of the climb, he stuffed her through the hatch hole. She was light, her weight making it easy for him to maneuver her through the opening inside the tunnel.

"We have only a little ways to go, but I have to close our escape hatch, so they won't find us. I'm very clever, aren't I?"

He dragged her to the wall and leaned her against it. Slamming the hatch shut, he took a deep breath and hoisted her over his shoulder again. "Where is my light? Ah, here it is." From his inside jacket pocket, he fished out the penlight. After turning it on, he jammed it into his mouth, so the small light lit up the path ahead of them through the winding tunnel.

After a short time, he forked right when he heard the roar of the ocean. The wind howled outside the tunnel exit to the cliffs. It was getting colder and the dampness clung to his skin. Laine was getting heavier with every step. He tripped, dropped her...and the light.

"Damn it, Laine." He was angry at losing his light, but he felt it under his foot and picked it up. At least it still worked. He stuck it back in his mouth and repositioned her on his other shoulder. Her shoe fell off, but he ignored it. He was in a hurry.

The cave room was around the next bend. He made it without further mishap. They slipped inside the narrow opening. Her head bounced on the rock-like bed when he dropped her from his shoulder onto it.

"Oops," he laughed. "Gonna have a little headache, honey, but you'll never feel it. We're in a hurry, so you'll have to stay here for a little bit. I promise, I'll be right back," he chuckled. "I have one more thing to do before we go." When he leaned over her, his penlight fell to the floor. He did not notice it. Placing his finger under her nose, he felt irregular breathing. "I think you need another dose to keep you quiet until I get back." He fished the cloth from his pocket.

At that moment Laine's eyes opened. She coughed and coughed again. Jack's arms held her down when she struggled to get up. Her eyes grew wide as she looked into his dark eyes. "John! It's me, Laine—your wife! What are you doing? Are you crazy? Let me up."

He took the cloth and reached for her face. Her head turned away from him, toward the wall. Raising her knees, she kicked at him but missed. He held her down and quickly clamped the damp cloth over her nose and mouth. She stopped struggling, so he rolled her limp body toward him.

"Good girl. Stay right here. This won't take long." Her head lolled to one side. "Always loved to watch you sleep, my dear wife, but I don't have time tonight." He laughed at his joke. "That's it. I'll be back soon to get you." He removed the cloth.

Her body was still, so he bound her wrists and ankles with rope. He thought about gagging her, but no one would hear her if she cried out, so he didn't bother. Placing his finger under her nose, he checked her breathing again. It was steady.

"Good you aren't dead yet. Too bad that scaffolding didn't take care of *you* instead of Murray. That stupid Rodriguez blew it. But don't you worry. You'll be going for a very long swim real soon. Call it your last boat ride, honey. The chloroform oughta keep you quiet for a while, or at least until I get back."

He took one long look at her, leaned down, and whispered in her ear. "Think of it as a late birthday present. This time, I won't be disappearing—you will."

With those last words, he covered her with the tarpaulin they had left on their last visit to the cave. Marla would be pleased, he thought, as he slipped into the tunnel. He lit a cigarette and threw the match on the ground.

Within minutes he climbed the cliff path to the top. Now all he had to do was find Marla and warn her about Miles and the old man. Peering over the edge, he scanned the area below for the men. He did not see them, but he knew they would be looking for someone on the island.

We'll have to make a new plan, he thought. She is going to be really mad, but that's too bad. She'll eventually be happy when we leave this place. And happier still when I inherit from my poor dead wife. He pulled his cap low on his forehead. His clothes were soaked through to his skin. And his leg where the cigarette had burned it felt like it was still on fire.

Taking one last look, he did not see them.

Maybe I should chance it and bring her with me now, he thought. Then he saw the men climbing down the stone steps to boats in the cove below him. He darted into the trees and headed down the path to find Marla.

CHAPTER 34

BLACKROCK ISLAND

Jack stumbled his way through the forest. He breathed in the strong smell of the sea and liked it. He thought about Laine, unconscious in the cave, as the heavy rain shower beat down on his back and soaked his clothes in the dark. Fumbling in his pockets, he realized he had dropped his light somewhere along the way.

I can't see. This is ridiculous, he thought. When I get back to the cave, I am going to make her pay for making my life miserable. He remembered the shock on her face when she realized he—her husband— had abducted her. It made him smile, despite the downpour.

Deep in thought, he ran smack into a large tree. "Damn it." He rubbed the side of his head and rounded the trunk as the rain slashed his face. Fighting to see the trail, he stumbled over the uneven ground. Tree roots made the going rough and he tripped several times. After he gained his balance, he ripped his shirt on a bush covered with thorns. The needles scratched his arms and tore at his face.

"What the hell!" he shouted into the darkness. The rain had thoroughly soaked his clothes. "This is nuts!"

By the time he got to the beach, he felt like he had been in a fight. Marla is going to kill me, he thought. He scanned the beach. Where the hell is she? Oh yeah, I bet she went to Plan Zero. Yeah, that's it. Plan Zero and out of here. I'll have to go to our next meeting place and see if she is there.

He maneuvered his way to the other side of the island through the underbrush. When he got to the beach, he called for her, but she did not answer. Where are you, Marla? I have to tell you to get the hell out of here before they find us. Guess I'll see if you left in the curragh.

He went to the boat's hiding place on the beach. Under the trees, he removed several branches that partially hid it from prying eyes.

"Well, it's still here. I'll get it ready, so we can get the hell out of here. You better show up soon, or I'll have to come back and get you later. I have to come back for Laine, so what's the difference."

He hurried to uncover the rest of the curragh. Just as he finished, a white beam of light swept the trees a few yards away from him. It was coming toward him from the ocean.

"Damn," he said, dropping to his knees. He crawled on his belly to hide behind the nearest tree. Peeking out from behind it, he saw the police patrol boat coming toward the beach. The white light ping-ponged back and forth along the shoreline.

Just my luck, he thought. They're looking for my boat. Damn it.

Taking a chance, he peered around the tree and squinted in the rain. He could barely make out the man standing in the bow of the boat, but he knew he was there. The floodlight pointed directly at his curragh. It was only a few feet from his hiding place.

"Got to get out of here before they catch me."

He ducked down and inched his way up the rocky cliff until he found a small ledge. Catching his breath, he slid onto it, peered over the edge, and watched the men investigate the area. Within seconds of flattening himself on the slab, he heard squawking noises close to him. He recognized the sound. The frigate birds were huddled in their nests deep inside the crevices of the cliffs.

Typical, he thought; even the birds are squawking at me. Just like Marla! The thought made him laugh. He laughed and laughed until he saw the white beam of light directed upward along the cliff walls. Shutting his mouth, he pulled his black cap low on his head and flattened himself on the rocky surface. Within seconds, the white beam of light passed over the top of him. He waited, holding his breath. It disappeared as quickly as it came. He sighed when he realized that he was not spotted.

"Safe," he whispered. He snuck a peek over the edge.

Several policemen were on the beach near the curragh. In the distance, near the cove, a band of men marched down the pebbly shore toward the boat crew. Their flashlight beams bounced along the sand and crisscrossed into the trees as they made their way to his boat.

A thought crept into his mind. I hope she has the sense to hide. She knows we have to go to our next plan. He frowned. I bet she hid in one of her caves. Yeah, that's it. She hid. I can't wait to hear all about it. Complain, complain, complain. That's all she is going to do. Guess I'll have to buy her off with a nice trip or something. I have better things to do than worry about her now. I have to get moving.

He scrambled slowly up the cliff. He hid on small ledges to make sure they weren't tracking him. So far, he wasn't sighted. He lost his footing and smashed his elbow on a rock that jutted out from the cliff on his left.

He stifled a cry and swore under his breath. "Damn, damn, damn." The icy cold rain made him shake. "I need a scotch."

He lost his footing and slid down a slight incline. At the last second, he grabbed a branch to break his fall and shifted his foot so it rested in a crevice. The wind and rain punished him. He flattened himself against the cliff surface and grabbed a rock with his other hand. After a few seconds, he shoved his other foot into the nearest niche. He realized he was on the climb he had taken earlier, but it became more treacherous as he went up the slippery slope. His hat blew off.

"Great, just great. Now they'll see my hat. I have to move. This is totally nuts!"

Finally, he reached the top of the cliff. When he looked over the edge, he saw dozens of lights—like sparklers— illuminating the area on the beach below him. He checked his watch. It had taken him more than a half hour to make the ten-minute climb. But they had not seen him.

He estimated it would take at least another half hour to get Laine to the other boat they had hidden earlier that day. If the men left. It would be too hard to carry Laine out of the cave without being seen. Well then, I am initiating our next plan. Marla hated it, he thought, but she would have to suck it up.

Without hesitation, he ran through the dense forest and made his way down the cliff on the back of the island to the beach. He had only slipped half a dozen times, but it was worth it. He laughed a guttural laugh when he thought of dropping Laine into the ocean.

His thoughts went wild inside his head. No one will ever believe I killed her. *I* will be dead soon, won't I? Drowned at sea. Yeah, that's what they will think. It was going to be the perfect murder and the best plan ever.

Going to the place he and Marla marked with stones, he pulled up the rocks and uncovered the plastic bags holding their wetsuits and extra life jackets. Good thing we hid these here, he thought.

He looked around. No one was watching. Pulling out the wetsuits, he muttered, "Here's Marla's suit. Now, where is mine?" He rummaged around in the bag. "Okay, mine's here." He pulled open another bag. "Ah, here are my gloves, hood, facemask, snorkel, and boots. Excellent."

He placed them on the sand and unzipped his wetsuit. Next, he ripped off his wet clothes, rolled them into a ball and stuffed them into the bag.

He shrugged quickly into the wetsuit. "This feels great." He placed the rest of the items back in the hole and shoved the rocks on top. "Marla can get her things later when I come back to get her. Hope she figures it out," he said as the rain poured down.

He dressed in the hood, boots, and gloves. Perched on top of his head were the facemask and snorkel. Scooting over to a stack of rocks near the first hole, he uncovered the oxygen tanks, fins, and weight belts from the hiding place. He strapped what he needed onto his body. The weight belt was heavy, but he knew he would soon be in the water. He placed Marla's equipment back in the hole. I'm ready. Now, I've got to get the boat.

The black inflatable boat and motor were quickly uncovered from under the branches. He unhooked the line from the tree that held the boat on shore and dragged the light craft into the ocean. In his other hand, he carried his oxygen tank and fins.

Wading into the icy water, he pushed the inflatable into the inlet. He hoisted his tank into the bottom of the boat. Next to it, he dropped his fins. He sloshed through the waves until the water was waist high; then he climbed into the stern. He slid the oxygen tank and fins by his feet and smiled.

The wind covered the sound of the engine when he turned the key. It sputtered and quit. A wave hit the boat broadside, tipping him backward into the bottom of the boat. He slammed his head against the oxygen tank.

"Shee-it," he said, rubbing his head. He got back up, grabbed an oar, and shoved off by pushing on the bottom of the ocean floor. He placed the oars in the locks and tried the engine again.

The craft pitched and rolled in the unforgiving waves and he was taken off guard. The bow slammed and went under a huge wave. The skiff leaned heavily on its side. He braced himself for the flip, but it stayed upright. He grabbed the oars and rowed hard until he was away from the beach. After a few minutes, he turned the key again. This time, the engine caught.

"I did it. I'll be back for you, Laine. You too, Marla." He looked around, but no one was in sight.

Pushing the throttle forward, he managed to maneuver the inflatable away from the shallow rough water. Waves tossed him from side to side, but the boat picked up speed. He rode the waves like a surfer, staying on top of the crests, so he would not overturn. He took in his surroundings again as the spray filled the bottom of the boat. Seeing the dotted lights from the mainland made him happy. The rain beat down on his facemask and obstructed his view — but he had escaped. He steered toward Blacksod Lighthouse.

After a while, the wind gusted around the Zodiac, making it hard for him to steer. He knew he was at the halfway point when he saw the red buoy just outside the lighthouse tower.

"I timed it perfectly. I am on target, Marla; my plan is working. Wish you were here to enjoy it with me," he shouted into the rain.

He shivered, despite the wetsuit. It was not the cold he was feeling as he rode the dark waves, it was the excitement of believing he could get away with murder. He went over it again in his head. Tomorrow was not soon enough, he thought. Maybe I should go back tonight.

The white glow from Blacksod Lighthouse mocked him in the distance. It was not far, but the journey was all but short. I made it this far, he thought. I'll make it the rest of the way. I am sure of it.

But the bright white light from a police boat shined directly on his boat, shattering the darkness. It came as a surprise, and it lit him up like the Fourth of July. Quickly, he jammed the throttle forward and crouched low.

"They couldn't have seen me! They're not going to ruin *this* plan."

Quickly, he dropped his life jacket overboard and slipped on his fins. Donning his oxygen tank, he strapped it to his back. The facemask was already down over his nose and mouth but he pulled the head strap tighter. The regulator fit easily into his mouth. Now facing backward on the side of the boat, he was ready. He checked the time on his watch and flipped over the side backward into the water—away from the light. He purged the dive valve in his mouth and descended below the waves.

I made it, he thought as he kicked his way down through the water.

When he dropped to twenty-five feet, he leveled off. He checked his depth again and began swimming toward Blacksod. His compass reading was dead on. He would make good time getting to the mainland in his underwater "tomb."

CHAPTER 35

BLACKROCK ISLAND

Laine lay on the stone slab and looked around the cave through partially open eyes. It's a miracle he left me alone, she thought. She gasped for breath. My ops training paid off once again, she decided. The room spun around her as she sat up. That extra dose he gave me could have been lethal. I guess I underestimated him.

She gulped in more air to clear her head. Within minutes, she worked loose the ropes from her wrists, tugged them off and did the same for her ankles. Keep moving, she reminded herself. I have to get out of here before he comes back.

She swung her legs over to the side and stood up. It took her only a second to kick off her single shoe. Her bare foot came into contact with the penlight he had dropped on the floor. She grabbed it up and ran blindly into the tunnel.

Where am I? She thought she heard the ocean. The sound directed her to it. She cut her feet as she stumbled along the jagged rock floor. At the end of the tunnel she saw an opening. It was the way to the cove. She hugged the wall and cautiously stepped outside the entrance. No one was in sight, so she flew down the stairs to the cove where Miles kept his yacht.

Quickly, she sped up the next set of stone stairs to the top of the cliff and ran across the grass toward the cottage. The going was slippery in the rain. She charged into the kitchen, where she found Patricia standing by the sink.

Patricia dropped the platter she was holding. "For the luv of Mary, you're a filthy mess. Look like you've seen a ghost."

"I did." Laine quickly locked the door. "Lock the other door. I'm getting my gun." She ran from the kitchen, leaving a stunned Patricia to pick up the china pieces that had shattered on the floor.

In a short time, Laine returned.

"What's going on?" asked Patricia.

"My husband is alive. He kidnapped me, left me unconscious in a cave. I got away before he could come back and finish me off."

Patricia stared at Laine then shook her head, charged to the pantry and came out holding a small metal box. She brought it to the table, opened it and took out a pistol. She slipped it into the pocket of her apron.

"You know how to shoot?"

"Aye. I'm calling the guarda." Snatching the cell phone from the table, she dialed the police.

"Tell them to come immediately." Laine placed her gun in the back of her pants and covered it with her shirt.

Pressing the phone tightly to her ear, Patricia dialed the police. "Tom, ye gotta come to the island. There's something terrible goin' on here. Laine's all beat up. Said it was her husband. Eamon found an empty curragh beached 'round the end of the point earlier this evenin'. Himself and Miles are searching the island and carryin' their rifles, so they are. Left half an hour ago. Aye, we've got our guns, we do, in case the bugger comes here. Donna have a good feelin' bout this. You'll be comin' by boat, you say? Aye, we'll be waitin' for you in the cottage. Bring all yer boys." She hung up and looked at Laine.

"I've got things to tell you about John."

"Aye, that you do. You can tell me while we be eatin' our meal. We may not get a chance later."

While they ate supper, she told Patricia what happened. "So now we wait."

"Glad you made it out alive. To think he wanted to kill you! The bastard."

"By now, he knows I've escaped. It's only a matter of time until he shows up again."

"We'll be ready for him. Let's do the cleanin' up. They'll find him, they will," said Patricia, crossing herself.

Laine nodded and stared out the window. "They don't even know he took me, let alone know he's on the island. It'll be hard finding him in the dark in the downpour."

"Hard work is what they know." Patricia wiped her hand on the yellowed towel. "He'll be gettin' what he deserves, so he will. Let the lads do their job. They're good at it."

"I suppose you are right. Next time I see John, I'm going to give him a piece of my mind." She watched the droplets of water stream down the window in thin lines.

All at once, the pantry door flew open and banged heavily against the wall. Laine and Patricia whirled around.

Grabbing the gun from the back of her pants, Laine pointed it at the doorway as Marla stepped into the room.

"Marla! What the hell are you doing here?" asked Laine.

"You have no business here." Patricia backed up against the kitchen counter behind the table.

"Shut up, old woman." Marla glared at Laine. "I'm here for her. Don't get in my way."

"He botched it, didn't he? Wouldn't be the first time. But then, you know that. You should be used to it. Bet you don't even know where he is." Laine leveled her gun at Marla. She cocked the hammer and positioned herself—legs apart—ready to shoot.

"You really are a dumb bitch," said Marla to Laine, ping ponging her own gun back and forth at the women. "Not so smart now, are you? I know exactly where *Jack* is. Think I didn't know where to find *you*?"

Staring into her cold, dark eyes, Laine said nothing and watched her every move.

"You think you're something, coming here and messing up our plans. We'll see about that." Marla's facial muscles tightened and her red lips formed a taut line as she squared her shoulders and took a step toward them.

Laine's voice turned hard. "Back off or I'll shoot you."

"You're coming with me. Yeah, honey, we're going to take a little trip together. Just you and me."

"Hardly. Took you long enough to get here. We've been expecting you for days. Sit down." She ordered her to the nearest chair with a nod of her head.

"Not in my plans." Marla moved toward the table that separated them from her.

"You don't have any plans anymore. The men are going to take you and John back to the mainland — to jail — where you both belong."

"Wanna bet? You're going with me now or the old woman gets it."

"Come to kill me, Marla?" Patricia piped up. "I always knew you were a bad one. Killed your own father, you did. We all know about it."

"Close your trap! He deserved it, the way he treated me and Ma. A man whore is what he was." An evil grin sprang from Marla's lips and her hands shook as she swung her gun at Patricia.

"Leave her out of it," Laine said. "It's between you and me now. John's left you to clean up his mess. How's that working for you?"

"Working out good, smart mouth."

"Not this time. Count on it."

"Oh, I'm counting, all right, but it's all about how much time you have left."

Laine thought, I'll kill her if I have to. She steadied her aim while her finger tightened on the trigger.

"Donna think we can settle this peaceful like, Marla?" said Patricia.

"Shut up, old lady. I told you I'm going to shoot you dead if you don't shut your damn mouth. Take a seat on the floor over there." Marla waved her gun at Patricia while she nodded toward the floor by the stove.

Laine blocked Patricia's path. "If you touch her, I'll shoot you right between the eyes before you even move a muscle. Count on it."

"Close your trap, bitch, before I blow your head off and hers too. Are you deaf, old woman?"

Patricia stayed where she was, gripping her apron.

"You're a slut. I think I'll have a little talk with the captain of the cruise boat." Laine knew that would get her attention.

"Not in this life. If I'm a slut, then you're a whore. Think Miles is going to go after someone like you? Right. You really are a dumb bitch. I see why Jack—John—dumped you. We've been planning to kill you ever since we saw you in Donegal. Coming here was a big mistake for you, *Mrs. Rafferty.*" She laughed.

So she's part of the plan, Laine thought. "I want to talk to my husband."

"You mean your *dead husband,*" she laughed. "He doesn't want to talk to you. Don't you get it? He hates you. It's about time you figured it out."

"I'll find out for myself."

"Yeah, you will whether you want to or not. You really are a dumb bitch, just like he said."

"You're not as clever as you think you are. She quickly flipped the table between herself and Marla. Patricia took aim, fired, and missed Marla's head by inches.

"*What the hell?*" Marla fired back at her. The bullet struck the table and splintered the wood. At the same time, Marla unlocked the kitchen door. Within seconds, she was in the mudroom as the door slammed shut behind her.

Laine shot out the door window. Shards of glass flew in all directions.

Marla screamed. "Damn you! I'm hit!"

"Lucky you. Give up while you can. So what's it going to be? Your time's run out."

"Damn you! Damn you!" Marla fired wildly into the kitchen through the windowless door.

Laine ducked behind the table and fired back.

"*Screw you, bitch. John's bitch!*" Marla returned the shots. They pierced the wall behind Laine.

"Nice try, but you're a lousy shot. Give it up." Laine fired again. For a moment, she thought she'd hit her. It was quiet for a few minutes, until the outside door banged shut.

Laine ran across the room and cautiously peered into the mudroom. Patricia had crept up behind her. "She's gone."

"Let her go. The police will be arrivin' soon—they can go after her."

"Wait here. I want to get a better look." Laine reloaded her gun, bent low, and hugged the wall of the mudroom while she scanned the room. It was empty.

"Are you okay?" asked Laine.

"Aye. Let's go inside."

"Thanks for backing me up. You're a good shot."

"For the luv of Mary, who be teachin' you to shoot like that?" Patricia stood next to the counter and laid her gun on top of it. "You been in trainin', you have."

"It's a long story. My father taught me how to hunt on the farm in Michigan."

"Must have been a good teacher, so he was."

"Yes, the best. Let's have a drink."

"'Tis a good idea. I'll be gettin' the whiskey."

Laine nodded and shoved the table against the door. John was not the kind of man she'd thought he was. By now, that fact was certainly clear. She needed answers, but he and Marla had disappeared.

Moments later, shouting from the front room of the cottage interrupted them while they sipped whiskey. Miles and Eamon ran into the kitchen, followed by the guarda Tom and Wilfrid.

"We heard shots." Miles fixed his eyes on Laine.

"That you did," said Patricia. "Takin' your time, you be, with the lads. Laine was keeping the peace, she was. Should have seen her."

"Marla just left. I shot her," she told Miles. He stared at her with a hard look, waiting for something that wouldn't come from her.

The men stopped what they were doing and listened.

"She's armed. I saw her head toward the woods." She pointed to the blocked kitchen door.

"We're on it," said Tom. He spoke into his walkie-talkie and updated the peacekeepers canvassing the island for John, and now, Marla.

Laine listened as he directed the troops to set up a perimeter near the woods.

"It won't be long. She can't go far. Police boats are looking for Jack—John—whatever name he goes by."

Wilfrid nodded. "We'll get them. Donna be worried. We have officers stationed 'round the house. Protectin' you, so they will."

"No worries," Patricia said as she reached for Eamon's hand.

Tom picked up the gun from the table, smelled the barrel. "It's been fired."

"Aye, that's me gun. Laine's got her own, so she does."

Miles's eyes widened when he looked at Laine. "You have a gun?"

"I do and I have a license for it. Do you need to see it?"

"No."

She watched him take her in. She felt uncomfortable under his cold gaze.

Wilfrid pointed toward the door. "Tom, let's go out back and track Marla down. She can't be far. Surprised she'd be out on a night like this."

"There's more. My *dead* husband kidnapped me a few hours ago. He wants to kill me. He surprised me in the map room and chloroformed me. I escaped through the tunnels when he left me alone for a short time in a cave room. He said he'd be back to take me on his boat and it would be my last ride. The room where he kept me is down by the steps leading to the cove. He might be hiding or meeting Marla somewhere on the island."

Eamon stepped forward, as if to comfort Laine. "Kidnapped you and tried to kill you? You poor lass. Are ye all right?"

"Yes, I'm fine."

Miles leaned on the counter, studying her, and she felt his eyes on her. He was waiting for her to say something more — explain herself — and the gun.

Patricia made a scooting gesture with both arms. "Aye, boys, go after them and be quick about it. Marla can't be far. She just shot her way out of here."

Tom gave Wilfrid a stern look. "Let's track her down. You take the rear of the house. I'll go round the front."

Wilfrid left after contacting the peacekeepers.

"Laine, did I hear you right?" Tom began. "You said your dead husband kidnapped you and wants you dead?"

"Yes, he's not dead. He's very much alive. He attacked me and drugged me with chloroform. He left me in the cave for some reason, but he said he'd be back to kill me. I pretended I was out of it. I escaped and found my way back here." She put her back to the wall, concealing her gun under her shirt. Miles raised his eyebrows but said nothing.

"Donna worry. We'll catch 'em. Lock all the doors after we leave. Miles and Eamon, search the cave. I know you know how to get there."

Miles opened a drawer and took out two flashlights. He handed one to Eamon. "I've got extra shells for the rifles." He dug into his pocket. "Here's a few more. We'll go through the tunnel. I'll get the shotguns." He left the room.

"Watch yourself. Marla knows how to shoot," said Patricia.

"Aye, so do I," said Eamon and gave her a peck on the cheek.

Laine kept quiet.

Miles returned. His eyes bore into hers. They were dark and uninviting. "Lock all the doors and tunnel entrance. Don't open any of them. We'll talk about this later."

Slamming the tunnel door behind them, they left the kitchen.

She wondered what Miles thought of her as she busied herself with cleaning up the broken glass. Patricia went to check the doors and returned to the kitchen.

"For the love of St. Patrick, donna be worried. The lads will find 'em. Let's go into the living room. We'll get the shotgun from the rack above the fireplace. Wait for them there."

After they entered the room, she lifted the gun from the wall and handed it to Laine.

"It's loaded. Somethin' tells me ye' know how to use it better than me, so you do. I've got me own gun in me pocket. This time, we'll be ready for 'em if they're comin' back here to surprise us."

"Good thinking. I might tell you a story to pass the time. One you want to know."

"Aye, you will, lass—in time—when you are ready."

Patricia pulled a box of bullets from a bureau drawer. She picked up a few and loaded them into her gun. Patricia spun the barrel in place. "Makin' us safe."

"I was surprised your shot missed Marla, but only by this much." She held her finger and thumb close, almost touching. "You've got a good aim."

"Aye."

"Good."

"We'll give 'em something to think about if they try again, so we will."

"Yes, we will."

Patricia made herself comfortable in a chair. She sat looking at Laine on the couch. "I'm here for the listenin', if you've got to get something off your mind."

"I do. I was deceived. I thought my husband and I had a good life. It was all a lie."

"Some things can't be explained. It's the way people are. Some are bad from the start. Marla's one of 'em — maybe that's what she saw in your husband and he in her. They're alike, they are, from what I've heard. Hard to be tellin' the good from the bad."

"It's the bad that's so hurtful. Making himself something he wasn't. Nothing he said was the truth. It was all show to get what he wanted. Finally admitted he married me for my money." She looked at Patricia. She found genuine feeling and wisdom in those elderly eyes.

"Someone high up was watching over you." She blessed herself. "Go on with you now. Make a better life. You have the talent. I saw it the first day you came to the island. You've got the chance to put things straight. I know someone who's been lookin' after you, but you hardly notice. You'll be happy if you find that new beginning, so you will."

Laine felt a peace she hadn't felt in a long time. Dark shadows fell away from her mind as she listened. She was right. She didn't need the answers. They were right in front of her all along. She had chosen to ignore them. Not any more, she decided.

All at once, an explosion rattled the windows and shook the house. Multiple gunshots rang out from behind the cottage. They ran to the kitchen window and saw a huge burst of orange flames shoot into the sky. Armed men ran toward the helicopter pad and the woods.

"Oh, no! Miles!" Laine shoved the table away from the door. They raced into the backyard.

"What happened?" Laine shouted to the nearest man.

Black smoke made her cough. She covered her nose and mouth with her hands. Patricia did the same. Multiple fires blazed in front of them, scorching the trees.

A plethora of voices came out of the smoke. Men in black uniforms, gas masks, and unslung rifles marched toward Laine and Patricia. They held masks toward the women.

"Them's the peacekeepers," said Patricia, choking on her words. "Fine troops, they are. Be wantin' a word."

"You there. Stay back. Put these on and don't take them off," shouted the armed man in the lead. He roughly placed the masks over their faces and tightly fastened the straps.

Laine heard more voices materialize out of the smoke. A group of soldiers surrounded them. In the distance, Miles's helicopter burned.

"Is Miles all right? Was he in the helicopter?" Laine shouted at the man.

"He? You mean she." He turned his back on them without another word and walked back into the haze.

Laine thought she heard him wrong, but he was gone. She'd ask someone else.

The soldiers encircled them within seconds of his departure. Laine felt stifled as the peacekeepers marched them back into the cottage without saying a word. Two men stood guard at the mudroom door.

"Is Miles safe? Please tell me." Laine asked a soldier. "Tell me!"

The soldier shut the door in her face.

"Something is very wrong. What the hell is going on?" she asked Patricia when she pulled off her mask.

Patricia removed her mask. "Never seen anything like it."

Laine knew all too well what it meant. It reminded her of Cuba — the day she almost died in her last mission.

CHAPTER 36

BLACKROCK ISLAND

The sea-worthy patrol boat sliced through the choppy ocean searching for the boat. The spotlight swept back and forth over the dark waves, skimming the surface. Several times the bow of the inflatable dipped under the curl of the waves, popped back up, and pounded down again as it surfed the waves. It jarred the teeth of the men on patrol and set them on edge. Wind howled in their ears.

"There it is! Thirty degrees off the starboard bow. Dead ahead," shouted Captain Robert. The flick, flick, flick of the wipers cleared the spray from the windshield as he turned the boat toward the dark shape in the water.

"I see it. It's sinking, Sir." Crewman Ogden peered through the binoculars.

"Then we don't have much time. Anyone aboard?"

"Hard to see."

"I'll get closer," he said and spun the wheel.

"Aye, it's taking on a lot of water."

"Beam the light on it." The captain ordered the man controlling the searchlight to illuminate the boat. Its bow jutted up into the black sky while the stern sank rapidly into the ocean.

"Give a shout. See if anyone answers. I'll get as close as I can. Look for survivors." Captain Robert ordered crewman Ogden to the stern. He pushed the throttle forward and steered his ship closer to the sinking vessel.

Ogden ran from the wheelhouse and slipped on the wet deck. He saved himself from a fall by grabbing the boat rail and steadied himself as the boat rolled from side to side.

"Anyone there?" he yelled. "Ahoy!"

"There's a life jacket near the engine. Don't see anyone, Sir." The salty water washed over the deck and drenched him.

"Affirmative." Captain Robert inched the throttle back, slowing the boat. "I'll get closer. Fog is closing in. Stay sharp."

"I see something! Portside, near the stern."

While they circled to the port side of the Zodiac, several huge waves crashed over the small boat. Within seconds, it had disappeared.

"It's gone under, Captain. It's no use."

"Affirmative," said Captain Robert. "We'll take a few more passes to check for any survivors, but I fear the worse."

"Aye, Aye, Captain."

The wind hummed. They patrolled back and forth, back and forth, and found nothing but dark ocean.

"I'm calling off the search. Make ready for the harbor. Crewmen went to their stations."

The Blacksod Lighthouse light guided them into the harbor. After they docked the boat, Captain Robert wrote in the leather-bound volume of the ship's log: "Unidentified inflatable vessel sinks in Atlantic Ocean." He wrote the latitude and longitude of the incident. "Extensive search reveals no survivors." He signed his name, dated it, and marked the time. He closed the log and patted the cover.

CHAPTER 37

BLACKROCK ISLAND

At the same time the police were searching the Atlantic, Jack, in his scuba gear, was swimming under the waves toward the mainland. It had been harder than he thought. Exhaustion crept in when he reached the first buoy marking the course for the Olympic Triathlon Swimming Competition.

Taking a moment, he rose near the top of the water and rested. He held onto the chain that secured the buoy to the bottom of the ocean.

He loved the darkness. He rested a moment then decided it was time to finish the plan. Letting go of the chain, he kicked his fins and pressed his hands tightly to his sides for a deep dive. He adjusted his mask, purged his regulator and sucked in air from his tank. He was ready. Down he went. He swam toward shore, making sure he stayed above thirty feet from the ocean floor, so he wouldn't get the bends. He kicked onward.

His watch glowed the direction on the compass. When he knew he was in shallow water he stood up, removed his weight belt, fins, mask and regulator, and lifted off his tanks.

I made it, he thought. It's a great plan. Marla will be fine for a night. It won't be that bad for her. He laughed, thinking about how she would scream at him for leaving her there. But it will be worth it, he thought.

What choice did I have? I'll have to go back and get her later. Then we can kill Laine together. It will be easy this time.

Yes, he decided, it would be simple. His new plan continued to take shape in his mind.

After hiding his diving equipment in his special place under the docks, he went to the nearby pub parking lot. He gazed inside the dimly lit pub window but walked on. Skipping the scotch was a feat, but he ignored the pull to go inside for a drink. He'd get one later. Undetected by anyone, he reached his car and drove away from the harbor toward Donegal. He reviewed his plan. He'd find a hotel outside of town and stay there for the night.

After a short time, he checked into a small bed and breakfast far enough away from the town so he would not to be recognized. I'm close to the harbor, he thought. I can take my boat back to the island early in the morning, before the sun is up and get the women. One alive, the other…not.

He slept badly and woke with a headache. His arms and legs cramped during the night and his dreams woke him. The clock near his bed read 11:00 a.m. He had overslept.

"Holy hell, it's late. Now, I'm in for it." Jack thought Marla would be raving mad at him. What could he bribe her with now? It worried him for a few minutes, but he promptly forgot about it. He had better things to think about. He stretched and searched the room for the refrigerator.

"Here it is," he said. "Ah, ice cold beer. Just what I need." He took two from the refrigerator. He pressed one to his forehead; the cold felt good. It relieved some of his headache. Uncapping it, he drank all of it and started on the next one, until he remembered he might have to dive again. He set it on the bedside table and got dressed.

He thought back to his new plan for Laine. Parts of it had formed in his mind while he swam underwater the night before.

"So what am I goin' to do with her? Let's see." He picked up the notepad and pen next to his phone. He sat on the bed and began writing. "First, go through tunnel to the fireplace hatch. Two, hmmm." He looked at the gray wall in front of him and took his time figuring out the next step. "Yeah, now I have it. Go to her bedroom. Then carry her up the stairs to the tower." He chewed on the pen and tossed a huge swig of beer down his throat.

"I have to start again. That won't work."

He sipped a little more beer. "It'll wear off by the time I have to go. Let me see. I got it. Go to her room and take the pillow. Yeah, that's it. Suffocate her! Great idea, Jack," he praised himself. "I don't need chloroform this time." He finished the beer and took a shower.

He liked the plan. Pulling on his pants and shirt, he thought, how can they catch a dead man? He laughed. "That's me—a dead man. Drowned at sea."

Studying his unshaven face in the mirror over the desk, he said, "Like it. I look like a paid assassin. Yeah, I'll kill Laine and she'll be paying me when I inherit her estate." He laughed harder. "I should be a comedian."

The knock on his door startled him. He wasn't expecting anyone.

He waited. The knock came again.

"Room service," said the maid.

"Come back later."

Flinging the curtain open, he stared out the window at the small town. People were walking along the sidewalks. Colorful flowers bloomed in window boxes of storefronts. Across the street he noticed the wood pub sign hanging from a wrought-iron post. It beckoned to him as it swayed in the breeze. Can't hurt, he thought. A man's got to eat.

A sudden thought made his head reel. Damn, I can't take my boat. I left the curragh on the island and the Zodiac at sea. Where can I get one?

It came to him. I'll take the old fisherman's boat docked near mine. He'll never know it is missing. I'll wait until tonight when it is dark. I won't go now. I'll eat and have a drink. Yeah, I'll go later.

He dropped the key on the unmade bed. Towels were thrown about on the floor of the bathroom. The maid can clean this place up. That's what she is good for, isn't it? He smiled.

Glad I paid cash. He remembered telling the man at the desk he was Mr. Marlatta from Italy. No, he did not have luggage. It was on his private plane. Marla will love it.

He walked out the front door of the hotel without paying his room bar bill. He knew he couldn't be traced. Laughing, he climbed into his truck and drove across the street to the pub parking lot.

He took a table in the corner of the dingy pub. He noticed men seated on the opposite side of the pub. They were dressed in long white robes, heads swathed in white turbans. Dark beards dotted their faces; black eyes looked at him then away. They were huddled together around the table, intent on their discussion. They ignored him.

"Dublin coddle today and a beer," he said to the gray haired, heavy-set waitress. He felt his stomach tighten. The men gave him a bad feeling. He looked over, but they were not looking at him. One man was shouting in a foreign language and the others nodded in agreement.

"Guinness?" She wrote on her pad and walked off after he agreed.

He knew he would not be there when she came back. I've got to get Marla off the island and take care of Laine, he thought. She'll be mad as hell if I wait until late tonight." He looked over at the men. They reminded him of the sheik and Kamal. He felt nervous. I've got to get out of here. He headed for the men's room, changed course and went out the back door.

Within a few minutes, he was in his car. I'll find someplace else to eat, he decided. He drove along the narrow road, threading through mountains on either side of him. They were blue against the brown, barren land. In some areas, patches of wildflowers grew in abundance in beautiful contrast to the brown land. It seemed the mountains closed in on him at times, sharp, hard, rugged and black. Goats stood on ledges and sheep grazed in the grassy fields. A donkey stuck his head over the fence at one turn, shook it. His long ears stood straight above his head. Sheep and dogs blocked traffic as they crossed the road.

He swerved to miss a capped old man in a tweed coat pressing his walking stick into the road, followed by a longhaired black and white dog. The old man's ruddy face peered at him, blue eyes bright, not smiling. He pointed and waved his stick at Jack, who zipped past him. His other hand fisted up in the air.

Jack laughed at him and pressed the accelerator to the floor.

He was hungry and his head pounded. I've got to get something to eat. I need my strength to take care of Laine. Marla will understand that.

In the next town, he found a pub and parked his truck in front of it. I think I'll have one drink, fish and chips, and hit the road.

He remembered the long white robes. It still bothered him. It was dark inside the pub when he entered it. He liked the dark. It made him feel good.

"Scotch. Make it a double. Got anything to eat?" He took a stool at the bar.

The bartender placed a scotch in front of him and a dog-eared menu. Jack ordered, sipped his drink, and watched television on the wall. I'm killing time, he thought and laughed. Yeah, *killing* time. He had another drink. I feel fine. I can do this. It's a good plan. I'll have one more drink before I head out. He ate, dropped the money on the bar, and left.

When he exited the pub, he walked by the shiny black car. It was parked in the corner of the lot near his truck. Men in white turbans talked on their cell phones in the car as he staggered past them. He recognized them from the other pub. He quickly climbed into his truck and started the engine. He ignored them as he pulled out from his space, but Kamal's face appeared in his mind. A few seconds later, they drove out of the lot onto the road in the opposite direction from him.

Sweat poured down his sides. He felt sick. Don't be silly, he told himself. You're just remembering that idiot Kamal. They're nobody. Nobody. They don't know you and you don't know them. It's all a coincidence. If they wanted to make trouble, they would have. He put the idea behind him.

The road was empty as he swerved back and forth along the coast highway that led to the harbor. It's a good day. I'll be on the island soon enough, he thought. Then the real fun will begin. He turned on the radio and hummed along with the American singer "On the road again. Driving places that I've never been..."

The landscape whizzed past him. He thought of Marla. We'll finally be together when we get rid of Laine tonight. Then we can start living.

CHAPTER 38

DONEGAL AIRPORT

onegal Airport was filled with activity as planes arrived and departed on the landing strip. In front of the terminal, the impeccably dressed Mexican boy with the smooth brown skin arrived with the chauffeur in a long black limousine. He sat and waited for his father's plane.

"Senor, Rodriguez, would you like me to get you something to eat while we wait for your father?" Fredrick asked him.

"No, we will eat later in town." He continued watching his favorite TV series, *NCIS*, in the back seat.

Fredrick pushed a button and the glass partition rose to the ceiling.

Within a short time, Rodriguez saw his father coming to the car. A heavyset man who carried the suitcases followed him. After the porter placed the luggage in the trunk, his father climbed into the car.

Rodriguez embraced him and kissed him on both cheeks. "Father, I'm happy to see you."

"Rodriguez, my son. I have missed you." He spoke in Spanish and gestured to the car. "Your mother sends her love from New Mexico. She is not at the Oklahoma Ranch just now. She decided to take a small trip to our la casa to make it welcome for me after this trip." Rodriguez saw his eyes light up as they closed the door to the car.

"Si, Father, I spoke to her this morning. I told her I was picking you up at the airport.

"What is this you are watching?" His father gazed at the small screen embedded in the back of the seat in front of them.

"It's my favorite show. *NCIS*. Oh, I like this part. Mark Harmon plays Gibbs, the chief officer. He is sanding the wooden boat in the basement of his house. I want to build a boat like that someday."

"Si, you will, Rodriguez." His father smiled, changing the look of his taut, pot-marked face. "But now tell me what you found out for me at Bourke's farm." He reached over and turned off the television.

"Bourke buys and sells the best racehorses in all of Ireland. He breeds only the finest stock. I listened to him talk to the men when I was cleaning up the stables. He is an excellent businessman. The men say he only deals with the top clientele. His employees revere him and keep the horses in top condition. His reputation surpasses everyone else's in the business — except you, of course. They thought I did not understand them, so they spoke freely."

"You learn fast, Rodriguez. I am proud of you."

"I studied hard at the University of Michigan for you, Father, so I could help you and our cousin in Mexico with the horse business. Someday, I will have my own stables and be just like you."

"Si, my son, you will be part of the business very soon. Tell me more about Bourke's horses and his relationship with his clients."

Rodriguez stared at the gold medallion on the thick linked chain around his father's neck. I will have one of those someday too, he thought. People will know I am rich.

"The horses are very expensive. Sheik Tariq bought many of them from Bourke over the years. They are kept at *Koolmoore Stables,* where he breeds them. It's not too far from here. He runs the horses in the most prestigious races in France and the United States. I hear he has hundreds of horses at the stables. The word is he is not to be crossed, and the men fear him. He will go to all extremes to get what he wants."

"This is very good information. It is useful to me. Did you do what I asked you to do? I sent the Phenylbutazone and the Sonata sleeping drug to the post office box you set up. Did you get them?"

"Si, I did. First, I put the sleeping drug in the guard's coffee at the small concession stand where I was working. I watched him go there every morning and evening when I worked at the racetrack. It hit him quickly that night when he entered the stables, and he forgot to lock the door. I snuck inside and was quick about my business. It was raining hard and thundering, so the storm covered the winnies of the horses. The guard dozed while I injected high doses of Bute into the muscle of each horse just like you taught me. I was certain they were the horses the sheik bought from Bourke. The horses I drugged did not finish the race — some died. I was successful. No one saw me do it."

His father turned his head toward Rodriguez. His black eyes wrinkled at the corners. "Ah, yes, our competition. You helped me very much to eliminate them. You learn quickly. That is very important in our business. You did an excellent job. Is there more?"

Rodriguez told him about Jack and how he wanted to sell horses to their cousin in Mexico. "He wants to get involved in the business. I know he will do anything if he is paid enough. He asked me to secretly get information about a woman who is designing a party room in Bourke's lighthouse on his island. I delivered her schedule to him. I couldn't tell him much because I left the job the very same day. I withheld important information that I knew you would want. He paid me well for my services. One night in the pub after he had too many scotches, he asked me about brokering horses for you."

His father's eyes darkened as he looked at him. "What did you say?"

"Nothing. I did not tell him about your horse business, Father. I said he might be interested in doing business with our cousin. I said I would have to let him know. I pretended I did not really understand what he wanted. Did I do the right thing?"

"Yes, my son. It was the right thing to say. Is that it?" His father arched his eyebrows and smiled at him.

"There's more."

He told him about Rex and the hunters who shot the horse by mistake on Bourke's property. Then he explained the scaffolding incident in detail.

"Murray, Bourke's foreman on the island, overheard me talking to Jack about spying on the woman on the island. She is the lead architect on the lighthouse. Jack wanted her daily schedule and said he would pay a lot to get it. I agreed. Murray, Bourke's foreman, was in the bar at the same time we were there. We did not see him until too late. He was in a booth in the corner with his back to us. He heard everything we said.

"After hearing our plans, Murray made trouble for me at work on the island. I tried to stay away from him, but he kept after me. Finally, I told Jack about it. He was furious. He said he had a plan to stop him, but he needed my help. He described how to loosen the screws on the scaffolding poles that were fastened to the catwalks on the outside of the lighthouse.

"I did it. No one saw me. The scaffolding collapsed the next day when Murray was on it. He didn't die, but he was badly hurt in the fall. I failed. I've been in hiding until now. I need your protection, Father."

"Put it behind you. I am here. We don't dwell on our mistakes. We get even." He laughed.

"I have a lot to learn." He shifted in his seat.

"Si, what else? Or is that it?"

"The party room in Bourke's lighthouse tower that I mentioned. It's going to be used for entertaining people like you. Important buyers in the racing business, I mean." He looked embarrassed.

"Yes, you are right, Rodriguez. I should meet this man Bourke. I will arrange it. You are becoming an excellent businessman."

"Gracias, Father."

The young man watched his father pull a cigar from his inside coat pocket. He gripped it with his teeth and opened his briefcase. There were several packets of one-thousand-dollar bills bound by thin white strips of paper with red numbers on them showing the amount in the pile. He picked up two packets. He placed them in a brown sack.

"It serves you well to be a good listener." He handed the sack to Rodriguez.

"Gracias, Father. I will invest wisely. I will buy my own horses."

"Si," he said. "You will ship the horses to your cousin for good keeping. In a few years, you will join me in the horseracing business. There are millions to be made—and spent, my son." He pulled another fat cigar from his coat, cut the ends off, and lit it. "Here have one. Today you are a man and a business partner." He handed him the cigar.

Rodriguez took the cigar. Inhaling the smoke from his first cigar burned his lungs. He coughed. His father laughed at him.

"You'll enjoy it more if you don't inhale," he said and went back to reading a document.

"Si." He felt the heat creep into his face. He called me a *man* and a *business partner*, he thought. I'll make millions like him and my cousin Jose.

He observed the lush green grass outside his window. He felt fine.

"After we reach the hotel, we'll eat and drink." His father puffed on the cigar.

"Si, there is a good restaurant in Donegal Bay. Brown trout comes from the sea every day. It es deliciosa. It is good with rice and fine wine." Rodriguez smiled his bright, shining, white teeth that were no longer stained by the ink he'd used to blacken them. He placed the cigar in the ashtray.

His father pushed the button to open the glass separating them from the chauffeur. "Fredrick, take us to Donegal, to the hotel."

"The *Abbey Hotel* in the *Diamond*. It is in the center of Donegal Town," said Rodriguez. He sat up straight in his seat. I am important, he thought, just like my father.

The chauffeur nodded and drove on. The coast road gave them a fine view of the yellow and white estates. The ocean was dark green and rough while the wind blew the waves away from the shoreline. Here the country was quite green and punctuated by black wrought-iron gates. Statuary surrounded by beds of colorful flowers and overhanging trees stood tall at the end of the long driveways leading to the mansions. A profusion of cars, mostly Mercedes, crowded the entrances.

They rounded a bend and found sheep farms blanketed the hillsides. Sheep went along eating the grass. The car flew up a hill and down the next, the farms going on and on, green land rolling over the hills. Rectangular stone hedges, covered in ivy, fenced in the sheep. They had a pleasant view of the blue and white-striped sheep grazing on the lush green grass.

As they sped along, indoor and outdoor horse arenas followed one after the other, along the road, sporting thoroughbreds and workhorses in the barnyards. The view was good and, after awhile, they arrived at a long sandy beach stretched outside the town. Anglers dropped their lines in the green water for saltwater fish. They fished in their wood curraghs. Old men were baked brown in the sun. White sails dotted the horizon.

The sun winked from behind the white clouds that skudded across the sky as they came into Donegal Town. Gray stone pavers whitened by the sun and cracked by the cold winter surrounded the square's sidewalks and made up the streets. A line of people coming from a bus walked through the town square, passing the sandstone Statue of the Four Masters.

"Father, we are here." Rodriguez opened the window and the sea breeze felt cool on his face. He felt fine. He sat forward in his seat as the car stopped in front of the *Abbey Hotel.*

He climbed out of the back seat and went into the hotel alongside his father. He was happy. That night he would have a good bed to sleep in.

CHAPTER 39

BLACKSOD HARBOR

Later that day Jack took the fisherman's boat out from his well and arrived on the island around 11:00 p.m. Slipping the line over his shoulder, he tugged the boat up the sand and into the trees.

It's a bit chilly here tonight, he thought, as he climbed the path that led him into the dense forest on the far side of the island away from the lighthouse tower. He slogged along a winding path at the top of the cliffs. This is good practice for carrying Laine, he thought. He looked at his watch. It read 11:30 p.m. It was still early. I'll go to the cave at midnight, he decided.

Waves crashed below him along the sandy shores. He knew the merlins slept in their nests inside the crevices of the cliff walls. After stumbling and falling several times, he made it to the tunnel. He crept inside and collapsed on the stone floor. He smiled. Laine is not far from here, but where are you, Marla?

"Marla?" he whispered. "Marla, are you here?"

There was no response. When she gets back from wherever she is, I'll have to tell her I have a new plan. She'll be a raving lunatic. Oh, well, she'll get over it when we are far away from here on our trip. She's probably spying on Laine and the men, so we can make a clean getaway without being noticed. When she gets back we'll take care of Laine. I'll rest a little until she gets here. I am tired. It's been a long day. Damn Laine. She's messing up all our plans. Well, she's run out of luck. I'll see to it.

Closing his eyes, he stretched out on the cold floor. After a while, he fell asleep and dreamt of lions roaming the fields.

* * *

It was only a short time later when men in long white robes moved silently into the cave where Jack lay sleeping. The lead turbaned man covered Jack's mouth with his hand while another quickly slit his throat from ear to ear. One of the men snapped a photograph of him before they wrapped him in plastic, placed him in a black bag, and zipped it up. Within seconds, another man slung him over his shoulder and carried him out of the cave. Taking the path through the forest to the back of the island, they found their way down to the shore. It was easy going. They'd marked the trail back to the boat they had pulled up on the shore. Dumping the body in the boat, they pushed away from the island and sped out to sea.

When the boat reached the deepest part of the ocean, they unzipped the bag and dumped the body overboard. It floated for a moment, bobbing up and down in the waves. They watched and waited under the full moon.

Within a short time, gray pointed fins broke the surface of the water. Swimming fast and smoothly through the waves, they zeroed in on the body. The sharks circled the floating man wrapped in plastic. They turned and attacked the black blob, thumping into each other. A frenzied dance began among them. A ritual of striking, ripping and tearing the flesh became their music as they fought over the body pieces.

The men smiled at each strike. A man in the stern took several photographs of the scene until the sea rose up and the water bubbled with dark red blood. They knew the sheik would be pleased when he saw the pictures. They followed his orders without question. Soon the sharks moved away.

Nothing was left.

The clouds covered the moon, leaving a starless black sky. Finished with their job, the men put the boat in gear and sped toward the harbor.

CHAPTER 40

BLACKROCK ISLAND

While the peacekeepers, Miles, and Eamon searched for John on the island, Laine followed Patricia into the living room. "I'd like to run a few ideas past you."

"We'll pass the time talking while we wait," said Patricia.

"I think Marla is dead. The soldier said—'she' not 'he'—burned up in the explosion."

"Aye, she knew how to fly that helicopter, she did. Miles, herself, and a few blokes from town took the lessons. If you are right—and I believe you are—she met a terrible death."

"Yes, I am sure it was her. The first day I was here, I saw her with my husband in Donegal Town. I knew he was alive. I doubted myself until I saw him again with Marla on the boat in the harbor. She avoided my questions about him, but you heard her tonight. He hated me." Laine walked over to the couch and sat.

"So she said, but she's nothing but trouble."

"I need to talk to John."

"So you will. The lads will find him. Remember the day you came to us? Rex was shot by them hunters, so he was. I remember Miles tellin' me later, a man named Jack was livin' on your land next door. He was probably carryin' on with Marla there."

"Yes, I agree. She was rude to me on the boat. Now I know why."

"'Tis a terrible situation, it is. She's just like him. Taking all she can get no matter who she's hurtin'."

"There's also Rex's murder. I think John arranged it with the hunters, so he could swindle the sheik out of more money. Remember, he replaced Rex with Duke, didn't he? He tried to blame Miles for it."

"So he did. The hunters also said he was livin' next door on your property, for some time. He told them they could hunt there after they fixed the roof. I remember it well."

"Miles and I saw his truck leaving the Sullivan property, but at that time, we didn't know it was him. What I can't figure out was why he avoided me. All I wanted to do was talk to him. I told Marla when I met her on the sightseeing boat that I wanted to talk to him. She denied knowing him."

"He was watchin' you, he was. All along he knew you were here. Sorry to be sayin' this, but he had no time for talk. Just the killin' was what he was after so as he could get your money and be with Marla."

"Yes, that makes sense. I knew he wasn't the man I thought he was, but I never figured him for a murderer. When I was in the cave, he thought I was knocked out. He said he only married me for money. He told me he and Marla were going away after they drowned me in the ocean. He was going to collect the inheritance. But after he disappeared on the lake last year, I changed my will. Took him out of it. He didn't know about the change."

"Aye, a surprise. He'd run off with Marla only to be broke."

"Yes."

"It's a terrible sickness—wantin' the money, that is. Do you think he was involved with Murray's accident?"

"Yes. Miles pieced it together from what Murray told him in the hospital. John was behind all of it. I think he involved the Mexican boy and had him do his dirty work on the island. It included spying on me."

"Maybe he had him rig the scaffolding so Murray would get hurt."

"I don't put anything past him."

"Eamon said he was going to fire the boy. He didn't feel right about him after Miles told him about the boy taking money from the man in the cove. The lad never came to work after that day, so it was over anyway."

"That boy puzzles me. I think he knows a lot more English than he led us to believe. Murray said he overheard him tell John he had a cousin in the horseracing business in Mexico. The boy wanted to do business with him. At first I thought he was bragging about nothing, but now I am not so sure. What was his last name? Do you remember?"

"Aye, when Eamon hired him he told me his last name is Diaz."

"Rodriguez Diaz. It sounds familiar, but I am not sure why." It triggered a memory. There was scuttlebutt in the U.S. newspapers about someone named Diaz who was involved in drugging the horses at the Kentucky Derby. They could never prove he did it.

She would ask Max to follow up on it. He always told her to follow the money. Of course. Rodriguez took money from the man down in the cove the day she and Miles observed them.

"The boy took money from the man in the cove. He took money from John in the pub. I wonder if he took money from anyone else."

"He was not who he said he was. Eamon said he was always sweeping close to them when he and Miles were talkin'. It was like he was listenin' to their conversation. Someone was puttin' him up to it. No lad hovers like that for nothin'."

"It makes sense. He was spying for John."

"We'll be ready for John, we will, when he gets here. You can question him." Patricia set the gun on the table next to her.

"I'm not who I say I am either." Laine stared into a face of wisdom.

"Aye. No one shoots like that by learnin' it only on a farm in Michigan. There's more, I'm suspectin'. Want to tell me about it?"

"It's not for anyone's ears but yours. I'm an undercover agent for a special agency in the United States government. I was sent here to find out why the horses were being drugged. I also needed to learn who is behind the money laundering on the racetrack. I came here to observe Miles."

"Have you found your answers?"

"Yes, some of them. I'm certain now that Miles is not involved. I am working on the rest. I have only my suspicions. That's why I wanted to talk to you."

"Aye. We'll be needin' you to clean up this horse business. Find out who is doin' it, lass."

"I am working on it. I need to make a phone call. Please let me tell Miles myself."

"That you will. I'll wait for you here. Go make that call."

She left her in the room and went down the hall to the bedroom. She closed the door and dialed a number on her phone. Max picked up on the first ring.

"Labrador," he said.

"Yellowbird reporting in."

"Confirmed. What do you have for me?"

She updated him on the helicopter explosion, John and Marla's plan to take her money and kill her, John's involvement with the sheik while brokering his horses, and the boy Rodriguez Diaz and his connection to John. "His name is familiar to me, but I am not sure why."

"You have good instincts. What can you tell me about him?"

She gave him all the information she had. At the end of the conversation she said, "Miles Bourke is not a part of it."

"We'll take him out of the equation."

"He wants answers as much as we do."

"Given what you told me, it's clear John figured he would inherit your money and the land in Ireland, if you were dead. He was skimming off the top with the sheik. I'm sure he had many more suckers on his list. It's easy to launder money on his end, because he's the middleman. There's no one to keep track of his transactions. It's a cash business."

"That's right," said Laine.

"We also discovered John was helping the Mexican cartel sell drugs in Michigan. He was moving drugs from Detroit to Canada near the Blue Water Bridge in Port Huron. He hired older people as dealers who rode on wave runners in the St. Clair River, where they brought the drugs into the U.S. They would make the drug runs back and forth between the two countries at all hours of the day and night. A white van operation would then take the drugs to the Detroit casinos, where they were transferred to the cartel for disbursement. We apprehended a woman high up on the food chain and she fingered him. It seems he cut her out of part of her commission."

"No surprise there."

"We are monitoring their movements. Before we set up a sting, we have to coordinate with the Border Patrol and the U.S. Coast Guard and find all of the locations on the lakes."

"It adds up. Ramming my sailboat on the rocks close to the Canadian shoreline makes sense. With his extended license, John could walk straight into the country. I don't think he was a part of drugging the horses on the racetrack. At least I couldn't find a connection, unless it's through his association with Rodriquez. Anything is possible."

"Yes, again you are correct. John was not involved in the 'milkshaking' incidents. The boy, Rodriguez Diaz, did that. I said your instincts were accurate. Diaz is a bad one.

We've confirmed that he took a job at the racetrack selling food at a concession stand near the stables. A guard who was protecting the horses identified him as the one who drugged him. The boy overdosed the horses by lethal injection. He's got no heart."

"He is dangerous. He's not been seen here for several days. He walked off the lighthouse job. I am not sure if he is still in Ireland. I know he and John were working together because I saw them myself. Is there any other way he and John are connected?"

"Yes, teaming up was a perfect fit. The boy has international connections with his cousin in the horseracing business in Mexico. We discovered something else, after you gave me the information. Rodriguez is not from Mexico like his cousin; he is from New Mexico. Jack—John—and the boy could have been involved in tampering with the horses at the races in Kentucky and in France. We looked into the 'milkshaking' episode. Yes, the cartel connection is there, but I don't think John did the drugging. I think he is into money-laundering."

"Wait a minute, it just dawned on me. Rodriguez might be the son of Don Juan Diaz, head of the Mexican cartel! I knew I'd heard that name before. The family is involved in money-laundering and drugs."

"Laine, I'll call you back. I'm contacting the FBI, DEA, and our own agents to get them up to speed. This is a breakthrough. Good job! I'll bring you in the day after tomorrow." He hung up.

Laine stared at the phone. She was not finished talking to him. She now knew for sure what she had begun to suspect: John had sold drugs in Detroit and he had used her—again and again.

How could I have missed it? I was so wrapped up in my work, I didn't pay attention. The signs were there.

Let it go, she told herself. He can't hurt you anymore.

My operation is over for me, but it's only beginning for other operatives, she thought. I'm going home. It's time to talk to Miles. I can't put it off any longer.

She went to the bedroom window. The helicopter was smoldering, flickers of flame bursting upward every now and then. The dark night and the lingering smoke obstructed her view of the ocean. She left the bedroom and went back to the living room, where Patricia had built a fire in the fireplace. The flames lit up the room, warming it.

"It's under control." She took a seat on the couch.

"You had a good talk, so you did," said Patricia.

"Yes. I have a lot to tell Miles and Eamon when I see them. I'll give you a run down while we wait. I know you will keep what I tell you confidential."

She crossed herself. "Aye, I swear it on me mother's grave."

She highlighted the conversation she had with Max but left out the classified information. The rest she kept to herself. When she finished, she felt exhausted.

"I'll be gettin' both of us a glass of Powers whiskey. I'm needin' it. The fairies are making mischief in this place today."

Laine chuckled. "I need it, too."

The fire burned white against the dark logs, sending warmth into the room. She touched the gun behind her back. It was snug in her waistband — ready if she needed it.

I am going to miss this place, she thought as she looked around. I'll finish my job designing the party room in the lighthouse for Miles. A party room for racehorse owners, breeders, and buyers — a good room with plenty of light. When that's done, it will be time to begin again.

Miles and Eamon banged open the front door; the smoke from the burning chopper filtered into the room. They hung their wet coats on the peg and set their rifles in the corner. Eamon went to Patricia and hugged her. The grim look on his face alerted Laine that something was wrong.

"What is it? What's happened?" asked Laine.

Miles's eyes darkened. "Marla is dead. She thought she'd get off the island in the helicopter. Instead, it exploded and she burned to death."

"I was afraid of that."

He stared at her, his mouth a thin line and his eyes hooded.

"Your husband escaped. We didn't find him. The peacekeepers are still looking on the island and setting out in the boats. They'll scour the ocean for him, but I have a feeling he is cleverer than we thought he would be. We have to be on alert." He leaned against the fireplace mantel.

"I have something to tell you." She looked into his cold, dark eyes. His facial muscles were tense. Tension stiffened her shoulders.

"It's about time. I've waited long enough."

* * *

The next morning, the Atlantic Ocean looked different from the map room window, as if she was seeing it for the first time. The black rock cliffs jutted up into the cloudless blue sky and the sun shined bright on the water. The sunlight danced, flickered, and skipped along the crests of the waves.

She heard the warbling of skylarks—not the ravens and the peregrine falcons. It was a cacophony of sounds mingling with the warm sea breeze. A gavia immer, which she knew better by the name great northern diver, with its heavy spear-like bill, circled above the green foamy waves, gliding low on the water. On the edge of the black rock cliffs, even the trees in the forest looked greener—more alive. She did not let her gaze wander to the helicopter site.

She was glad she'd told Miles what she was doing on the island. He understood her mission and the need for secrecy—so did Eamon. It was unusual for her to be able to talk to someone like him, she thought.

It's too bad I have to leave soon. I could really fall for this guy.

"Laine, everything all right?" Miles entered the map room and went to her. He put his arm around her shoulder and kissed her.

"It's a good day. Miles, it's perfect. Let's have a party." She took in the view from the tower room. Sunlight filled the room.

CHAPTER 41

BLACKROCK ISLAND

Laine stood in the mudroom doorway and watched the helicopter wreckage carted off the island by the men. The clean up was quick and what was left of the incident were the black, scorched earth and charred trees near the helicopter explosion site.

"What a mess," she said to Miles. "Such a shame that the guarda's shots destroyed that beautiful helicopter."

"Insured, so I'll get another one. Come on, I've had enough of this. Let's go to Donegal. I think a change of scenery will do both of us some good. If you want, we can stop by Margaret Hogan's office and look up your property deed and then grab some lunch. What do you think?"

They stood, looking at each other in the sunlight.

"Yes, Miles, I'd like that. It's a good idea." She held her teacup in her hand, but the liquid was cold. I think I'll get rid of this, she thought.

"The Trumpy is all set to go. When would it be convenient for you to leave?" He followed her into the kitchen and set his mug of coffee in the sink.

"Soon. I'd like to go by boat. I can be ready in fifteen minutes." She squeezed his hand. "Guess you have to get a new helicopter."

"Something I do often." He laughed and kissed her.

"I liked that," she said.

"There's more where that came from."

"Oh, Miles, we could have a good time."

"We don't have to leave, if you don't want to."

"It would be better."

"Only if you want to."

"Yes, I want to," she said.

"There'll be other days."

"But not like this one. Yes, let's go and have a good time. We can pick up things for the party."

"I'll meet you down at the boat." He laughed and left the kitchen through the back door.

"I think I'll drink Patricia's black tea from now on. I've had enough of this." She picked up her favorite tea tin and threw it into the trash. She emptied her teacup in the sink.

After grabbing her handbag from her room, she headed down the stone steps to Miles's boat. The crew was ready, and cast off as soon as she boarded. The breeze was warm on the stern as they pulled away from the island. The sun was high in the sky. They sipped wine and looked at the horizon on the way to Donegal Harbor.

"I feel good. And happy." Laine snuggled up to Miles on the seat.

"It is a good day."

"Yes, it is, but I wish I knew how John escaped."

"That's still a mystery."

"I've been meaning to ask you something."

"I'm not sure if I'll answer." Something tightened inside her. She stared at the boat's wake.

"It's about the gun. How did you get it into the country?"

"It's nothing. I have a permit. It's part of my job. I told you enough last night. You'll just have to trust me." She felt her face muscles tighten and knew he was watching her.

"Yes, you did. It's nothing. You did tell me some of it last night. But there's more, isn't there? Things you can't tell me."

She smiled. Then nodded. "Yes, you're right."

"I won't press you."

"So we won't talk of it. Ever."

"No, we won't. Ever."

"I like you, Miles. You're a good man." She leaned over and kissed him.

"I like you too." He smiled and threw his arm around her shoulder. "Feels right. I think we should go to Cong tomorrow. We can visit Ashford Castle and fish for brown trout. I'll hire a guile—that's 'guide' to you. We can go out on the water in the early morning and take a curragh, before it gets too warm on Lough Corrib."

"I'd like that."

"That's what we'll do tomorrow. Fish. Fish on Lough Corrib."

"We'll have a good time."

"Yes, we'll have a good time. "

"And we'll talk of pleasant things."

"That's the plan. By the way, my ancestors built Ashford Castle on a beautiful piece of land along the Cong River. It is a good place to fish."

"Lovely."

"You'll be all right."

"I am."

Before noon, the yacht pulled into Donegal.

"The flag is flying half-staff on the *Morrigan* waterbus."

"I see that."

They walked the short distance to Margaret Hogan's Real Estate office and entered the white room. Margaret was behind her desk. She looked up in surprise.

"Afternoon, Margaret," Miles greeted her. "I thought we'd come and see you today."

"Good afternoon to you both," she said, rising from her desk. "Won't you have a seat?"

They sat in the two chairs facing her.

"We saw the flag at half-staff on the *Morrigan*."

"Captain's wife Marla died in a helicopter crash, they say. 'Tis no loss."

"What do you mean *his wife*?" said Miles.

"They were married, so they were. I'll not be mournin' the likes of her. Didn't you know she married the captain of the *Morrigan* 'bout a year ago?"

"No," said Miles.

"Marla was married?" Miles looked surprised. "She was going out with John."

"Don't know about no John. Carryin' on with some Jack fella, she was. 'Twas a blessing for the captain to be rid of her. They was sayin' she met her end in a bad way, they did. Not sure what all the fuss was about." She returned to her desk, sat, and began flipping papers.

Miles was silent.

Laine said nothing, wondering how she had missed it. She would update Max. There was more to the story.

"Well, then, sorry for the captain." Miles cleared his throat. "On a happier note, you mentioned you have the deed for the Sullivan property?"

"I've gone and found the deed, but there's a bit of a problem. *I* can't be givin' it to you, Laine."

"That's all right," said Laine. "It wasn't really mine to have."

"Aye, it is, lass, but it is!" Margaret stood up.

"I'm confused. I thought you said I can't have it."

"All right then, I did." She smiled and shouted to the back room. "Bring the deed out here, will you, Norbert?"

A white-haired man entered the office. He was smiling. His cheeks were red and his eyes were blue and bright. "Here 'tis, Margaret. Miles, it is good to see you again. You must be Laine."

Laine stared at him. She couldn't speak. She was taken aback by the looks of him.

Miles stood up. "Norbert! So glad to see you, I heard…" Miles pumped his hand.

Laine bolted up from her chair. "My God, it can't be. You look exactly like my father!"

"That I do. This may come as a shock, but I'm your father's brother, I am."

"Brother?"

"His twin brother, as a matter of fact… Had a fallin' out when we was young."

"This is crazy. I had no idea."

"Aye, I'll be needin' to make up for not telling you sooner. You're all I have left of family, Laine. The rest of us is gone."

"Norbert, I am so happy to meet you." She threw her arms around him and hugged him to her. After a moment, she stepped back and studied his face. "I really can't believe it. You look just like him." She clutched at his arms, examining his face with her eyes.

"That I do." He smiled into her eyes.

"Margaret told us you went to Michigan. We heard you disappeared and never came back home."

"Aye, but not in the sense you're thinking of. I couldn't remember who I was for quite some time. There was an accident on the lake."

"What happened?" asked Laine.

"It may be a bit hard on you, if I tell you, lass." Norbert wrung his hands and shook his head.

"I'd like to hear it."

"I almost drowned on Lake St. Clair."

Laine's heart jumped into her throat. "What do you mean 'drowned'?"

"I was in Michigan sailing with your husband John. We were cruising the South Channel when the wind picked up. It wasn't in me plans to go with him, but that's what happened."

"You went sailing with John?" Pure insanity, she thought. John tried to drown this lovely man. What kind of a sadistic person had she married? She should have seen through him long before now.

"Aye, I was with your husband. He tried to kill me."

"Tell me what he did."

Norbert told them the story of his near drowning, the amnesia, and his rescue by the Gudefins, the French Canadian couple who lived in their summer home near Squirrel Island.

"This is shocking." Laine clutched at her stomach, willing the sudden nausea to pass.

"Aye, there's more. I went to your Grosse Pointe home, Laine. I wanted to give you the deed to me property in person. Surprise you, but John told me you were out of town. He said you were in New York and he didn't know when you'd be back. 'Tis a bad man, that husband of yours. Hope you know it." He pushed his hands through his white hair, smoothing it back. "Really bad, he is."

"Yes, I know. I am not with him anymore."

Norbert smiled. "Glad to hear it. He invited me to go sailing with him that very day I was at your house. I told him I couldn't swim, I did. Convinced me it was no matter. Like a fool, I went with him anyway. He's a clever man, he is."

Margaret gave him a loving look. "Yes, I was worried sick for months after you didn't come home or call, Norbert. I'll be remembering it for a while now, I will."

"Oh, Margaret, let me tell the lass the story." He gave her the same sweet look.

"Go on then. Tell it."

"I got knocked in me head by the boat beam when we gibed. It tossed me overboard, it did. I was callin' John for help, but it made no difference to him — he didn't come back for me. I screamed to him to pick me up, but all he did was sail away. He left me in the water hanging onto the sail and part of the rigging."

"I am so sorry. He's an evil man. I feel responsible."

"It's not your fault. It's in him — the evil is in him. It's not in you, lass."

"John can't hurt anyone anymore," Miles offered. "We think he drowned yesterday at sea. The police saw an inflatable boat sink into the ocean by the Olympic buoys. It's not confirmed, but they are pretty sure he went down with it. I got the report this morning."

Margaret blessed herself. "I'll not be mournin' the likes of him."

No one said anything for a few minutes.

"Well, here we are, Laine." Norbert took her hand in his.

"It feels good to know I have family."

"Aye, that it does."

"So glad you're back on Irish soil," Miles told Norbert.

"I'll be forgivin' you, Norbert, but you best be watchin' your step in the future," said Margaret and took his hand.

"That I will."

Laine wiped a tear from her cheek. "It means a lot to me to know you are here."

"Donna be worried. I am going to be here for a long time. I've something for you." He reached into the breast pocket of his coat. "Here, this is for you. It's the deed to the Sullivan property and I want you to have it. It's the original. Donna forget you're a Sullivan, lass."

"I'm overwhelmed. Thank you... and I won't forget it."

"Good to know. Anyone tell you that you look like your mum?"

"I'm a lot like her. And my father."

"That I'll be seein' for myself." Norbert laughed.

Miles coughed and stood up. "Let's celebrate this happy occasion, everyone. I'm buying lunch and drinks."

"I'm having a chocolate martini," said Laine.

Norbert rubbed his hands together. "Sounds good to me. I'll be havin' a Guinness, so I will. Comin', Margaret?"

She followed them out of the office and locked the door behind them.

Near the pub, a crewman from the Trumpy ran up to Miles with an envelope. "Sir, a man left this for you. He said it is important that I deliver it to you now."

"Everyone, I'll catch up to you at the pub," said Miles, taking the envelope.

Laine said, "I'll wait with you."

The others agreed and walked on, leaving Laine and Miles with the crewman.

"Did he leave his name?" asked Miles.

"No, but he was dressed in a white turban and a white robe, if that helps you. He ran off as soon as he delivered it. We had no chance to talk to him."

Miles nodded. "Thanks for delivering it. We'll be down to the boat after lunch and then head back to the island."

"We'll have things ready, Sir," said the crewman and left.

"What could be so important?" Miles opened the manila envelope and slid out a typed piece of paper. He read the word: "A broker's commission"? That's strange."

"What does it mean?" said Laine.

"I don't know. There's more in the envelope." He dug out a photograph. "This looks like my horse Duke in front of my stables. That's odd. Why do I need a picture of a horse I sold to the sheik?" He handed it to her and brought out another photograph from the envelope. "Bloody hell! What's this all about? I don't want you to see this."

"Why not?" She leaned in and took a look. "Oh, no! It's John! His throat is cut from ear to ear!" She dropped the typed paper and the picture of Duke.

Miles shoved the picture back in the envelope, picked up the photograph and paper from the ground and placed them inside the envelope. He quickly wrapped his arms around her and held her close. "I'm sorry. You shouldn't have seen that."

"It's horrible. Even if he was a psychopath." She put her head on his chest.

"Yes, awful. Try to forget it."

She stepped back from him and looked into his eyes. "I'm sure he's really dead now. But how horrible. Why would someone murder him?"

"I don't know. We know he swindled the sheik. Maybe it's revenge."

"You could be right. He was playing a dangerous game."

"Yes, he was. Someone wanted me to know what happened to him. I need to take this information to the police right away."

She nodded at him. "The sooner the better."

"Why don't you go on and meet the others? There's no reason for you to go with me. I'll walk you to the pub and then drop this off."

"No, you go on ahead to the police station. I'll wait for you with the others."

"Will you be all right? I'll walk you there." He took her hand.

"No, I'm fine. It's important you take them to the police now." She let go of his hand and waved him off.

"I'll be there as soon as I can." He gave her a kiss and walked briskly toward the center of town.

Laine moved slowly down the street to the pub. For the second time that day, she felt sick. It's better to know the truth, she thought. *John is dead. I won't be seeing him again in Donegal—or anywhere.*

Now I can move on with my life.

CHAPTER 42

LOUGH CORRIB AND THE RIVER CONG

They ate a fine meal at *Donahue's Pub*. Later, they strolled along the docks in the sunset. Laine knew they were good people. Maybe this time it would be different, she thought.

Margaret and Norbert left them after a short time.

"Don't forget. We're going fishing tomorrow," said Miles, placing his arm around her shoulder.

"Sure," Laine said. "Bet you I'll catch the biggest fish." She nestled close to him.

"You're on."

He took her hand as they ambled to the harbor beach area. The sand felt good on their feet. The water was clear and the sun was a warm orange glow on the horizon.

"To fishing," said Miles. He leaned in and kissed her.

She smiled up at him. "And — to the catch and release on Lough Corrib and the River Cong."

She watched the sunset with him. It shut out the darkness. She felt fine in his arms.

THE END

J. Lee Burke

J. Lee Burke wrote as a student reporter for The Michigan Journalist at University of Michigan and for The Villanovan at Villanova University.

She edited Simon and Schuster's *Handbook for Writers*, and revised *Literature and the Writing Process* for Prentice Hall. An example of the way she uses dialogue in her writing was aired on CBS-WWJ Newswatch, during the filming of Clint Eastwood's *Grand Torino*. Her articles are featured in the Grosse Pointe Magazine.

She is working on her next novel that takes place in Key Largo, Florida.

We hope you have enjoyed J. Lee Burke's *Blackrock Island*. If you enjoyed the story, please take a moment to peruse the other great titles offered by going online to www.bluewaterpress.com in order to check out other great stories.